The Meadows

CYNTHIA KEYES

BOOKS

Vinci Books

vinci-books.com

Published by Vinci Books Ltd in 2025

1

A CIP catalogue record for this book is available from the British Library.

Paperback ISBN: 9781036702601

By Cynthia Keyes

Regency Romance

The Meadows
The Smuggler
The Spy
The Heiress
Bride of Montrose

This book is dedicated to my mother, Martha, and my mother-in-law, Edna. Two women whose fierce determination was exceeded only by their ability to love.

Chapter One

BEWARE THE IDES OF MARCH

Kate shifted forward on the coach seat, peering into the darkness as the carriage passed the twin towers of Reculver, searching the beach for signs that the galley had made the shore. The steady beat of the horse's hooves as they trotted along the seaside road was the only sound. The channel itself was uncharacteristically silent as if it too were waiting for the arrival of the smugglers.

"Er now, ma'am. The boys will come in using the towers to guide them, true, but they'll not land until they're well past and out of the eyes of the Watch. There is a wharf they are using on The Meadows, near the village. Twill be a mile or two yet." Old Tom gave the reins a brisk snap, and the horses quickened their pace.

The March air chilled, clinging damply to her skin. Straight ahead, to the north, sheet lightning periodically lit up the skies promising a quick end to the stillness of the night. A storm rolling into the channel from the North Sea could be brutal and treacherous this time of year.

Kate pulled up the hood of her cloak and wrapped it more tightly across her body.

Dealing with the 'free traders' had its risks. If the authorities intercepted this load of French goods, all would be lost. England had barred all trade with Napoleon's France. If activities on the beach were detected this night, the entire shipment would be forfeited to the Crown. Even worse, Kate could be arrested for smuggling, along with the crew of the Po, Old Tom, and anyone else who had braved the beach tonight. But if one wanted the luxury items that only the French could provide, and Kate did, then the risk was worth the reward.

"Lanterns ahead, ma'am," Old Tom said, pointing into the dark, "just there on the shore."

Kate squinted into the night. A faint amber glow was soon joined by another and another as they neared the landing site. Shapes began emerging out of the dark. Loaded pack horses meandered up a sanded trail in a steady stream to the carts and carriages waiting on the lane.

"Whoa girls." Tom pulled on the reins, coming to a full stop behind a wide wagon.

The night had become a hub of activity. At least thirty men worked the site. Horses were unloaded and headed back to reload, men hollered, horses neighed as barrel after barrel was hoisted into the waiting carts. Somewhere, a donkey heehawed in a bellow and came bucking down the lane with two men in hot pursuit. As it passed the coach, the beast gave a kick, sending a precariously balanced barrel from its back flying to the ground.

"Hold, girls, hold." Tom held tight the reins.

Kate watched the commotion with wonder. She had grown up in the neighborhood, only five miles beyond the village of Herne, just down the lane, and knew well the smuggling life of the community, but this was the first time she had seen it. All the village men were in one way, or another connected to the trade. Everyone knew of it. The landing dock was located on her land, The Meadows. Her father had, like everyone else, ignored the activities at the landing.

Even the Vicar collected his tithe from the free traders.

Smuggling jobs paid well, as they had for the last 300 years. The latest ruckus with Napoleon in Europe had only increased the crossings at the channel. The coast of the county of Kent was an ideal landing site for the galleys. It was close to London, where the goods—brandy, wine, silks, and luxury items—disappeared quickly into its maze of shops only to reappear in the homes of the wealthy.

It was time to collect her treasure. Kate gathered up her skirts in one hand and climbed down the side of the coach. "I'll not be long Tom. The captain will see to my goods, and we will be on our way."

She made her way down the beach, careful to avoid the pack horses. A sudden gust of wind blew the hood from her head. The north sky lit up once more as a rumble of thunder announced the storm's eminent arrival. The loading crews worked with a renewed urgency, and shouts of, "Heeya, heeya," encouraged the horses with their heavy loads.

The boat was tied broadside to a wharf entrenched parallel to shore. A seafarer yelled orders to the crews, a lantern swinging from his left hand while he directed the men with his right. He wore a sash across his lower face and its ends flapped wildly in the winds, where it tangled with strands of long dark hair that had escaped a knotted tie at the back of his head. He was a svelte figure in tattered jacket and trousers, and not at all Kate's vision of what a ship captain should be.

"Keep them moving, Saul. We'll beat the rains. That is the last of the barrels. We will hit the silks and be soon done," he hollered.

"Aye, aye, Cap'n." The men began to heave the long crates to the wharf.

One crate hit the deck beside Kate and splintered wide. She opened her mouth to protest when a burly crewman moved forward, and without a glance in her direction stomped the lid back in place. No one seemed to notice her standing on the wharf, or if they did, they were not interested in dealing with her. The men kept working. Kate stood awkwardly at the edge of the dock, trying to keep out of the way of the crew.

When the last of the crates had been loaded, the captain whirled about and faced her although he had given no indication earlier that he was aware of her presence. "And what can I do for you, ma'am?"

The shock of his appearance stunned her. He was young, with the clear complexion of a dandy, not a seasoned shipman. His eyes belied his youth for they were black and hard.

"Well?"

Kate realized she had been staring rudely. "I have come for the pattern books."

The wind picked up and seemed to drown her words. A crash of thunder echoed through the cove.

The storm had arrived.

"Pattern books," she hollered and leaned in close enough to be heard. The wind was now carrying bits of hard rain which seemed to be slicing into her face from the side. "Ugh, it is the Ides of March... the pattern books from the supplier, Rheames."

"What's that? Repeat that."

She yelled into his face, "Pattern books. The books from the supplier Rheames. On this galley."

"No. No, the other. Repeat the other."

The rain was coming down hard now.

The captain shifted his body to break the wind and rain, "Repeat it!"

"The Ides of March? I was just—"

The captain spun around and jumped lithely to the galley deck.

"I've got your goods. And it is glad I am to be rid of them," he hollered into the wind. He disappeared below deck and returned almost immediately with a wide leather satchel which he lobbed up into her grasp. "Your books, and you will find your prize inside."

A half a dozen deck hands hustled up the wharf.

"Below deck, boys. We'll ride her out below. This squall will be gone in a flash, and we'll be getting our pints when she's past."

Kate opened the bag to see that it contained at least two scrapbook sized pattern books. These were the prized gown patterns for the Empress Josephine, Napoleon's outrageous and fashionable wife. As a dress designer, Kate was fascinated by what these books might contain, but more than that, these fashion plates would make a fortune for her salon, the LaFontaine.

She tucked the awkward leather bag beneath her cloak to shield it from the rain. When she looked up, she was alone. The galley rocked in the wind; the beach was deserted. A flash of lightning lit up the path to the lane and the single carriage waiting there. It was like the scenes of action and chaos from moments ago had never happened. The horses, the carts, and the men had all melted into the darkness. She stood in confusion.

"Well, not exactly the dashing sea captain of my dreams," she muttered.

Facing the wind and the driving rain, she trudged up the slippery path to her coach.

After squeezing the satchel beneath the cushions of the coach seats, she eyed the resulting lump dubiously. It would have to do. The next stop would be to pick up her lady's maid, Milly, and Old Tom's grandson Ned, who would act as a footman for this trip, from her friend Clarissa's residence. After all, she was Lady Kate, and no lady could travel alone.

Kate sighed. This smuggling business had not been all that it was cracked up to be. She had imagined an air of romantic chivalry about the whole business. Perhaps a wild ride through the night with the constables at their heels. But her night of excitement, such as it was, was over. She had her pattern books and that would have to be enough.

And now she owed Clarissa, an old friend from the neighborhood. She had relied on her for accommodation on this trip from London. The Meadows, her childhood home, was closed for the season. Clarissa had both welcomed Kate's visit and accepted her rather curious departure plans. She had giggled when Kate told her she must take a jaunt to the beach, when the coach had been packed, and all was ready for the trip home. Clarissa was sure a clandestine meeting meant a love affair and a man. Nothing could have pleased her more.

The coach came to a halt. Kate pushed aside the curtain. The rain had abated; it was now a drizzle.

The front door of Clarissa's townhouse opened. Milly

lumbered down the broad staircase and hoisted a picnic basket and a cumbersome bag into the coach, while young Ned climbed up to join Tom.

The flame of the carriage lamp fluttered as Milly pulled tight the door.

"Well, now. That was a short visit. Lord knows nothing good can come of romping around the countryside. Heading off at this time of night is nothing but trouble. Thank goodness Clarissa packed you a little snack for the road." She opened her basket and examined the contents. "Bit on the cheap side, that woman. It's going to be a long, wet journey from what I can see. And heaven knows what kind of mess we will be in before we're home. No comfort on this trip, no comfort at all. I can't see why we are leaving this time of night when the trip could be done in a day's journey tomorrow."

Kate winced as Milly plopped down on the seat and wriggled her bum into the cushions. "For all this is a grand coach it's not very comfy now, is it?"

"It will be fine, Milly. Think of it as an adventure." Kate had not considered staying another night with Clarissa for two reasons. First, she was eager to get home with the patterns, and second, the idea of spending another night sharing a room with Clarissa was too much for her to bear. Clarissa was a friend, but she was a friend that could only be handled in small doses.

"Cavorting around the countryside. No good can come of it, I always say. And here we are heading off into gad knows what. Can't say as I didn't warn you. No good can come of it, I always say." Milly wiggled her generous behind into the coach cushions again.

The coach swung right down the east road towards London five hours away. A short trip to Maidstone, where they would spend the night, and a morning's ride would see them home again.

Kate glanced again at the cushions on the opposite bench, now almost completely covered by the generous folds of Milly's skirts. She thought of the exchange at the wharf. The captain had been strangely focused on her few words about the weather. It was as though he had waited for her comments before handing over her prized patterns. It was odd. She shrugged off her reservations and smiled to herself. She had managed to get the pattern books. That was all that mattered.

Chapter Two

Ambrose pulled up his soaked collar and turned to Theo. "My guess is that the crew of the Bella will be up at the Old Bailey."

Riding double on Thorn, his favorite horse, was not exactly the mode of transportation he had envisioned for a meeting with the smugglers. But Theo's horse had gone lame and there had been little time to make other arrangements.

"We certainly have missed the rendezvous." Theo grimaced. "The galley is moored. My guess is you are right, and they have anchored for the night. No one is on board. They must have transferred the goods."

"The Bailey it is then. Let's hope they also have a horse to purchase." Ambrose was thankful for the cover of night. He was uncomfortably aware of the sight they must be, two grown men, drenched through from the rains, sandwiched on the back of Thorn.

The raucous sounds emanating from the pub poured into the street before Ambrose had even swung open the doors. The loading crew had obviously been paid and were eager to celebrate the night's work. Theo pushed through the heavy oak door and held it wide for Ambrose. Indeed, the place was packed.

Ambrose was certain that two strange gentlemen, even wet and bedraggled, were not a welcome sight at The Bailey, especially given the night's work. Silence descended like a thick wave over the crowd and all eyes turned to the door. Ambrose was uncomfortably reminded that just two weeks ago two constables tasked with an investigation of the activities of a similar coastal town, had been set upon by a mob of townsmen and forced to barricade in a shop, where they had eventually been rescued by the magistrate, who then charged them with disrupting a business.

"We are looking for Captain Ara, of the Bella." Ambrose announced in his firmest military voice. The words seemed to echo in the stillness.

An infinity of seconds passed. From across the room, a chair scraped loudly on the planked floor and a slim figure, with his head wrapped in a red sash, stood.

"I be he. How can I help you, sirs?"

A sea of suspicious eyes followed Ambrose and Theo as they weaved their way across the room. As they approached Ara's table, a half a dozen hulking seafarers stood, each with a hand resting lightly on the cutlasses at their sides. The biggest of the gang, a giant of a man, stepped forward, partially shielding the young captain with his body.

"I am here on a matter of business. I believe you have something for me," said Ambrose, attempting to ignore the big man as he addressed the captain.

The crowd seemed to exhale, and a spattering of conversation could again be heard. The captain raised his eyebrows but said nothing.

Ambrose continued, "I have been told the expression is, 'Beware the Ides of March.'"

"Ah." The captain looked at him with eyes as black as coal. "But your package has been delivered. She picked it up at the docks."

"What! Who picked it up at the docks? But I just gave the password! A she—"

The captain's massive protector stepped forward. The captain put a gloved hand on his arm. "The package has been delivered," he repeated. "The password was given. Now I have no further business with you."

With that the captain sat down, leaned back in his chair, and picked up a trencher of ale. His crew closed ranks around him.

Ambrose eyed the smugglers, each of them ready and waiting in deadly stillness. The big man with a face that looked as though he had had a career as a prize fighter leaned slightly forward.

"Ye heard the man," he rumbled at them.

One wrong move and they would both pay dearly and painfully. A glance around the room assured him there would be no help from that quarter.

Theo tugged at Ambrose's great coat. "We are done here," he said, shifting nervously, as he sent the captain a scowl. Ambrose could have sworn that the buccaneer smiled beneath his makeshift mask, the arrogant bastard.

"Ambrose, it is time to leave." Theo repeated, giving his coat another quick tug.

Ambrose reluctantly followed Theo to the door.

Standing across the cobbled street, once again listening to the shouts, and singing from the hotel, Ambrose's frustration burned.

"We must find this woman, Theo. The stakes are high.

That package as you know contains the code keys for all of Napoleon's dispatches past and present." Ambrose shook his head. "I cannot understand how someone else was able to give our password and collect the package. There is nothing more important to England than that book of codes. There has to be a way to find out who this woman was and where she is headed."

"Not much chance of that here. I cannot envision much assistance from anyone in this village. Maybe we can pick up her trail—"

He was interrupted by shouting and hollering emanating from across the street. The door to the pub burst open and a fellow born aloft by a bunch of angry patrons was tossed into the street. The man tumbled onto the cobblestones and the doors closed again, muffling the cacophony inside.

"And here is that chance, Theo. Get out the coins."

Both men hurried across the street and helped the man to his feet. He swayed drunkenly.

"T'ank you, sir, much 'preciated." He gestured with his arms as though to brush the mud from his coat but lost his balance.

Theo grabbed his shoulders and held him upright.

"You look like a man who knows a lot about his community. Just the kind of man I need to do business with." Ambrose jiggled a sack of coins and, after opening the tie, began to run the coins back and forth through his fingers while Theo held the old sot steady.

"There was a woman at the docks today—"

"Oh, aye. The Lady Kate." He licked his lips and watched the stream of coins. "Fine young woman she be too. We all loves her. Loves her. Sad day when she left for London. Sad. Not be knowing what she be doin' at the wharf today. Strange sight 'twas. Pulled up in a coach I 'eard."

He shook his head, eliciting another stumble, which kept Theo occupied with his task of holding the fellow upright.

"Wasn't there meself. 'Eard about it rightly." Ambrose pressed a coin into his hand. He brought it to his mouth and bit it. "Ah, t'ank you kindly."

"And where might I find the lady?" Ambrose slipped another coin into his hands.

"Dat's the thing. Kate is of The Meadows, but the big 'ouse's been boarded up by Count Serves since Yuletide. Knows it 'cause my girl worked the big 'ouse, she did. Right good girl, my Rosie. Gave her pa a little cozin money now and agin. Sad shame that ol' Serves be. Can't stomach a man 'oo closes the place jus' for the season. Shouldn't be allowed. How's a man to make a little gin money if'n even the girls can't make a little dough for the ol' da—"

Ambrose dropped another coin into his hand. "Where would the Lady Kate be living now then?"

"S'pect she be in London, with the ol' lady. Carstairs, I t'ink."

"And one more thing. Where might I find a horse?" Another coin made its way into the old man's hand.

There were two main routes to London. Less than an hour later Ambrose and Theo were mounted and at the crossroads. Though they had missed the rendezvous at the docks to attain the precious codes and somehow a Lady Katherine had given the password, absconding with them, they had at least some idea of who this woman was, and where she might be headed. But they could not trust the word of a drunk with such vital information. It was imperative they find her, confirm her identity, and retrieve the codebook.

Ambrose pulled out another coin. "The Lady Kate will take one of these roads to London. Either way she will likely stop for the night. It is late. Hopefully one of us will be able to intercept her. Heads, I take the East Road, through Maidstone. Tails, it is yours, Theo, and I am for the route through Canterbury." He flipped the coin. "I am heading east."

Chapter Three

Ned opened the carriage door and helped the ladies down. Kate adjusted the package beneath her cloak and juggled her reticule as she pulled open the door of The Running Boar. Milly waddled behind her with the carpet bag while Ned and Old Tom saw to the horses. A lone rider followed the coach to the stables. Kate glanced at the horse but thought nothing of it.

The inn was not the best of places, but it would do for a warm meal and a few hours' sleep. In front of her was a counter, behind which an open doorway led to what she assumed was the keeper's residence. She rang the bell which sat beside an open register and turned to look about her. Left were the stairs, presumably to the rooms above, while to the right was a common room, with a welcoming fire. Placed before it was a single stout table and heavy benches. The place was not the cleanest, but it was warm, and the scent of fresh baked bread permeated the room.

The proprietor stood before Kate.

"I am needing accommodations for myself and my

company." After much haggling it was agreed she and Milly would share a suite, while Tom and Ned would take a place above the stables. Each would receive a hot meal, Kate in the common room and her servants in the kitchens, provided the entire bill was paid up front.

In her room, Kate tucked the satchel under the mattress and freshened up for supper. The evening had not been the grand escapade she had hoped for. Sadly, the most exciting part had been riding up top on the coach. The smugglers had been a disappointment. They were a rag-tag crew who looked more like villagers on a job, than her romantic version of sea pirates. And now she was obliged to spend the night in accommodations which were questionable at best.

So much for adventure.

"Well, missy, I am thinking we best sleep this night atop the sheets." Milly crinkled up her nose in distaste as she ran a brush through Kate's hair. "I am not trusting the sheets have been laundered. Here we are, in a fine mess. I won't be getting a wink of sleep. And who knows what kind of ruffians are hanging about the place? I can't think that Lady Elizabeth allowed this trip. I told her nothing good could come of it. But no. Here we are. Not an ounce of comfort to be had this night. Warned her I did."

Kate glanced around the room. It was basic at best. There was a pair of single beds, a cot, a washstand, and a fireplace. A lantern sat on a rickety side table next to the bed. While she agreed the room was less than expected, at this point her only option was to make the best of the situation.

"Do not worry so, Milly. Everything will be fine, you will see. It will do for a few hours' sleep. We will be up and gone early."

Milly twisted Kate's hair into a quick braid, muttering her disapproval.

"Thank you, that will do, Milly. It has been a long day and I think a little food will do us both some good."

Kate was pleasantly surprised by the delicious chicken stew and fresh bread waiting for her by the fire. She had just begun to enjoy her tea when the sound of footsteps on the stairs announced the arrival of another guest to the common room.

What had been intended as a glance at the newcomer became a lengthy stare as Kate took in the sight of the man at the bottom of the stairs. His black hair was wet and had been freshly combed into a queue. He was tall. He wore a fine riding jacket, pulled tight over wide shoulders, opened to reveal a white shirt, without a cravat. His lean hips were fitted into snug trousers tucked into tall boots, the clothes of a gentleman.

He is a fine specimen of a man, Kate thought as she raised her eyes to his face. As their eyes met, Kate realized with shock that he had been returning her appraisal. He gave her a slow smile. She turned away, a blush staining her cheeks.

The proprietor arrived with a supper tray.

"I'll just put this here then." He set the tray down at the end of the sole table. "Will there be anything else?"

"A bottle of your finest Claret would do nicely. And two glasses."

The gentleman seemed to stand as though assessing his next move. Kate was thankful to have taken the time to freshen up. She wore her perfectly tailored travelling suit. It was, as was most of her wardrobe, stylish and elegant despite a long day's journey. While she knew she was not beautiful, her looks were nonetheless pleasing, with soft brown eyes, clear skin, and a thick coiled braid of chestnut hair.

He sauntered across the room until he stood directly across the table from Kate. "I realize we have not been introduced, but you must agree it would seem a bit awkward to be sharing a meal in silence at the same table. Allow me to rectify this situation. Lieutenant Ambrose St. Claire, British Royal Navy." He gave a deep bow, waving his left arm with a flourish. "If you allow me to eat with you, I promise to be the perfect gentleman."

Kate's heart skipped a beat as she gazed up into the face of the handsome stranger. His eyes were a dark blue green in a swarthy face. He had chiseled features, with full lips currently curled into a questioning smile. She realized her mouth was agape and quickly snapped her lips shut.

"Uh...I suppose we could. I—"

"Wonderful." Ambrose slid his plate of food across the table before she could change her mind. "And to which beautiful lady do I have the privilege of addressing?"

"Er...Lady Katherine Blythe."

Ambrose performed a second bow. "Honored to make your acquaintance, ma'am," he said as he slid deftly into place across from her. "I am the most fortunate of men to meet such a charming woman in such an unexpected location. And now that we have been properly introduced, we can dine together in this splendor."

He swung his arm about indicating the limited expanse of the common room. "And how was the meal?"

Kate looked at him with a half-smile. "The food is fine. Though the company may be rather fast, and I am not yet sure if it is to my liking."

He ignored her comment. "Ah. This is delicious, perfect

after a chilly night," he said as he attacked his stew, ignoring her trepidation.

Kate watched in amazement as he ate his food with relish. He looked up from his meal to smile at her with sparkling eyes. Her heart skipped a beat. He was obviously aware of the impropriety of the situation. He seemed to dare her to object. Who was this man and how had he managed to insert himself so comfortably into her presence?

"So, tell me, my fair lady, what brings a lovely woman out on a night such as this? Where might you be heading?"

"I am returning to London after a short visit with a friend." Kate gave him a smile. It would be a pleasure to watch him attempt to continue this conversation with his ease. After all she was a stranger to him as well.

"A friend. And here I thought you had just come from the sea. Your cheeks have the fresh windblown blush of an appearance at the shores."

Kate laughed. "My friend lives by the sea. Near Hernes, in fact. So, you are part right, lieutenant."

"Some wine, my dear." Without waiting for a response, he poured her a glass. "We must have a toast."

He handed her a glass and picked up his own. "Now what shall we toast to? Let me see. I have just heard the most wonderful laugh. Let us toast to hearing it many times this evening."

Despite her efforts at restraint, Kate found herself laughing again. "Oh, but you are good sir. Quid pro quo. How did you find your way to this inn tonight?"

"I purchased a horse. By the oddest coincidence, also in the village of Hernes. It seems we were destined to meet." He gave her the biggest grin.

"In Hernes? Never say so! But why not? The livery

stable of Sir Noyes is one of the best in the country, or so my father said. Tell me, did you by chance, purchase one of the new breeds, the thoroughbred?"

"Why yes. It was a bit of a surprise to find such a treasure there. And quite by accident. What do you know of the new breed?" Ambrose leaned forward with interest.

"My father and Sir Noyes had been working to breed the finest horses in the land. Their new stallion, Byerly Turk, was to be the father of a whole new line." Kate smiled. A memory of her father's enthusiasm flitted through her mind.

"Yes! The Turk. It is quite the horse. I do believe your father is right. This horse will be the beginning of the best of horses. I purchased an offspring, a mare, just tonight. Is your father still raising horses? It would be interesting to talk with him." Ambrose could not contain his excitement.

"Sadly, my father passed some time ago." Kate waved off his polite condolences. "But it is good to know Sir Noyes is still in the business. I would love to see this horse."

"Well, my dear, you are in luck. She is here in the stable. I would be honored to show her to you." Ambrose stood, walked around the table, and held out his arm. "And besides, it is past time I checked to see that she is properly bedded down."

Kate hesitated only a moment. It would be quite improper to be touring a stable with this man. She pushed her apprehensions aside. She had wanted a little adventure, and it was right here in front of her.

"Thank you. I would so enjoy that," she said as she took his arm.

The rain had stopped, but the night air was cool and damp. Kate shivered as they walked toward the stables.

"Ah, how rude of me. Of course, you must be cold. Let

me give you my coat." Before Kate could object, he had removed his jacket and was wrapping it about her. As he pulled the lapels close, he again flashed her his brilliant smile. His hands lingered on her shoulders.

Kate was mesmerized by that smile. The jacket had been warmed by his body heat and the musky scent of maleness overwhelmed her. There was the spicy quality of cologne blended with his unique manly odor. She gazed up at him and slowly raised both her arms to pull the coat closed herself. For the second time tonight, her cheeks flamed.

"Thank-you, that is most kind of you."

Ambrose grasped her arm securely as they walked across the inn yard. Something about his touch felt comfortable and secure. Once in the stables, he led her to the rear stall and his new mare.

Kate glanced up at his face. He seemed to have lost his military countenance; his eyes sparkled with anticipation in his eagerness to show her his newest prize.

"Her name is Starling. When you see her forehead, you will see the name suits her well."

The mare leaned forward from her stall and gave a soft whinny of welcome.

Ambrose stroked her neck. "Ah, my beauty. I see you have settled in well."

Kate gave a gasp. "She is lovely my lord."

The horse was a chestnut mare, with white boots and an elongated star on its forehead. Kate stroked her soft nose.

"She is part of my dream. I want to raise horses someday. I intend to have a horse ranch with the finest breeds. So far, I have four of the best." Ambrose smiled. "Actually, as of today I have five. This latest horse may be my greatest investment. For now, all of them are housed in my brother,

21

the Earl of Suffex's stables. But very soon I hope to buy a piece of land and breed my beauties on my own estate."

Ambrose reached for the brush on the wall next to the stall and began stroking Starling's front shoulder.

"It is a fine dream." Kate sighed. And a familiar dream. It had been her father's greatest wish to bring the new thoroughbred horse to the attention of all of England. "At one time I too hoped to raise horses, but alas, I have had to leave that dream behind. Now I seldom even have a chance to ride."

Kate smiled wistfully, remembering rides across the fields at The Meadows.

"May I ask why?"

"I guess it was more my father's dream and now that he is no longer with us—" Kate again waved away Ambrose's sounds of condolence and continued to pet the downy nose. The horse nudged her in appreciation. "I have new dreams now and I must work towards those."

Ambrose paused, suddenly alert. "Ah, and what might those be?"

Kate gave a little laugh. "Now that is a secret. And a woman must keep her secrets. Don't you agree?"

"A lady with secrets. What could be more enticing?" Ambrose flashed another smile. "Sometimes a secret is more delicious if shared."

Kate laughed again. "You are persistent. No, I think this secret is best kept." Kate thought of the outrage he would express if he knew she was engaged in trade. For a woman of her class an occupation would be scandalous. Upper class persons did not participate in business.

"There must be a way to uncover that particular secret." Ambrose smiled as though sure he would enjoy the efforts.

He patted Starling's shoulder. "We will give her a treat."

He reached for a pail of oats and poured a little into a trough in the stall.

"There you go my beauty," he said as he set down the pail.

Ambrose stepped back from the pen and turned to face Kate who just at that moment took a step towards Starling. They bumped. Ambrose put his arms about her to steady her. The scene seemed to freeze in time. Kate gazed, hypnotized, into his blue green eyes; eyes which stood out sharply against his swarthy complexion and coal black hair. His arms were warm and inviting. His scent appealing. Looking at his lips, and finding them lush and enticing, she leaned forward, wanting a taste of him. His lips had just grazed the softness of hers when she stepped back quickly.

"I..." Kate reached up and covered her mouth with her hand. "I must go."

In one brisk movement, she shrugged off the jacket and draped it over the rail.

"Thank you, thank you for this," she said, indicating the horse. She turned and hurried from the stables, back to the safety of the inn.

Ambrose lay back on the bed. He had decided to catch an hour or two of sleep before heading into the stables to search her coach. By that time, he could be sure everyone would be soundly asleep. He was glad for a few hours rest. It had been a full day; wet, uncomfortable, and exhausting. If he could not find the codebook tonight, tomorrow he would offer to escort her to London. But hopefully his search would produce the codes.

He believed he had made progress on the Katherine

front. She was an enigma. She had projected an air of inno-cence, yet if she was a courier, or worse a French spy, she must be a particularly good one. He was impressed at her portrayal of wide-eyed innocence. She had played her part rather well. Remembering her laugh, he smiled—it was a clear and joyful sound, heartfelt and without inhibition.

Tomorrow promised to be an interesting and enlight-ening day. Oddly, he had enjoyed his time with her, had even confided to her his dreams, something he was not wont to do. He smiled to himself. Perhaps he should have been one of Admiral Hews' spies after all, instead of a mere code breaker. He certainly had a talent for it.

He crawled beneath the covers and closed his eyes. A vision of soft wet lips, and deep brown eyes lulled him to sleep.

———————

Kate pulled her cloak over her as she lay back on the bed. She looked across the room at Milly who had also chosen not to risk the comfort of sleeping beneath the covers. When she had returned to her room it had been a relief to find Milly snoring softly. Kate had not wanted to give expla-nations. She was sure her cheeks still burned.

It had been a wondrous evening. The lieutenant was the stuff of dreams. And though she may not have behaved like a proper young lady it had all been worth it. At any rate, she was not young. At twenty-four, she was just a few short weeks away from being officially on the shelf. She smiled. She would grab what adventure she could. It was unlikely she would ever be in contact with him again.

As Kate snuggled down beneath her cloak, she realized the scent of him had lingered on her clothes. She pulled her short suit jacket up over her mouth and nose to inhale deeply. She sighed, decided to leave the lantern burning, and rolled over to try to go to sleep, a smile on her lips. It had been a successful trip.

Kate grinned with satisfaction. Never once had she thought she be there on the beach, a part of the age-old smuggling tradition. She had lived her early life on their family estate, The Meadows, enjoying the quiet life of the country gentry. Her father, the Baron of Ellesworth, was a widower who had indulged his only child. No expense had been spared in her education, clothing, or well-being. Kate had not known the responsibilities of finance, the worries of money—particularly the lack of it. As for the smuggling, like everyone, she was aware of it. Though her wharf at The Meadows was often in use for clandestine activities, it had simply not been an issue which affected her sheltered life.

But everything had changed six years ago, when Kate was eighteen. Her father had died in a fall from his horse. Kate had been left in the joint guardianship of her father's brother Edmund, the Count of Serves, and her mother's sister, Lady Elizabeth Carstairs. Until Kate married, or reached the age of twenty-five, Uncle Edmund was to handle the estate, arranging for allowances and costs, while Aunt Lizzy was responsible for her actual care. The problems had begun after the funeral when Uncle Edmund announced that the estate was near bankruptcy and no funds could be spared until he had set affairs to right.

And that was when Kate had learned about, 'The Secret.' It seemed Aunt Lizzy had done what no gentleman or lady of the ton could do without risking total ostracism and complete exclusion from the social world. She had gone into trade.

LaFontane, a dress salon, had covertly financed Lady Carstairs' household for years. It was exclusive, expensive, and most important of all, it was French. The shop had been responsible for helping to bring to England the revolution in clothing which had recently swept the continent.

Kate was proud to be a part of it. She had a talent for drawing fashion. She had, with her aunt's encouragement, created fashion plates and pattern books. Her designs were worn by the elite of London for they were exhibited not only by the LaFontane, but by most of the town's exclusive shops. And tonight, Kate had achieved a coupe which would keep her creations on the lips and bodies of every woman of London. She had acquired the dress patterns of the Empress Josephine herself! Just thinking of the pattern books, tucked carefully under the mattress, made her smile. It would be the most exciting innovation in fashion of her generation.

Meeting an interesting man and enjoying his company tonight had been an unexpected boon. Overall, it had been an exciting evening. Kate took another deep breath, hoping to catch his scent once more as she faded off to sleep.

"Oh Lord! Kate! Turn up the lantern. Oh, my lord!" Milly jumped out of bed and began to hop around the room.

"What is it? What has happened, Milly? For heaven's sake, calm down. You will wake up the entire inn." Kate rubbed her eyes and looked at Milly with annoyance. She turned the lantern to its highest lighting. "What in heaven's name are you doing?"

"Oh, my lord! The place is crawling with bedbugs!" Milly pointed an accusing finger above Kate's head at the headboard. "Look!"

Kate looked behind her. All along the railing the bugs

marched two by two, a steady stream of vermin, moving precisely like a platoon of French soldiers heading off to battle. Kate scrambled out of bed with a shriek.

"Oh! My heavens! What in the world?" She joined Milly in the middle of the room, frantically examining and brushing her arms and legs. "I have never seen so many bugs! Enough of this. We are out of here, Milly. We are leaving this minute. Down you go to wake up Tom and Ned. Have them harness the coach. Whatever rest they have had will have to be sufficient. I will pack up here and meet you in the coach."

Milly stomped to the door to retrieve her cloak. Her face was flushed with anger.

"And what did I say? Gallivanting about the country-side. No good could come of it. Here we are then. What a mess. And didn't I say just that. Oh, my lord, my lord. It is no comfort at all..." Milly continued to mutter as she straightened her clothes and headed for the door.

In less than ten minutes, they were in the coach and ready to go. Old Tom rubbed the sleep from his eyes and slapped the reins. "Gee up, girls, hey yah."

They were off to London.

Kate looked back at the inn, now shrouded in darkness and sighed. How unfortunate she would never see her dashing lieutenant again. She shifted her satchel, with its precious contents onto the seat beside her, leaned back and tried to catch some sleep. The man had given her one night of excitement and that would have to suffice. The chances of her meeting him again were slim indeed.

Chapter Four

It had been a difficult journey into London and the worst was yet to come. Ambrose walked up the steps to the offices of Admiral Hews. The last two days had been a complete disaster. First Theo's horse had gone lame, then they had been caught in a blistering storm, missing the rendezvous at the docks and losing the book of codes to a woman. He had found her, only to have her slip away in the dead of night. He had been duped. And worst of all he had been attacked by bedbugs, a situation he blamed entirely on the Lady Katherine. After all, anyone who chooses an inn named, The Running Boar, should expect the worst.

When he arrived at the Home Office, he was met at the admiral's door by Sergeant Ames. He nodded a greeting. The sergeant gave him an arrogant smirk before opening the door to the admiral's office. He let Ambrose in, then slipped inside and stood at the door.

"Come in, lieutenant." Admiral Hews motioned him to a chair. "From what Theo has had to tell me the mission was not entirely a success."

"Yes. We had a few difficulties." Ambrose glanced at Theo who flashed him a grin. "But all is not lost. I was able to track down the codebook to a Lady Katherine Blythe who resides here in town with her aunt the Lady Carstairs."

"Well done." The admiral smiled. He had the look of a portly country gentleman, with bushy eyebrows and extended sideburns on a face which looked almost jovial. Yet as head of Homeland Security he was a force: astute, wily, and unflappable. "I know the Lady Carstairs. Hmm, I believe I also know her address."

He rubbed his hand across his chin. "Interesting, her niece you say. Well, we will retrieve the codes without delay. I will put Boucher on the task for tonight. He is the absolute best. He will be able to break into the Carstairs house and hopefully retrieve the notebook immediately. I am afraid there can be no delay. We dare not risk the codes returned to France."

The admiral rose from his desk and walked to his window. For a minute, he seemed captivated by the view.

"It would be intriguing to discover the connections in this enterprise. In fact, I do believe the war office must know." He returned to his desk and sat down with a sigh. He addressed Ambrose. "Can you put together a false set of codes, say in twenty-four hours or less?"

"I suppose I could. I certainly have a storehouse of discarded attempts."

"Good. Then that is what we will do. Make up a book of codes. Tonight, Boucher will enter the Carstairs' house and bring you the actual notebook. Copy it. Match it. Replace the pages. Whatever it takes to make your copy look like the original. Then we will find a way to slip it back in place. Perhaps if the enterprise runs smoothly, it will not be noticed that the notebook was ever exchanged."

The admiral rose again and began to pace the room. "I'll put a few men on surveillance to watch her every move. At some point one of two things will happen. Either she will approach us with a proposition, or she'll meet her French contacts. This could be an opportunity to ferret out a few of our enemies."

Theo added, "As Lord Pembroke, and a man with a certain reputation with women, I am sure I could get an introduction, escort her about, court her, discover her contacts—"

"No!"

Both men looked at Ambrose with surprise.

"No," he said more softly, "I have been introduced to the lady. I believe I could easily infiltrate her life. Let me do the honors."

Ambrose held his breath while the admiral debated his proposal. He was not sure why the idea of Theo courting Katherine disturbed him, but it did. If anyone were going to pursue the lovely Katherine it would be him. Besides, he owed her. Quid pro quo.

Ten minutes later Ambrose flagged down a hack. "Shall we share a cab, Theo?"

"Excellent idea. You can drop me at my club." Theo looked at him curiously as he settled into the coach seat. "Quite unlike you to volunteer as a suitor. I would not have thought it."

He gave Ambrose a grin. "Does not seem to be your usual line of work at all. I believe I will enjoy watching your progress."

"I do what I can in the service of my country." Ambrose straightened his shoulders, giving his best impression of the dutiful soldier.

Theo gave a bark of laughter. "Yes, quite. She must

have made an impression on you. I am eager to meet this woman. Let me know if you need my assistance."

"I believe I have it well in hand." Ambrose replied. Theo had been his best friend since their school room days. He knew well his talent with the fairer sex. Ambrose did not want him anywhere near Katherine. Not this time and not with this woman.

Theo looked at him with a more serious expression. "Ambrose, there is no one I would prefer, over you, to be at my back should I ever need assistance. You are loyal to a fault. Furthermore, you are the best swordsman I have ever encountered, and no slouch with your fists either. But as a lover you are a babe in the woods. You are an innocent in these matters. I do believe you have leapt into the fire in this instance. I am serious when I say I can be of assistance. Retreat man and leave this to me."

Ambrose pressed his lips together stubbornly. He squared his shoulders, looking very much like the commander of men he had been. He replied, "She is my concern. As I said, I have the situation well in hand." Ambrose thought of the auburn beauty he had met at the inn. He intended to see her again. And this time he would be sure she did not escape his clutches.

Chapter Five

Milly arranged the tea tray on the settee. "Hoodlums everywhere. Imagine. Housebreakers here at Grovner Square. Our very home invaded. I never thought I would see the day. It was lucky Old Tom was able to make them skedaddle. What a mess. What this world is coming to I don't know. It is getting worse every day. I just don't know."

She clucked and shook her head in despair.

"Thank you, Milly. I will have my tea here at the desk." Kate slid her pattern books to the side and set the satchel on top.

"That will be all, Milly." Lady Carstairs sipped her tea, leaned back in her chair, and sighed.

"Can't say as I haven't warned you. Even here in Mayfair." Milly frowned sadly. "Ruffians everywhere. Hoodlums. I cannot believe our home was the target of scoundrels, housebreakers! What is this world coming to I ask you?" Milly continued her tirade as she left the library.

"It was a stroke of luck that Tom was able to scare off the intruder before he absconded with my patterns." Kate glanced at the satchel. She was convinced the intruder must have been after her pattern books. It was too much of a coincidence that a break-in had occurred the first night she had them in her home. Yet it seemed the housebreaker had missed her great prize, or perhaps he had not had the time to do a thorough search, as Milly claimed. Either way she was much relieved to see the patterns safely tucked in the satchel on her desk.

"Yes. Fortunate indeed. Though I think it more plausible to assume he was looking for other valuables. Nothing appears to be missing and there was no harm done." Lady Carstairs changed the subject. "By the way, have you thought more about the notebook you found, and what it might be? "

Kate smiled. Tucked between the pages of one of the pattern books she had found a small notebook. She assumed someone in the French court must have hidden it there and then forgotten it. The little journal contained several pages of encoded lettering. After scrutinizing it carefully she had been unable to discern the complicated messaging. She had finally given up her attempts and placed it back in her satchel. Someday, when she had more time, she would attack it again.

"Given the French court, it is probably a collection of love letters, misplaced amongst my patterns. It is encoded so we will never know." Kate laughed. "With the reputation of the Empress Josephine, they could be very steamy. It is too bad. It would have made an interesting read."

Lady Carstairs chuckled. "Katherine, I am quite scandalized."

Old Tom stood at the door. "A gentleman to see you, ma'am. Gave me his card."

Lady Carstairs rose and examined the card, a puzzled

expression on her face. "Do we know a Lord Ambrose St. Claire, Kate?"

Kate felt her cheeks flush. "I believe I may have been introduced to him, uh, this last trip."

"Hmm, interesting." Lady Carstairs tilted her head to the side and examined Kate's blushing face. "Very interesting indeed. Send him in, Tom."

Kate's heart skipped a beat at the sight of Ambrose entering her domain. He cut a fine figure in the blue dress jacket of the Royal Navy. She had forgotten how tall he was; he filled the room with his presence. This time his jacket was conservatively buttoned, with a simple white cravat at his neck.

Kate squashed the tingles of anticipation. Why and how he had found his way to her residence she did not know, but she mustn't read too much into it.

Lady Carstairs swept across the room to greet him. "Lord St. Claire, do come in. I am Lady Elizabeth Carstairs, and this is my lovely niece Katherine Blythe, who I assume you have met."

"An honor to meet you, ma'am." Ambrose took her extended hand and raised it to his lips in an elegant gesture. "And Miss Blythe, it is a pleasure to see you again."

He executed a perfect bow.

Over his bowed head, Lady Carstairs shot Kate a gleeful look. "St. Claire, that sounds familiar. Have you relatives here in town?"

"My brother, the Earl of Suffex, is in residence at the moment." Ambrose scanned the room.

The library doubled as a parlor. It contained a settee and chairs for receiving. Further into the room, two desks were placed symmetrically at each side of a tall window, flanked on either side by bookshelves.

Katherine stood behind the desk on the right. The shock of seeing her lieutenant standing in the parlor had not quite worn off. Looking down to hide her reddened cheeks, she flipped the flap on the leather satchel on the desk nervously. She could feel Ambrose's eyes on her. She took a deep breath, resolving to regain her composure and enjoy this interlude; how ever it had come about.

Lady Carstairs said, "Ah, the Earl, of course." She gave Kate a triumphant smile, which Kate returned with a roll of her eyes. "But you must join us for tea. I will just slip out and ask Milly to lay another place. Katherine, please join us at the settee."

Katherine picked up her teacup and made to move into the sitting area. Ambrose rushed across the room.

"Allow me," he said grasping the cup.

"It is quite alright."

Ambrose gave the teacup a quick tug and let it slip from his fingers. It hit the desk; it didn't break, but a stream of tea spilled towards her papers.

"How clumsy of me," he said as he pulled out his handkerchief to stop the flow. "Perhaps you could get a cloth. I believe I can hold this off before it reaches your papers."

"Oh, dear. Yes, yes of course." Kate slid her books to the very edge of her desk and hurried from the room, leaving Ambrose alone at her desk.

Milly hustled into the room, followed by the ladies. "Here now, where is this mess?"

Ambrose was bent over Kate's desk, one hand holding his handkerchief against the tea, the other on Kate's satchel. He quickly straightened as they entered the room.

Millie shot Ambrose an accusatory look as she marched to the desk, cloth in hand. "Nothing worse for mahogany than the damp I always say." She punctuated each word with a swipe at the spill. "A person needs to take more care—"

"Milly," Lady Carstairs said firmly, "that will be all." Her look warned that no further comment was to be made. Milly satisfied herself with a dark scowl in Ambrose's direction as she left the room.

"Now then, have a chair, and let us get more acquainted." Lady Carstairs smiled graciously at Ambrose, handing him his teacup. "Sugar?"

"Thank you, no, this will do."

"I believe I know your mother, Violet. We came out in the same season." Lady Carstairs smiled as she proffered Ambrose a tray of delicate biscuits with jam. Ambrose took two and popped one into his mouth whole. "How does she fare?"

Ambrose swallowed before answering. "Rather well. She has stayed at the country house these last few years I believe. Now that I am home, I intend to spend more time with her."

"Home? Have you been away?"

"I have just returned from my third tour of duty in the Caribbean with the Royal Navy. I am afraid it has been more than a decade since I have spent any time in England."

Lady Carstairs held out the tray of biscuits. "Your dedication to country is to be commended. And do you intend to enlist for a fourth?"

Ambrose again took two biscuits. "I've decided to remain at home. I recently transferred to an office position here in town, though how long I will retain my commission is unsure. I have other pursuits in mind." He turned towards Kate with a smile.

Lady Carstairs too turned towards Kate; her expression

could only be described as that of a cat that ate the canary. Ambrose was fitting her requirements in a suitor for Kate quite nicely.

Kate's gaze travelled from one to the other. It was clear she was expected to contribute to the conversation. "I, ah... I am sure you will much appreciate a return to polite society, my Lord. There are many entertainments this season."

She was still a little overwhelmed by his presence. It was disconcerting to know he was as handsome as her daydreams had portrayed him.

His eyes sparkled as he smiled in her direction. "And that is precisely why I am here this afternoon. As you know, riding is one of my favorite entertainments. I find it is much more enjoyable with a companion. I wonder if I might interest you in a morning ride in the park. If we are early enough, it may also be quiet enough for a gallop."

Lady Carstairs was quick to interject. "What a wonderful idea. Katherine is an accomplished equestrian. Sadly, we do not keep our own stables here in town..."

She made a helpless gesture with her hands and looked at Ambrose hopefully.

"Not a problem. I have the perfect chestnut mare. I will mount up a groom as well. Would ten o'clock be too early?" Ambrose helped himself to another couple of biscuits.

Lady Carstairs clapped her hands together. "Ten o'clock will be splendid, an excellent time for a morning ride! Do you agree, Katherine?" She smiled at Kate expectantly.

"As it appears to have been already decided, I suppose it will suit."

Ambrose rose. "Thank you, ladies, for a most enjoyable afternoon tea." He gave a short bow. "Until tomorrow then. I shall look forward to it."

Both ladies stood, inclining their heads in the appropriate half curtsy. "It was our pleasure, my lord. Katherine will see you to the door."

Katherine took his arm as they entered the foyer. "It seems I will have a ride on the beautiful Starling after all. Thank you, sir. I too shall look forward to tomorrow." She smiled mischievously. "I believe I have something for you as well, if you could wait just a moment."

She left him at the door and returned a moment later to hand him a jar.

Ambrose held up the jar and gave the mysterious green contents a confused look. "I, ah, thank you of course. What is it?"

Kate gifted him with her widest smile. "It is a balm. It works wonders on bug bites and the like."

Ambrose emitted a loud guffaw. "You minx!" He laughed again. "I will take it. It will definitely come in handy."

He raised his jar of ointment in a toast and was gone.

When Katherine returned to the library, Lady Carstairs met her, barely able to contain her excitement. "A suitor, Katherine! How marvelous. I had no idea your trip to Hernes was so eventful. You should have told me."

Kate returned to her place at the settee. "Please do not make too much of this, Aunty. You know my history with suitors. I am sure this one will be the same. He will fade away like all the rest." Kate picked up the last biscuit, leaned back in her chair, and munched thoughtfully. "This time I think I will handle it differently. I am going to enjoy every moment, take what I can get as it were."

"Oh, Katey, I understand it has been a struggle since the Damien scandal, but I am sure this time will be different." Lady Carstairs walked around the settee to sit beside Kate.

"No. No, it will not. Damien called off our engagement all those years ago. It was a scandal, true. But the incident was years ago and still I cannot seem to hold a suitor for more than a few weeks. I am not sure what it is... but if I indeed have a suitor, I will enjoy every minute. After all, I am almost twenty-five and this may be my last."

"There is always your cousin Jeremy, my dear. He has been endlessly persistent. Perhaps you should consider him?"

"Half cousin. Lord Serves and father were half-brothers, and no, that I will not do." Kate rose, patted her aunt on the shoulder, and returned to her desk. "Do not fret, Aunty. I have my work which has kept me happy and occupied. Work which I must get back to. I am hoping to copy these patterns and have them in the salon this week."

"Yes, our shipment of silks will also be in this week. With your exciting new patterns, we stand to make a tidy sum this season."

Kate reached for her satchel. How strange, she thought as she glanced down. The little notebook was lying on top of the flap. She could have sworn she had tucked it into the case. She shrugged and slid it back in place.

Chapter Six

Kate was the opposite of everything Ambrose had imagined she would be. She exuded a freshness and honesty he not expected. If he had hoped for his image of the spy—a sultry seductress, whose conversations were rife with double entendre—he was to be disappointed. Instead, like his meeting with her at the inn, she confused him with her exuberance and obvious enjoyment of his company.

He looked at her admiringly. The brisk spring air had made her cheeks glow beneath a pert riding hat, from which a few curls escaped. Her riding gear fit her snuggly, and like each time he had seen her, she emitted a sense of style. She was made to ride Starling.

"Your hair exactly matches the coat of my mare."

Kate laughed. "Thank you, I think." Her eyes sparkled mischievously. "And that, I believe, is the first time I have been compared favorably to a horse. You, sir, cut a fine figure yourself in your navy uniform atop your mighty stallion. He is a beauty. An Arabian, is he not?"

Ambrose patted his horse's neck. "Yes, I call him Thorn.

He was my first investment in my horse farm, and a favorite. I purchased him after my second tour of duty."

They walked the horses in silence until they rounded the curve and now faced the full expanse of the park.

Kate looked at him curiously. "What is it like in the West Indies? Yesterday you said you had spent a decade there?"

"Hmmm." Ambrose considered the question. He smiled. "The sky is very blue, the water aquamarine, the forests intensely green and thick, and for the most part the sun is shining. I remember once thinking that while initially one is overwhelmed by its beauty, it is hard not to long for a dreary gray day in foggy London."

He thought about the battles he had fought and the hardships he had endured. Perhaps it was time to lighten the mood. "You promised me a gallop. I propose a race to the duck pond."

She grinned. "Only if the victor can choose her prize."

"You are on!"

Without waiting, Kate spurred Starling forward. She soon found her advantage challenged as Thorn lunged towards her. Starling was no match for the stallion's superior stride, and Thorn was in no mood to allow the new horse to dominate. As they rounded the curve, Thorn pulled into the lead. By the time they reached the duck pond, he was the undisputed winner.

Ambrose swung from the saddle and, laughing, turned to assist Kate. He guided her carefully to the ground, his hands lingering on her waist. "And now my prize. I claim a kiss."

He had planned to kiss her lightly but when he tasted her, she was agonizingly sweet. He held his lips close to hers and breathed her heady scent. His lips brushed hers tentatively at first. She smelt of crisp lemons, fresh air, and a soft feminine essence which was uniquely her own. He felt his body respond to her nearness. Their eyes met briefly, then in unison, slowly lowered to their lips. He deepened the kiss.

Her hands found his shoulders as he pulled her close. Ambrose let his hands slide to her hips. He pulled her tight against his body, allowing her to feel his desire for her. Her body trembled. When she gasped, his tongue found her mouth. Ambrose was suddenly lost to his desire for her. Their teeth clashed as they came together with a wild passion.

Starling took a quick step to the side and did a welcoming whinny as the groom rounded the corner at a brisk trot. Ambrose had forgotten him. He stepped back quickly, feeling a spasm of instant regret. He had lost control, manhandling her in the most ungentlemanly way. Furthermore, he was supposed to be close to her to find her contacts, not seduce her.

Realizing his arms remained on her hips, he pulled them back quickly. "I believe it may be best if we remount."

He avoided her eyes as he assisted her back onto her side saddle.

"Yes," Kate replied. She looked flustered and slightly flushed. She stole a glance at him.

Ambrose cursed himself for losing control. He had completely forgotten his task in his enjoyment of her company. Perhaps Theo was right. He did not seem to be able to concentrate on anything but her when he was in her company. He loved her laughter. And more than that, holding her and kissing her had been a revelation. She belonged in his arms.

The playful mood of the morning had dissipated, leaving an awkward silence between them. They circled the park and approached the gates. The ride would soon be over. It was time to return to his assignment,

Ambrose looked straight ahead. "You have not told me much about yourself or your pursuits here in town."

His stoic expression belied his interest in polite conversation. Kate appeared to be at a loss.

"There is not much to tell. I live a quiet life with my aunt," she replied in a soft voice.

He searched his mind for something to add, a way to alleviate the tension which had grown between them but could find nothing. They reached the steps of her town house. Ambrose dismounted and was quick to assist her to the ground. This time his touch was business-like and efficient.

"I must apologize for my behavior in the park. It was most ungentlemanly of me. Please forgive me."

Kate let out a sigh. Taking his hands in both of hers she said, "I am not the least offended. You forget, sir, I am not a chit fresh out of the schoolroom. I am almost five and twenty, a mature woman. I am not without some experience in these matters."

She flashed him her brilliant smile and squeezed his hands reassuringly.

Ambrose looked at her skeptically. He gently pulled his hands from hers. "Though that may be true, it is no excuse for dishonorable behavior on my part. Again, I must apologize. If you consent to a ride with me tomorrow, I promise to make amends by being the perfect gentleman."

"I would love nothing better than a second chance to ride the beautiful Starling."

Ambrose lifted her hand to his lips. "Until tomorrow."

He decided a visit to the admiral was in order. Perhaps he could shed some light on the situation. His connection with Lady Katherine was troubling. She was not what he had suspected. In truth she was quite the opposite. She was open to the point of bluntness.

Ambrose groaned aloud as he remembered her heartfelt assurances that he had not offended her. The whole situation was out of hand.

He wanted her. He recalled the taste of her, the feel of her body pressed against him. She was lovely. But more than that, with her he was at ease, able to enjoy her company completely. He grimaced. Perhaps too at ease; kissing her this morning had been a huge mistake. It was a mistake he would not repeat.

It was time to discover more about his mysterious Lady Katherine. He knocked at the admiral's door. Sargent Ames opened it. He looked Ambrose up and down as though assessing the risk of allowing him into the room. Ambrose nodded a greeting. As always, Ames did not acknowledge his gesture. He stepped to the side, closed the door behind them, and stood like a sentinel next to it. There was something disturbing about Ames. He was always formal. Ambrose found himself forever extending courtesies which the man pointedly ignored. He shook off his distaste and turned to the admiral who sat behind his desk as usual.

"Come in. Come in, lieutenant. I am glad you stopped in today. We have much to discuss." The admiral opened his top drawer and laid a file open on his desk. "First of all, let me commend you on a job well done with the timely switch of the codebook. As you know this information will be essential in the months, perhaps even the years to come."

Ambrose smiled at the admiral's acknowledgement of his quick work in returning the notebook to Lady Katherine. He was much pleased with how he had taken the opportunity to spill her tea, giving himself a few seconds to slip the faked codes into her bag. He was proud of how deftly he had managed it. Kate had not suspected a thing.

Hews continued, "With luck no one will have noticed the little notebook ever disappeared. Yes, I must say you did an outstanding job lieutenant." The admiral smiled at him before continuing. "Now then, my lads have been terribly busy on this case. Time is a factor here. If we were able to track the codes to Miss Blythe, I am sure our enemies would have as well. Her appearance at the docks was memorable. After all, the free trade business does not see a lot of females." He shifted several papers in his file. "First, I want to share our financial information. Interesting indeed."

He cleared his throat. "We knew the Lady Katherine was an heiress. Her late father, a Baron, left her an estate called The Meadows in Kent, near Hernes. However, there appears to be little or no money entering the household from that quarter. That is odd and warrants closer examination.

"But what is more interesting is the affairs of Lady Carstairs. She receives a small stipend from her late husband, but the majority of her funds come from her interests in the fashion market. She is the owner of a shop called the LaFontane. She also has an interest in several other shops in town. Lady Katherine spends a great deal of time at the LaFontane. It can be assumed that she plays a role in its operation."

The admiral chuckled. "I must say Lady Carstairs has not changed. As I said, I am acquainted with the woman. She was always an audacious female. Her descent into trade under the very noses of polite society is a bold move indeed."

He let out a long sigh and leaned back in his chair. "We have been unable to find a trace of seditious behavior on the part of either woman. Other than their business enterprise, there appears to be no suspicious connections now or in the past. The two ladies live quietly. They seldom are out in society." Admiral Hews lowered his thick brows and gazed expectantly at Ambrose. "And you sir. What have you to add?"

Ambrose shifted uncomfortably in his chair. "I too have seen nothing that could cause alarm. In fact, if anything, I find myself questioning the likelihood of these ladies being involved at all. As I get to know them, the possibility seems outrageous. Yet the password was given, the codes were collected."

The admiral tapped his fingers on the desk. "Hmmm. As of today, there has been no move to transfer the booklet. My agents have kept a close watch on the home. Nothing." He leaned back and rested his hands on his protruding belly. "But very soon the vultures will have gotten word of the book. It is certainly a commodity England would have paid dearly for. If they believe the Lady Katherine has the codes, they will make a move."

The admiral closed the file. "We will wait. If possible, stay close to the household. Something may turn up in the next few days."

Sergeant Ames opened the door, indicating his dismissal.

Ambrose left the offices of Homeland Security feeling more confused than he had upon his arrival. Katherine was an unlikely traitor, yet she had taken the codebook from the smugglers. She was open and straight forward, yet she was secretly involved in trade. He would keep close to her, but not too close.

Chapter Seven

Kate completed a sketch of the Empress Josephine's patterns and reached for her colors. She hoped to finish this book today. It was time to announce the arrival of innovative designs at the LaFontane. The news of these treasures would travel quickly through the ton.

She smiled with satisfaction. By the end of the week, the LaFontane would be inundated with orders for the fabulous fashions. Only when the shop had its capacity in orders would Kate allow the other shops in town a chance at the designs. And then, there would be a steep price to be paid.

It had been the busiest of weeks. She had spent many hours at her desk completing the copies, interrupted only by the persistent presence of Lord St. Claire. He had arrived each day, sometimes for the morning ride and sometimes for afternoon tea.

Kate allowed herself to daydream for a few minutes about her Ambrose. His aquamarine eyes were enough to send a shiver down her spine. Since the kiss in the park, he had been the perfect gentleman. It was disappointing. She longed to feel his arms around her again.

She glanced at the clock. There was still plenty of time to complete the page before she would need to change for her ride with Ambrose. The thought of it made her stomach twist in nervous anticipation. She pushed these intrusive thoughts aside and refocused on her work.

A commotion erupted in the hall.

"What in heaven's name?" Kate rose from her desk to investigate the disruption.

From the doorway of her library, Kate watched in dismay as Ned and Old Tom loaded cases into the foyer. Lady Carstairs stood amidst the chaos speaking to Miss Clarissa. Kate had promised Clarissa an invitation to town in exchange for staying with her while securing the patterns. Clarissa had lost no time in collecting her favor.

Kate grimaced. That she would now have to tolerate her old friend for some time was apparent by the number of cases littering the room. This was a busy time for her. There would also be the expectation they would take in the social scene in town.

Lady Carstairs looked at Kate over the shoulders of Clarissa and raised her brows. Kate made a helpless gesture with her hands.

"Katherine, it seems we have a house guest."

Clarissa turned towards Kate as she approached. "Oh, Katey, it is so exciting to be here in town at last." She took Kate's hands. "A chance to enjoy the season. Mama and I were so pleased with your invitation. I just could not wait to get here."

She turned to Lady Carstairs. "And Mama said I was to thank you kindly. She just knows I will be properly chaper-oned to all the events in town. It will be so exciting, won't it,

Katey? It will be a grand opportunity for me, I am sure. Mama told me to thank you both for this opportunity. She was most pleased, most pleased."

Kate tried to smile. "Yes...well, we do live rather quietly...but we can discuss a schedule later."

"Yes, I am sure you must be fatigued from your journey." Lady Carstairs turned to Ned who had set down the last of the cases. "Please ask Milly to come at once. Now then, Clarissa, we will get you settled in."

Milly appeared in the foyer. "What is this then about a house guest? I haven't had no notice of a house guest." She turned towards Ned. "Don't you be leaving yet, Ned, my boy. I will be having all this lot hauled up to the green room. No notice at—"

Lady Carstairs interrupted. "The green room will be perfect, thank you, Milly. If you could show Miss Clarissa to her room, I am sure she would like to freshen up."

Milly snatched up a valise and a hat box before heading for the stairs. She grunted. "Ned, the trunk, please."

Milly's displeasure could be heard in each step on the staircase.

Before heading up the stairs, Clarissa snatched Kate's hands once more. "Just think of all the fun we will have! Balls and soirees. The season!"

She giggled. Despite the long journey, Clarissa skipped up the stairs after Milly.

"Oh dear. I am sorry, Aunty. I neglected to tell you that I had promised Clarissa a favor. I just had no idea she would be collecting it so soon." Kate sighed. "Nor did I expect to escort her through the social scene this season. You know I have given all that up."

Kate gave a long-suffering sigh.

Lady Carstairs contemplated the now silent staircase. "I

think this may be just what we need. You have been reclusive of late, my dear Kate. Perhaps it is time you started returning to the social world. Yes, I think a few balls and soirees will be in order this season."

"Oh, Aunt Elizabeth. Must we? I am quite beyond the eager debutant. I am almost five and twenty. Surely that ship has sailed. I certainly do not want to begin the search for a proper suitor again."

The knocker sounded at the door.

"Oh, no. That would be Lord St. Claire. With all this fuss, I have forgotten. Please keep him company while I run up and change."

"Run along, dear. I will keep him entertained." Lady Carstairs went to greet a most welcome visitor. She thought aloud as she crossed the foyer, "Whether you want it or not, Katherine, I believe you may have found your suitor at last."

The park was busy. Horses with riders dressed in their finest riding gear promenaded amidst open carriages. The object was to see and be seen by prominent members of the ton. Kate and Ambrose walked their horses, followed discretely by the footman.

"I am afraid it is much too late and thus too busy for a gallop today. I apologize again for keeping you waiting this morning. With our unexpected visitor, I was quite set off my schedule." Kate patted the neck of Starling, "Though I must admit it is a joy to spend time with this beauty even at a walk."

Ambrose nodded at a passing carriage. "Yes, it is too busy to gallop, but this will give us an excellent chance to get to know each other better. You still have told me so little about yourself. Why, for instance, has someone as lovely as you not been claimed?"

Kate laughed. "Thank you for that. I am not, nor have I ever, except possibly in my first season, been considered a good catch I suppose."

"So, no love affairs then. I am not sure I believe that. Someone as beautiful as you would be much pursued."

"I was engaged once." She debated confiding the whole sordid tale of her engagement. Perhaps he too would decide there must be something wrong with her to have been rejected the way she had. Certainly, the polite world had for some time turned their backs on her.

There had been some reprieve in recent years. After all, it was an old story. But it still loomed its ugly head each time Kate attempted to begin a new relationship.

Kate looked down at her hands and then glanced at Ambrose. "You have been away from London for a long time and have no doubt missed some of the gossip about me." She let out a breath she was unaware she had been holding. "It is no secret, and I am sure someone will be happy to tell you the sad tale. Damien, my fiancé, cried off after a year's engagement. He neglected to tell me or anyone else, as far as I know, why. He said only he had decided we did not suit. It was a scandal. After that unfortunate event, I became a social pariah. A girl who has been rejected in that way is not likely to recover socially."

Kate kept her eyes firmly on the saddle horn, waiting for his reaction.

"May I just say that this Damien character must have been blind and slightly dull. I am sorry to hear it. I am sure those tales are long forgotten, and you are swarmed with eligible young men."

"No. I have had suitors, but nothing has ever come of it." Kate laughed. "My only persistent suitor is a half cousin, Jeremy. And I assure you that is a relationship I do not encourage. I find I am more and more satisfied with the life I have made for myself. A woman of the world, as it were."

"Ah. And what does that mean?' Ambrose spoke softly. "You must tell me what has you so satisfied? It cannot be society as you have assured me it has not held your interest. What is your secret interest?"

Kate laughed. "It is not so exciting as you may think."

She paused. It was certainly a morning for spilling her secrets. First, she had told him about Damien and now she was on the verge of revealing her business interests.

How much could she tell him? Drawing fashion was a lady-like endeavor but selling it was not. A Lady was not to be involved in trade. A single woman in business would be even more frowned upon. Ambrose would quite likely distance himself from her if he discovered her secret. On the other hand, she had relished spending the time with him in part because she had given up the machinations required to catch a husband and simply enjoyed being herself with him. For once she had genuinely loved the time spent with a man.

Kate took a deep breath and decided to take the chance. She would throw caution to the wind. She did not want to play the coy innocent. He was not to be a suitor, like the gentlemen in her past. Ambrose was different. With him she had allowed herself to be Kate; twenty-five, independent, and interested in his company, but not in making him a husband. She chose to be completely honest with him. Let him see her for what she was. If he opted to end their budding relationship, then so be it.

She plunged ahead. "I draw fashion. I create original designs for the beauties of the town to wear." She looked at him carefully to see how he would react. "I sell my drawings; indeed, I have made a comfortable business for myself."

His face was impassive.

She pressed on. "I also assist with the day-to-day operations of a clothing salon."

Kate searched his face. There was not the slightest hint of disapproval or acceptance. To her frustration she saw he had cloaked his face in his stoic military countenance.

A horse and rider approached.

"Oh dear. My cousin Jeremy." Kate scowled. How like Jeremy to make a nuisance of himself and destroy what time she may have with her Ambrose. Her Ambrose—it had only been a few days and she was already thinking of him as her Ambrose. She would have to be more careful with her feelings. She, of all people, was aware of the danger to her heart in that line of thought.

Jeremy approached astride a sleek Barbary mare, the Spanish breed of horse popular in London. His pale blue riding coat was matched by a series of tassels of the same tones decorating his saddle. His head was held stiffly by an elaborate neck cloth, looped, and starched into a firm cascade beneath his chin. His hair was dirty blond, twisted into the tossed curls made popular by Byron. A waistcoat of bright yellow flared between the lapels of his fitted jacket. He was all that was fashionable among the young bucks of the town.

"My Katherine, it is good to see you out at last." He tipped his beaver hat in greeting. "You look fashionable as always. And who might be your distinguished friend? I do not believe we have been introduced."

He pulled his horse up to ride next to Kate.

"Lord St. Claire, may I present my cousin Jeremy Blythe."

"Pleased, I am sure." Jeremy gave the expected bow. "And it is Lord Blythe, Baron of Wardern and heir to the Viscount of Serves."

Jeremy raised his chin a little higher and looked at Ambrose. "Though I cannot say that I am pleased to see you escorting my very special friend this morning. May I ask how you met?"

"I, ah..."

Kate interjected, "My Aunt, the Lady Carstairs, was an acquaintance of Lord St. Claire's mother. Is that not so, lieutenant?"

Ambrose smiled at Kate. "Yes. It seems our connection is intergenerational. We are destined to be friends."

Kate could not suppress a wry smile as she watched Ambrose assess Jeremy. His gaze took in the dandy from his polished Hessians to the riding hat adorned with a pale blue ribbon accenting his outlandish riding costume. The entire effect was grossly overdone. That Ambrose smirked at her cousin indicated he too had identified Jeremy as the dandy that he was.

Ambrose's appraisal had only served to make Jeremy raise his chin even higher. Jeremy leaned back in his saddle. "Is that so? Well, my connection is much closer, I am sure. Lady Katherine is my esteemed cousin." Jeremy nodded as though scoring a point in a great debate.

"Half cousin," Kate muttered.

"In fact, it should be noted that Kate and I have been inseparable for many a year. An understanding so to speak. Is that not correct, Katherine?" Jeremy smiled expectantly at Kate.

"It is true we have known each other for some time, however that there is an understanding is certainly not the case," Kate said firmly.

"Not yet. But soon, Katherine. We do not want to wait too long, do we?" He looked at Ambrose, assessing his navy dress uniform with a sneer. "Lieutenant, was it? In his majesty's service, are you? I suppose you are a soldier boy on leave?"

Ambrose chuckled dryly. "I suppose a lifetime ago I could have been called a 'soldier boy,' but after a decade of battles on land and at sea in defense of my country, I find the label a trifle inadequate." Ambrose laid his hand lightly on the cutlass at his side. "Though my weapons are for show here in town, I am fortunate in that I have learned how to use them."

Kate added, "And actually, Lord St. Claire has transferred to Homeland Security. Thus, we can expect he will be in town for some time. He is the younger brother of the Earl of Suffex who I am sure you are familiar with. My friend, Lord St. Claire, will naturally be eager to take his place in society."

Kate gave Jeremy a saucy smile. She watched Jeremy shift uncomfortably with satisfaction. That Ambrose was the son of the Earl of Suffex seemed to have made him uneasy.

Ambrose met Jeremy's eyes with a cool stare and held them there while he replied to Katherine, "Thank you, Lady Katherine, for all your kind recommendations. If you will excuse us, my lord, I believe our exit is just ahead. A pleasure to meet you, I am sure."

Ambrose nudged his horse into a smooth trot, a maneuver matched by Kate on Starling, leaving Jeremy to contemplate as they headed toward the exit.

Upon reaching her residence, Ambrose helped her down from Starling and walked her to the door.

"Please come in for a moment. I will see to a little refreshment for us."

"Only for a moment perhaps. I do need to speak to Lady Carstairs if she is about?"

Old Tom greeted them in the foyer.

Kate turned to Tom. "Please have Milly bring tea and jellied biscuits, if she has them, to the library. And ask Lady Carstairs if she might join us. Thank you, Tom."

Lady Carstairs entered followed by a breathless Clarissa. Lady Carstairs smiled in greeting him.

"Lord St. Claire, or do you prefer Lieutenant? Such a pleasure to see you again. Please make yourself comfortable." She gestured to Clarissa. "I believe you have yet to meet our dear friend Miss Clarissa Dumont."

"A pleasure to meet you, Miss Dumont." Ambrose gave Clarissa a short bow. Turning to Lady Carstairs he said, "And you may address me as you wish, my Lady."

Clarissa stepped forward, took Ambrose's arm, and led him to the settee. "A soldier boy. How very exciting." She ignored his wince and settled in next to him. "You must tell me all about your travels. I do so love to meet a man in the King's service."

"Ah, and here is the tea. Thank you, Milly. I will pour." Lady Carstairs served the tea. She was about to offer biscuits when Clarissa snatched the tray.

Clarissa leaned into Ambrose with her best smile. "You must try these, my Lord. They are simply divine."

Ambrose helped himself to a pair.

"I do love a man with an appetite."

"Thank you." He turned to Lady Carstairs. "I was hoping to speak to you today. My brother the Earl of Suffex has an opera box for the season. I would be honored if you and your party could join me tomorrow night."

Before Lady Carstairs could reply, Clarissa let out a little squeal. "The opera! How marvelous! My absolute favorite! Oh, we would be thrilled to accept, I am sure!" She grasped his arm. "How very gracious of you."

Ambrose reached for another biscuit, dislodging Clarissa's hand in the process, and looked at Lady Carstairs inquiringly. "My Lady?"

"Yes, very gracious of you indeed. But only if Miss Katherine agrees."

Katherine, who had thus far been completely ignored, suddenly found all eyes turned in her direction; Clarissa and Ambrose with hopeful expressions and Lady Carstairs slightly amused. She was feeling annoyed by Clarissa's obvious flirtation and found herself tempted to find some trivial excuse to decline.

"Well..."

"Oh, Katey, you must! Only think of the lieutenant's disappointment. A soldier boy in the King's service. How could we say no." She grabbed his arm again and appealed to Kate.

It was the grimace on Ambrose's face which decided her. She turned to Ambrose with a merry grin. "It is decided then. We will not disappoint our 'soldier boy.'"

Ambrose laughed. He carefully pried Clarissa's hand from his arm. "Wonderful. I will bring around my coach at eight. And now I must take my leave. Ladies." He rose and gave his formal bow.

Clarissa hurried to his side. "Let me see you out."

Kate and Lady Carstairs stood and watched as Clarissa took his arm once more and led him to the door.

Kate kept her eyes on the two of them and said, "I

believe I will go to work at the shop this afternoon. I find I need to remove myself from the house for a while."

"Feeling a little irritated, are you, my dear?" Lady Carstairs smiled knowingly as she watched Clarissa and Ambrose through the library door. "A little competition is good for you. I had no idea Clarissa could be so... determined."

"It is exactly the kind of competition I despise." Kate sighed, turning to her desk.

The idea of competing once more for the attentions of eligible men was repugnant to her. Too well could she remember the evenings with a pasted smile on her face, tilting her fan, the elegant perfection of the three quarters curtsey, conversing with the exact balance of interest and decorum. She was beyond the delicate flirtations required by the young women who hoped to snag a husband. At this point in her life, she was uninterested in the battle, for battle it was.

She had forged a life for herself and was satisfied to live it. If there was an opportunity to enjoy male company, such as her friendship with Ambrose, she would take it, and she would enjoy it, but she was never going to be on the marriage mart with one objective in mind. Those days were over. Thankfully.

Kate gathered up the books and tucked them into the leather satchel. It was time to return to her work. "I do need to bring in the patterns and match up several with swatches of the new silks. Hopefully, we can have the news of the Empress's designs released today."

"Not to worry, my dear. Once you have announced their existence, the gossip will travel across town in record time. I predict that by nightfall, every lady of the ton will know of them. Are you hiring a hansom today? The fog is rolling in and I do so hate you walking that distance to the shop."

"Not to worry. It is only a few blocks. The walk always does me good."

Kate regretted her decision not to take a cab. As she walked along, she had the uncomfortable feeling she was being followed. The streets seemed unusually quiet. The afternoon fog had rolled in, shrouding the buildings and lanes, enhancing the isolating effect. Several times she stopped to peer behind her but each time she saw nothing.

The hair on the back of her neck prickled. She could not shake the unsettling feeling that someone lurked in shadows waiting to pounce. When she last looked behind her into the fog, she was certain she had seen a dark shadow slip between the buildings. She tried to dismiss her apprehensions. Just one more block and she would be safely in her shop.

Chapter Eight

She quickened her pace. Her footsteps rang hollowly on the cobbled walkway. After one final glance behind her, she slipped into the alley behind her shop. Her heart began to pound. She found herself running the last few feet to the back door of her establishment. Using her keys, she opened the alley entrance of the shop, scrambled inside, and locked the door. Leaning against its solid frame, she gave a nervous giggle.

How silly to allow her imagination to take hold of her as she had. It was unlike her. Kate shook off her feelings of unease, deciding that what was needed was a bracing cup of tea, and a full schedule of work.

The alley entrance opened to her office which connected to the hallway. One wing led right to the work-rooms, the other directly ahead with its dressing room doors on either side, finally opening to the showroom and recep-tion area. Madame Bouvier, the head modiste and manager, was hustling about between rooms to help her assistants in accommodating clients.

Kate smiled when she heard the strident voice of Lady Merriweather from the foyer. She was a valued customer with three girls on the marriage mart, but more than that she was a resolute gossip and exactly the woman Kate hoped would arrive this morning. It was time to send Madame Bouvier out to work her magic.

Kate stood in her office doorway. She could not resist hearing the launch of her new patterns. She moved a little closer to the foyer to better hear the conversation. If all went well, Madame Bouvier's announcement of the new fashions to the busybody would have the news of Empress Josephine's designs all over town before lunch.

Madame Bouvier's accented voice greeted her client. "Ah, Madam Merriweather, so wonderful to see you. I have a glorious surprise just for you. From France. But it is the greatest secret, my dear. For your ears and eyes only..."

Kate slowly closed her office door. Madame Bouvier was an expert in her field and knew exactly how to maneuver the situation. Lady Merriweather would be the first to see the dresses of the Empress. In hours, Josephine's fabulous wardrobe would be on the lips of every upper-class matron of London.

The time passed quickly as Kate continued her task of copying the patterns. Occasionally, she would head to the storage room to cut swatches of material to add to her patterns as suggestions. Sometimes, she would bring a bolt of cloth back to the office and unroll a length or two to get the flow of the material and compare it with the sketches.

She marveled at the designs. The new body movement in clothing emphasized the shape of a woman. Fabrics were light and flowing. Gone were the heavy brocades and thick quilting of the previous era. Short, puffed sleeves were worn with long gloves to emphasize the length and curvature of the arm. The dresses were tight to the bodice, but then draped gracefully to the floor. A filmy layer of opaque silk could be added or removed to change the style of the gown and provide versatility. An optional floor length pelisse could also be added to further alternate the style when a fresh look was required. Each dress could be adapted. This versatility allowed a woman to wear the dress several times.

Cassandra, an assistant, appeared at her door. "A gentleman to see you, ma'am. A Mister Bentley Brown. He assures me you will want to talk with him."

"Ah yes. Send him in." Kate smiled. The news of The Empress Josephine's gown designs had indeed travelled fast. The fact that Bentley Brown, owner of a competing company, was at her door was proof of that.

Kate lifted the broached watch on her bodice. Only three hours. It was better than even she had anticipated.

She reached for the widow's hat on her desk and placed it on her head, adjusting the veil. It was scarce protection against anonymity. But it would serve. Wearing the working clothes of the widow had served her well: a dark skirt and jacket over an equally dark blouse provided her with the degree of disguise she desired. People seldom looked beyond their first impressions. Furthermore, Mr. Brown was a tradesman and not likely to ever be in the presence of polite society, nor would he expect her to be. He knew her as Mrs. Servile, a widow and entrepreneur.

Her disguise protected her in two ways. First, as a married woman, she would be more acceptable as an entrepreneur. And second, it protected her from the scandal of a Lady involved in trade. That too was not tolerated. Her persona as Mrs. Sevile was a necessary one.

Bentley Brown entered the room. "Mrs. Servile. I could not resist coming to visit my most gracious competition today. Always such a pleasure to see you." He removed his bowler hat to display his greasy light brown hair and stood before her desk. She did not rise to greet him.

He was a little man. Despite owning a shop, he seemed unable to apply design principles to his own wardrobe. His suit was at least one size too small. It was an unfortunate shade of light brown, showing numerous stains. Kate could not help but think he was fortunate to have a modiste to manage his business, because surely no one would purchase from him.

"I had to come down and see how you were faring." He walked over to the desk and peered across it, in an obvious attempt to glimpse her work.

Kate quickly closed the book, laying her arm over it protectively. "How can I help you, Mister Brown? Shall we skip the niceties and go directly to the point? I am sure this is not a social call."

Kate had had dealings with Mr. Brown in the past. He was as slimy as his hair. Though she often sold her work to many shops in town, and not all of them partially owned by her aunt, she had vowed that he would never receive a design from her again. In fact, she felt he still owed her from her last contract, a contract she had neglected to have previewed by a lawyer to her misfortune. Kate did many of her deals on the honor system. Bentley Brown did not recognize honor.

He gave her a wide smile. "To business it is then. Rumor has it that you are displaying some innovative designs from the French court." He pulled at the thin ends of his waxed mustache looking at her thoughtfully. "I might be willing to pay a great deal to be one of the first to get a copy of those patterns."

He leaned forward as if to impart to her a great secret. "I could certainly make it worth your while."

"Well, now, I do believe you have made this little speech before. And to my misfortune I believed you. This time I assure you there will be no such bargain."

"Yes. That was unfortunate." He lifted his arms and shrugged with a helpless expression. "But what could I do? A contract is a contract, and one must follow the rule of law. But let us leave that unfortunate incident in the past. There is opportunity here for us both. If I can get these patterns for my shop before they are copied all over town, I will see a substantial profit this season."

"No."

"No? But what do you mean no? You have not heard my offer. When you—"

Kate stood, carefully placing her hands on the oversized book. "No. There will be no deal between us no matter what the offer. I am afraid your last contract has cost you more than you bargained for. Now you may leave, Mister Bentley Brown. I believe our conversation has been concluded."

Madame Bouvier appeared in the doorway. "Can I help with anything, ma'am?"

"Mister Brown was just leaving. Perhaps you could show him to the door."

Bentley Brown stared at the closed books under her braced hands. He seemed to debate grabbing them and making a run for it. His gaze travelled from Kate to Madame Bouvier who swung the door wide for his exit.

He glared at Kate. "You will regret this decision, Sevile. See if you don't. You have not seen the last of me."

With that, he was gone.

"I am afraid you have made an enemy there. He does

not appear to be much pleased," Madame Bouvier said, shaking her head. "Such a disagreeable little man."

"Yes, very disagreeable. Do not be allowing that creature through our doors. He is no longer welcome in our establishment."

And that, thought Kate, is that.

It was closing time when Kate decided to quit for the day. Though she did not usually lock up her patterns, tonight she decided to secure them in the vault for the night. She put the copies in her safe and tucked the originals back into her satchel along with the day's notes and cash sales.

She considered a walk home, but the fog was thick upon the streets and carrying the deposit home, after this morning's fear, was not a trip she relished. She shivered when she thought of the morning's trek to work. After her meeting with Bentley Brown, it did not seem as ridiculous that someone may have stalked her. The expense of a hansom cab would be well worth the money.

She forced herself to think more pleasant thoughts. Ambrose would be escorting her to the opera. She had given her relationship with Ambrose some thought in the last few days. If this was to be her last opportunity to enjoy a suitor, then she did not want to be held back by society's restraints.

She grinned mischievously. She had not let society dictate her actions in any other aspect of her life and resolved that her relationship with Ambrose would not be the exception. She was a mature woman after all. Perhaps it was time to see her relationship with Ambrose from a new scandalous perspective.

Chapter Nine

The morning was a hectic one. Clarissa had dug through all of Kate's closets, hoping to find the perfect dress for the opera later in the evening. It seemed her wardrobe was inadequate for the season. Although Clarissa was opposite to Kate in appearance—she had the classic looks of the English beauty, with her blonde hair and light blue eyes—they were close to the same height and dress size.

Kate looked at the heap of discarded dresses on her bed with annoyance. The cost of the season for a young woman was hugely expensive, driven for the most part by the wardrobe required. It seemed Clarissa and her mother had found a way to mitigate those expenses. It was with some relief that Kate greeted the news that a gentleman caller awaited her downstairs. Clarissa let out a little squeal and rushed to her room to freshen up.

As Kate entered the library, it was hard to mask her disappointment when she saw it was Jeremy who was waiting for her, seated comfortably by the settee with her aunt.

"Katherine," He rose to do his formal bows as she entered. "How pleasant to see you this morning. I had not realized until recently that I have been neglecting you."

"Jeremy. How kind of you to visit." Realizing Clarissa had entered the room behind her, Kate continued, "You must meet my friend, Miss Clarissa Dumont. Clarissa, my esteemed cousin Lord Jeremy Blythe."

"Oh, but we have met. Lord Jeremy and I are acquainted from County Hernes. We were introduced at The Meadows. Such a pleasant surprise to find you here in London. My visit to town is ever more exciting now that I know you are here." She took his hand and settled him down on the couch, seating herself securely beside him. "You must know how pleased I am to know you are here in town. As a country girl, I will surely need the guidance of someone as worldly as yourself. Such a joy, is it not, Kate?"

"It certainly is."

"Why, thank you, Katherine." Jeremy addressed her but gave Clarissa his smile, blushing slightly at the pleasure of her compliment as he removed his hand from her grasp and turned again to Kate. "This is precisely why I have stopped by today. To assure you, Katherine, that should you decide to venture out more frequently into society, I will be here for you."

He nodded as though to emphasize his commitment.

Clarissa was quick to respond. "Oh, how gracious. You are indeed a gentleman of the highest order. Why, Katherine and I could not be more pleased. To have a man of your caliber at our side while we find our way through society's perilous waters is the very thing."

Clarissa gave him a brilliant smile.

Jeremy basked in her compliments. "Yes. Well. I believe there is no one more able than I to assist in this matter." He surveyed the room. "You ladies may rest assured you are in the most capable of hands."

"More tea?" Lady Carstairs offered with an amused smile.

"I believe I will. Thank you," Jeremy replied, holding out his teacup. Clarissa promptly offered biscuits, but he waved them away, saying, "No, I must watch my weight. It takes some effort to maintain the perfect gentlemanly figure. I would hate to have to discard my collection of waistcoats."

"But that would be a terrible shame. I noticed your interesting waistcoat immediately. Tell me, is that a gold thread woven into the fabric?" Clarissa reached out to caress the gold fabric of his vest.

Jeremy preened under her compliment. "Why, yes. It gives it just the sparkle it needs, I believe. I have several in alternating colors with the same woven threads. My tailor insists the waistcoat is the statement piece of any wardrobe."

"I quite agree. It is dashing. I love the gleaming color. It is so up lifting to find a gentleman attuned to fashion, and so rare." Clarissa gestured to his cravat. "And such an elaborate neckcloth! Have you seen the latest neckcloths tied in the cascade? I believe Brummel has outdone himself with this latest fashion."

"Why, yes. Very exciting indeed. I assure you my valet is practicing it as we speak." Jeremy blushed with pleasure. "It is indeed a happy surprise to find you here this morning, Clarissa. I say, the season will not be the bore I had thought it would be now that I know you, and of course, Katherine, will be about."

He tore his eyes from her just long enough to flash Kate a smile.

He stood to take his leave, and the ladies rose. "Before I

depart, may I enquire if you have received invitations for the Hargrove masquerade this weekend?"

Lady Carstairs replied, "I believe we have, however we not yet decided to accept."

"Oh, but we must. We must! It is my favorite, my absolute favorite entertainment!" Clarissa clapped her hands together in excitement.

Kate raised her eyebrows; she could not resist. "I thought the opera was your most favorite entertainment?"

Clarissa was not the least phased. "Oh, but it is for tonight. For the weekend it is definitely a masquerade." She smiled happily. "I so seldom get the entertainments of town that every bit of it is my favorite."

"Then I believe we will attend, Clarissa. If only so you may enjoy it." Lady Carstairs smiled graciously.

"The opera you say. Tonight?" Jeremy interjected.

Clarissa took his arm to escort him to the door. "Why yes. We will be in the box of the Viscount of Suffex. Is not that exciting?"

"Hmmm." Jeremy could not hide his chagrin as they made their way to the door. Clarissa, however, did her best to charm him as she showed him out.

"Well, this is an interesting development." Lady Carstairs leaned back and sipped her tea. "It seems Miss Clarissa may have a beau."

She looked across at Kate.

"Nothing could suit me more. Though I know Jeremy is harmless, and he definitely has been persistent, he is not for me."

Milly appeared in the doorway.

"A message for you, ma'am," she said, handing Lady Carstairs a note. "The boy said it was urgent. He's waiting for your response."

Milly hovered nearby while Lady Carstairs read the message.

"Oh, my dear." Lady Carstairs let the note fall to her lap. "Not again."

Kate snatched up the note. After a quick scan she turned to Milly.

"Tell the lad we will be at the salon directly, Milly." Kate waited until Milly had snorted her disapproval and left the room before turning to Lady Carstairs. "Another break-in. This cannot be a coincidence. I am sure it is that nasty Bentley Brown. He was at the shop yesterday after my patterns. Heavens I hope they are safe!"

Thirty minutes later, Kate stood with Lady Carstairs amid the ruins of her office. Every shelf had had its contents swiped to the floor. The drawers of her desk had been removed and lay haphazardly about the room. The floor was strewn with the remnants of her possessions. A bolt of cloth had been unraveled and lay in a heap in the open doorway. Even her pictures had been taken from the walls, and their frames maliciously ripped off.

Kate stepped gingerly around a patch of broken glass and made her way to the wall safe. Its front panel had been pried open and hung precariously from one hinge.

"So much for the assurances of the salesman who promised complete security with the Carson2D model safe," Kate said with a scowl.

"Yes. I see that. What a dreadful mess." Lady Carstairs picked up a bronze statuette and set it on the shelf beside her. She frowned thoughtfully at the figurine. "There is something not quite right about this business. Why, for instance, would a thief leave behind this little gem?"

She scanned the floor and found the matching sculpture,

half covered by a sheaf of papers, and arranged the pair carefully on the shelf.

"I am sure it was only the patterns they were after." Kate reached out and grasped the safe door. Its final hinge gave way as she twisted it open; she found herself holding the front panel in her hand. She peered into the enclave. "Just as I suspected. Cleared out! Thank goodness I still have the originals."

"Thank goodness you brought the deposits home," Lady Carstairs replied wryly.

Kate reached down to set the heavy door on the floor. She gasped. "The patterns!"

There under her right foot was the pattern book, its large scrapbook-sized pages open and crumpled. She hurried to the desk and spread it out, carefully smoothing it.

"Heavens! It seems to be complete." She flipped through the broad pages, then finally closed her precious book, and straightened out a crease on its cover. Her eyes met Lady Carstairs's. Something was very odd indeed. "What could they possibly have been after if not the pattern books?"

Madam Bouvier appeared in the doorway. "It is a bit of a disaster out front. Every drawer has been dumped to the floor. All the pattern books have been tossed about and some of the silks were unrolled, but so far, nothing seems to be missing. I have the girls putting things to rights. It will be a job, but it will come together faster than it first appeared. We will be back in business in a couple of hours."

She glanced around the room. "Your office has taken the worst of it I'm afraid."

She looked at the gaping hole that had been the safe. "Cleaned you out, did they? Well, it could be worse. The silks are still here. Some will need to be cleaned, like this lot,

I am sure." She nudged the pile of cloth in the doorway with her foot. "But all in all, you have been quite fortunate, *nes't ce pas?*"

"Yes, madam, I believe we have," Kate replied, slowly rubbing the prized pattern books. "Strangely, we have been lucky indeed."

"Well, then, no need to fret. I have everything in order." Madam Bouvier reached down and bundled up the awkward pile of silks.

Lady Carstairs helped her gather it into her arms. "Thank you, my dear. You are a tower of strength as usual. I do not know what we would do without you."

As Madam waddled away with her heavy load, Lady Carstairs turned to Kate. "So what, my dear, do you suppose has gone on here? We have a monstrous mess, yet nothing appears to have been taken."

"It is odd. Let us not forget that we had the same occurrence at the house. In that case little had been disturbed yet the similarities remain. Nothing has been taken." Kate began picking up the empty drawers and reassembling her desk. "I was sure someone was after the patterns. I came here ready to accuse Bentley Brown of theft. But it cannot have been him. He would have left with those copies. I am at a loss."

The ladies worked in silence, putting the desk drawers back in place and arranging the scattered papers and numerous receipts.

Lady Carstairs held up a destroyed picture frame and its ripped print. "Why would a robber take the time to demolish this picture? It makes no sense."

"Perhaps it does. It could be that this housebreaker was interested only in cash. The safe was opened and many people hide cash in desks or behind pictures. Mayhap this fellow saw no profit in anything but what he could carry. Cash or valuables."

"You must be right. And the break-in at the house must be pure coincidence." Lady Carstairs arranged the last of the books on the shelf. "However, I do believe we need added security, for the shop as well as the house. I will be working on it immediately. It is time we took some precautions. And of course, we will need a new safe."

An afternoon of setting the shop to rights had left little time to prepare for the opera. After a quick early supper, Kate was dismayed to discover her closets and room were in an upheaval almost equal to her office. It was apparent Clarissa had had some difficulty deciding which of Kate's clothes would most suit her. Gowns were layered out across the bed in a heap. Several others were draped over the chairs. Amongst it all Clarissa stood, elegant in Kate's new jade silk and smiling radiantly.

"It is perfect. I look lovely, don't you think? And the color is ideal for me. It really sets off my blond curls." She tilted her head back and forth to display the masses of curls escaping a perfect coronet. "I really cannot thank you enough. Tonight, I will dazzle a beau! Mama would be so proud!"

She gave a little twirl, and it became evident she had found the new satin slippers to match.

Kate rubbed her hand across her forehead. She could feel a headache coming on. In a quiet and even voice she addressed her, "Clarissa, this room is too much. I am going to wash up to prepare for tonight and when I return, I want to see that my room has been put back together."

Clarissa hurried to make amends. "Oh, no. Do not worry. All will be well. You cannot be annoyed with me, Katey. This can be put back in a moment." Clarissa rushed to the hall. "Milly! Milly, you must come help me at once. Milly!"

Kate ignored the yelling and continued down the hall to the warm bath that awaited her. It was to be her first night in public with Ambrose. She was determined to set her tiresome day behind her and enjoy the evening. True, she would not be wearing the new jade silk as planned but she had to admit it suited Clarissa.

As she bathed, she thought about Clarissa and her prospects. Clarissa was younger than her. She was a girl with good bloodlines but modest means, and that meant that she was the hope of her family. A good marriage was her duty and must be her goal. A season in London would have been the greatest boon for her entire household. Though Clarissa was an irritant, Kate was determined to do all she could to help her achieve that goal.

But not with Ambrose. Ambrose she selfishly wanted for herself. She had given up on the idea of marriage. It had been many years since Damien had destroyed that dream. Nothing had worked out for her in that direction, and she had resigned herself to a single life. She had a prosperous career and her independence.

But lately an idea had begun to take root. If she was considered on the shelf at twenty-five, a birthday that was fast approaching, then maybe it was time to consider other options. Perhaps it was time for a lover.

"I wonder," she thought aloud, "how a woman approaches a man with a proposal for an affair?"

Chapter Ten

The opera house was packed. Tonight's performance was by a new European artist named Beethoven. The overture, Fidelio, had opened to rave reviews. Kate looked forward to the evening since it had been some time since she had attended. While she was not wide-eyed with the wonder of it all like Clarrisa, she still enjoyed the pageantry and splendor. Ladies were dressed in their best, in a rainbow of colors, displaying an array of sparkling jewels. Men wore the latest fashion; trousers had become the rage, with black tails, colorful waistcoats, and beaver top hats.

The Suffex box overlooked the stage, giving them a fine view of both the audience and the performers. One of the best parts of attending the opera, in Kate's opinion, was people watching. A world of drama occurred off the stage.

Ambrose graciously helped them to their seats, Aunt Elizabeth first, then Clarrisa and herself, seating himself at the end. A raucous burst of laughter erupted directly across from them.

Lady Carstairs was quick to turn her opera glasses on

the disturbance. "I see the prince is in attendance tonight. And in fine form as usual."

"Where? Oh, the Prince of Wales! How exciting!" Clarissa trained her glasses on to the box across the way. "He certainly has a full box. Who is that with him? Please tell me one of them is Brummel and point him out."

Lady Carstairs focused her glasses on the scene once more. "On the extreme left. The gentleman in a tuxedo with the fuchsia waistcoat. I believe the other gentlemen are his favorite cronies, the Duke of Bedford with Lord Alvanley on the extreme right."

"Oh, he is indeed an arbiter of fashion. How grand! And the ladies. Why look at that red dress. Who might they be? My goodness, their bosoms look ready to spill out." Clarissa glanced down at her more conservative neckline. "If that is the fashion, I wonder if we are a bit—"

Ambrose interjected, "I do not think you will be introduced to those particular ladies. And in my view, I have the three most fashionable belles in my box." He continued in an obvious attempt to change the topic, "I heard Angelica Catalani is in fine form this evening. We can expect an excellent performance."

Kate placed her hand upon his arm. "Why thank you for your compliment, my Lord." She gave him a wide smile. "I wonder if Angelica has had a row with her latest paramour. One hears she performs her best after a bit of a tussle."

Kate chuckled.

"Why, how interesting. Look Katherine, your uncle, the Viscount of Serves is in attendance tonight," Lady Carstairs said, peering through her opera glasses. "With the Earl and Lady Hargrove. Now that is a rarity. He has never been a fan of the opera."

"Where? Oh yes, I see them." Clarissa bubbled with excitement. "And Jeremy! And they seem to be looking our way."

Clarissa lowered her glasses and frantically waved in their direction. The gesture elicited no response.

"I hope they saw me."

Kate sighed, "How could they miss it."

The lights dimmed. The performance was about to start.

Kate sat mesmerized by the performance. It was uplifting to see a female character in a commanding role. Catalina's portrayal of the heroic Lenore had indeed been inspired. Intermission seemed to arrive in a blink. The crowd rose to their feet as the curtain fell to rousing applause.

Kate turned to Ambrose. "Thank you for this. I am quite enjoying it."

Ambrose smiled, remaining on his feet as the ladies settled back into their seats. "May I get you ladies some punch? Or champagne?"

Lady Carstairs replied, "That would be lovely. I think punch would be best."

Just then the curtain at the back of the box was pushed aside and a gentleman appeared. He was astoundingly handsome, with blond hair pulled back into a queue and pleasing features.

"Ambrose, my old friend. What a surprise to find you here. And with three so beautiful ladies. I demand an introduction. You must not keep such jewels to yourself."

Ambrose seemed annoyed. "May I present my friend Theodore, Lord Pembroke. My Lord, Lady Katherine Blythe, Miss Clarrisa Dumont, and Lady Elizabeth Carstairs."

Theo elegantly kissed the hand of each Lady in turn beginning with Lady Carstairs. Clarissa appeared to be struck dumb and could only gaze at him open-mouthed. He lingered over the hand of Kate.

"At last, the beauteous Kate, of whom I have heard so much." Theo kissed her hand, extending her arm to the side to further admire her person. "And even lovelier than I have been told, if that is possible."

He flashed her a winning smile, "How rude of my friend St. Claire to keep you to himself for so long. And you must call me Theo. All of my true friends do."

"Ah, you are a fine flatterer, sir." Kate pried her hand from Lord Pembroke, who seemed reluctant to release her.

"And may I ask if you are enjoying the performance? Myself, I love to see a female character with the intelligence and wit to manipulate her enemies. Quite intriguing. Would that I could find a female like that. Or have I? Are you my Lenore at last?" He again flashed her his most charming smile, tilted his head to the side, and assessed her with sparkling eyes.

"How very gallant." Kate tentatively returned his smile. While Kate would normally have found his excessive compliments overdone, she could not resist his boyish, mischievous charm. Lord Pembroke was definitely a heartbreaker.

"Yes, gallant indeed." Ambrose stepped forward and shouldered Theo back a pace. He gave him a hard look. "And speaking of gallantry, perhaps you could bring the ladies each a punch."

Theo laughed. He accepted Ambrose's obvious attempt to dislodge him from their presence with good humor.

"It would be an honor," he replied, and with a bow to the ladies, he withdrew.

Kate turned to Ambrose. "An interesting character. Is he a good friend then?"

"Yes, he is that." Ambrose sighed as if the admission was a difficulty.

Before he could take his seat, the curtain again parted to reveal a breathless Jeremy, who had somehow managed to cross the theatre in record time.

"Of course," Ambrose muttered.

Kate put her hand to her mouth to suppress a giggle.

Clarrisa rose to meet him and took his hands in hers. "My Lord, you cannot know how pleased I am to see you here. What joy!" She turned as though to present him to the others. "Look who has arrived."

Jeremy seemed to expand beneath her praise. He gave Clarissa a grateful smile.

"My Lord, it is indeed a pleasure. And I see your father, the viscount, is also in attendance. It is a rare occasion to see the two of you at a performance." Lady Carstairs offered her hand which Jeremy took in greeting.

"Yes, and it is my father who sent me over to address you." He turned to Clarissa who gave him her widest smile. He flushed a little and quickly added, "Not that it took much persuading."

Jeremy seemed to struggle to return his gaze to Lady Carstairs. He cleared his throat to continue. "Father asks if you, and the young ladies, would be interested in joining us in attending the Dunstun soiree after tonight's performance. He has brought the coach and you can be assured there is room for all."

"Oh yes! Yes!" Clarissa turned to Lady Carstairs. "You must accept. What a perfectly lovely idea. I am sure, I am sure."

"Well, what a gracious invitation." Lady Carstairs was

clearly pleased that her charges had received so much attention this evening. "I see that Miss Dumont is in favor. And Katherine? Does this idea appeal to you?"

Katherine glanced at Ambrose. His grim countenance and stoic expression told her that he was not pleased to see that Jeremy was attempting to pirate their first evening out. And Jeremy, sure of his victory, had leaned back on his heels having shot Ambrose a triumphant grin.

"It has been a dreadfully long day for me. I find that my head aches. I am afraid I must pass on the invitation." Clarissa gasped as Kate continued, "But please do not stay back on my account. Indeed, I insist that you do not. You must go. I am sure I can depend upon Lord St. Claire to bring me safely home."

Ambrose executed a short bow from the neck. "I would be honored, My Lady."

Lady Carstairs leaned forward to look directly at Kate. "If you are sure, Katherine?"

"Yes. Perfectly sure."

"Well, it is settled then." She turned to Jeremy. "You may tell your father that Lady Carstairs and Miss Dumont will be pleased to accompany him. We shall await your coach at the entry."

Clarissa let out a little squeal of excitement and reached to grasp Jeremy's hand. "We shall have a wonderful evening."

Jeremy stood dumbfounded. He blushed a dull shade of red before turning blankly to Clarissa. "Yes. Yes, of course."

He turned to leave.

From the stage below, a porter bellowed out the three-minute warning just as Theo entered with his tray of drinks. "The lineups were outrageous. Who was that just leaving?"

"No one important," Ambrose said, as he handed the ladies their drinks.

Whether from the giddy relief at having thwarted Jeremy's plans so easily, or from the sheer joy of knowing she would have time alone with Ambrose, Kate found herself bursting into laughter at his remark.

Theo looked at her quizzically. "My guess is that he was just another bee to the honey."

"Enough, Theo." Ambrose gently turned Theo's shoulder toward the exit. "You will need to hurry to get back to your seat."

The second half of the opera passed in a blur for Kate. She had considered her options carefully and determined that if she ever were to embark upon an affair, now was the time. Time alone with her Ambrose was hard to find. She was not interested in a lifetime of regrets and missed opportunities. It would be an adventure. Kate spent the second half of the show with her eyes focused on the stage, but her mind concentrated only on how to go about beginning an affair.

At last, the performance ended to resounding applause. To her annoyance, the buzz in the lobby was that the evening had been the performance of the century, with a musical score not to be matched. The consensus was that the new composer, Beethoven, was a genius. She had somehow missed it entirely.

Once Lady Carstairs and Clarissa had been seen on their way, Ambrose assisted Kate into the coach. She sat back on the cushions, adjusting her skirts carefully around her on the seat. She could feel Ambrose's eyes upon her but dared not look up.

"Did you enjoy the evening, Katherine?"

"Yes. Very much, thank you." She had planned to

approach the subject of an affair but now that the opportunity presented itself, she had no idea how to go about it.

Just how did a lady broach the subject? She felt her cheeks burning at the prospect. She began fiddling with her reticule, tightening and loosening the drawstring as she considered her words. She was at a loss.

"And your headache, does it bother you?" Ambrose enquired in a soft voice.

"Headache? Oh yes. I mean no." Kate tried to gather her thoughts. "My head is fine, thank you very much. I wanted to remind you tonight, ah ...That is, I wanted to remind you that I am a mature woman. Not without some experience, you see."

Kate was sure her face glowed with embarrassment. She continued to work the cords on her retinue. "I am trying to say...Oh—"

Ambrose reached across and stilled her nervous hands. He held them gently in his. "Look at me, Katherine."

His eyes were dark and luminous. Kate found herself unable to look away. He leaned forward until their lips were almost touching. His breath caressed her skin.

"May I kiss you, Katherine?"

"Oh god, yes."

His lips met hers, softly at first then with greater urgency as their mouths opened. His hands squeezed hers gently before sliding over her hips to her back. With a groan, he pulled her close and deepened the kiss.

"So beautiful," he muttered against her lips. He began placing small kisses on her cheeks, moving slowly towards her neck.

Kate gasped at the warm heat of his breath and lips. She pushed her body tightly against him, devouring his scent. She reached up to hold him. Running her hands frantically up and down the length of his back, she relished his strength and power. He leaned back and pulled his jacket from his shoulders, shifting back and forth until it was off.

Kate felt consumed by a kind of madness. She slid her hands forward to unbutton his shirt, desperate to feel his skin against hers. His shirt fell open. She slid her hands across his chest, touching his downy hair. She was overwhelmed by the mixture of cologne and his male scent. A moment later she felt his arms beneath her legs as he shifted her to his lap. He had her sprawled out across him.

Raising his head, he asked softly, "Do you want me to stop, Katherine? You must tell me for I fear I cannot unless you do."

"Please do not stop," she responded breathlessly. "Not now."

He laid her gently across the carriage seat, sliding out from under her. Reaching up, he pulled the shoulders of her dress down. Her breasts glowed white in the soft light of the coach lamp. Her arms were trapped by her sides for a moment as he bent over her and kissed each breast.

Kate gasped as his teeth closed carefully over her nipple. The sharp moment of pain sent a shock wave through her body. She began to twist with an insatiable, desperate need. While his mouth caressed her breasts, his hands slid up her legs to her thighs, pushing her gown before them.

She felt a moment's alarm when she realized that her body was wet to his touch, but soon forgot it as he stroked her. He began to rub her in a circular motion. Kate heard herself whimpering as an incomprehensible anticipation became unbearable. Then the world seemed to stop as she felt wave after wave flood across her body. She closed her eyes and allowed the feelings to overwhelm her. She could vaguely hear Ambrose whispering her name as he pressed his body to hers. A lethargy consumed her.

"Oh Kate, you are so ready for me." He lifted her, and seconds later he was pushing into her body.

"You are so tight, Kate," he breathed into her neck.

She felt his body arch, then he thrust into her in one quick motion.

Kate squealed as a sharp pain reverberated through her body. All the lethargy from a moment ago had evaporated as her body tensed with pain. Her eyes were wide open.

Ambrose held himself completely still. He looked down at her with an expression of shock and confusion. "What the hell, Katherine? You are a bloody virgin!"

Kate began to wiggle away from him. She was no longer in pain but was confused by his reaction. Things were not progressing as she had foreseen.

"Do not move, Katherine."

She continued to squirm. He swore before he arched his back and pumped several times into her body. He pulled out quickly and, grabbing his coat, held it against himself, falling back against the coach seat.

He looked at her, his stern military countenance solidly in place. "You could have told me, Katherine. This would never have happened had I known."

All was still. Kate could think of nothing to say. She stared at him wide eyed. This whole business had been a massive disappointment. It had started well, but everything had quickly deteriorated. And to top it all off Ambrose appeared to be angry with her.

So much for all the grandiose talk about the joys of having an affair. It was obvious that the whole experience was overrated. So much for her great adventure.

To add to her humiliation, she realized she was spread-eagled across the coach seats. She began to attempt to put herself to rights. For some reason, she felt a disturbing urge to cry.

"One moment please." Ambrose had put his hand on her thigh, stopping her progress. He took the sleeve of his coat and carefully wiped her. He appeared to be concentrating completely on his task. Kate remained perfectly still. She was too confused and upset to react. "I never did like this jacket anyway. There."

Kate scrambled off the seat, pulling her gown back into place as best she could. Ambrose had rebuttoned his shirt and was attempting to tuck it into his trousers. The coach came to a stop.

Ambrose reached over and quickly slid the latch into place, allowing them a little time to put themselves together before the coachman opened the door. He seemed calm, with an aura of quiet contemplation. He plucked her small hat from the floor and handed it to her.

"Oh, my goodness, my hair!" She felt the sides of her head gingerly.

"Here, let me help." Ambrose placed the small hat on her head, then using its hatpins carefully anchored it into place.

Kate watched his face. He wore an expression that could only be described as resigned.

He arranged her curls and, holding her chin, examined the results. "Perfect." He leaned in and kissed her softly on the mouth. "You will do."

Kate blushed. Ambrose reached over and lifted the latch, opening the carriage door. He leapt down and held his hand out to assist her. Her legs felt rubbery as he led her to her entry.

To her dismay, Kate found that her trembling fingers would not work for her as she attempted to unlock the door.

"Allow me." Ambrose took her key, reached behind her, and opened the door. He turned the handle with a push. The door opened wide. Kate turned to him to thank him for the evening but found herself speechless.

"I will be visiting you tomorrow before afternoon tea. Sleep well, my dear." With that he tipped his hat and headed for his coach.

Katherine watched as he walked to the carriage, jacketless, with his shirt not quite properly tucked into his trousers.

Chapter Eleven

Ambrose walked into his club. After a sleepless night, he welcomed the comforting smell of leather and polished wood. At this time of day, the sitting room was a place of quiet repose. Men breakfasted, then read the paper, or spoke in soft tones to acquaintances over a cup of warm brew. He made his way to his usual table near the fireplace.

A waiter appeared. "Can I bring you something, my Lord?"

"The usual will be fine, Jenkins. The admiral will be joining me. If you could direct him to my table when he arrives?"

"Very good, sir."

Ambrose thought about his meeting with the admiral. This morning he had sent him the invitation, only after a long night of self-reflection and debate. He had decided to resign his commission. It had been a part of his plan for many years to start a horse breeding enterprise. Now was the time. The admiral had always been aware that he planned to work for the Home Office only temporarily. This choice would not come as a surprise to him.

Ambrose had lived frugally, carefully investing both his allowance from his brother the Earl, and his pay. While he could expect some financial difficulty initially, after all it would be some time before he would be able to reap the benefits from the sales of his new breeds, he also had his brother's commitment to assist him by investing in a property. The interlude with Katherine had been the catalyst which had driven him into making this move. He was looking forward to beginning his dream at last.

Ambrose grimaced as he recalled the disaster in the coach. He had bungled the entire affair. Katherine had been a virgin. What should have been a sweet introduction to love making had turned into a sordid fiasco. It could only have been a shock and a disappointment to her. He realized that on some level he must have been aware of her innocence, which only served to enhance his guilt and regret. His course of action concerning her was limited indeed. One did not take the virginity of a lady. He was honor bound to marry her.

And marry her he would. It had taken him most of the night to sort through his options and come to this final decision. He had even considered the possibility that he may be tying himself to an enemy of England. He was at heart a patriot, having served his country for the past ten years.

But the more he contemplated the idea of Kate as a master of espionage and intrigue, the more ludicrous the concept became. Kate had been open and honest to a fault; at one point, she had surprisingly confessed her involvement in trade. Her interactions with him had lacked even the social duplicity common among young women in search of a husband. Indeed, it was that quality which Ambrose found most attractive in her. And in reality, he reasoned, it had been he who had come to her under false pretenses. He had courted her as part of his assignment from the admiral. He had punctuated their conversations with questions designed to trick her into some sort of misstep.

He enjoyed her company. With her, he could be himself and share his true feelings. The more he had thought about marriage to Katherine, the more the idea appealed to him. It was time he married. He was ready to pursue his dreams. With Katherine at his side, he could see his future clearly. A wife, perhaps children, and his horse farm; it was the future he had dreamed of all those lonely nights aboard his ship. She was a lady. He admired her and enjoyed her company. It was more than most marriages of the ton had begun with.

He was a soldier. A soldier trained to deal in facts, not feelings. He knew he wanted her and was satisfied to leave an analysis of his feelings at that.

Ambrose looked up to see the admiral speak briefly to Jenkins and then make his way to his table.

Ambrose rose to greet him. "Good morning, sir. I hope it was not inconvenient for you to meet me this morning."

"Not at all, part of my routine to breakfast here. Sit down, sit down." The admiral made himself comfortable, smiling up at Jenkins who had appeared with a steaming cup of coffee.

"Your breakfasts will be only a moment."

"Thank you, Jenkins," the admiral replied. He took a sip of his coffee and leaned back in his chair. Then addressing Ambrose, he asked, "So, what has you up and about at this hour?"

He smiled, adjusting the lapels of his uniform. "It has been my experience that young men of your age prefer more sedate hours unless it cannot be helped. Not too much of an emergency I hope."

The admiral sipped his coffee again, examining him carefully over the rim of his cup. Ambrose became aware once more of how the man's fraternal appearance masked a keen mind.

"No. Not an emergency at all." Ambrose cleared his throat, unsure of how to proceed. He decided he might as well go directly to the point. He pulled his letter of resignation from his inside pocket and handed it to him. "I have decided to resign my commission. Effective immediately if possible."

The admiral unfolded the document, quickly scanned it, and placed it into his inside jacket pocket. His face betrayed no hint of his thoughts when he replied, "Though you had informed me of your future intentions, I perceive this to be a rather abrupt change in plans for you. I presume this has something to do with your current assignment?"

Jenkins appeared with their meals. After refilling their coffees, he asked, "Can I get you anything else, my Lords?"

"No, thank you. This will do fine." The admiral adjusted his napkin and addressed Ambrose. "May I ask what precisely has precipitated this choice?"

Ambrose considered his answer. He decided his best course of action with the admiral was complete honesty. "I have concluded that Lady Katherine Blythe is an innocent in the matter we have been investigating. She does not appear to have the connections, or the character required to be an operative."

Admiral Hews looked at him as though waiting for him to continue. Ambrose felt his cheeks flush.

"And it seems I have developed a tendre for her." He struggled to continue, unsure how best to explain his intentions. "I find that this change in occupation best suits my future."

The admiral chuckled. He did not answer Ambrose immediately but attacked his meal instead. The men ate in silence. At last, the admiral placed his napkin upon his plate, leaned back, and looking at Ambrose with a distinct twinkle in his eyes, he said, "That is the way of it then."

"Yes. I wanted to assure you that should the service require my assistance at any time, I will make myself available."

The admiral folded his hands on his belly. "It is not without regret that I accept your resignation, lieutenant. But I see the time has come for you to move on. There are a few things I should share with you at this time. First, I suspect that your conclusions regarding the ladies involved may have some validity. Despite an intensive investigation my men too, were unable to find evidence to connect your young woman to espionage. What mistakes occurred in the transfer of the codes I do not know, but like you, I am inclined to think that mistake it was."

The admiral leaned forward and placed his hands on the table. "And second, you should know that we have discovered the ladies may still be in an awkward position. It seems my men have not been the only ones watching the movements of Miss Blythe and her aunt. On several occasions, my men detected the surveillance but have not yet determined the parties of interest. And this is of course, further evidence of the ladies' lack of knowledge in the affair. One can only assume other parties remain interested in the codes."

The admiral cleared his throat. "And finally, the shop

owned by Lady Carstairs was the site of a break-in two nights ago. Nothing was taken. However, the place was thoroughly searched, leaving it in a shambles. One can assume that the faked codes were not found because the surveillance of the home and its residents continues. We believe this surveillance has been conducted by one individual, at least so far."

Ambrose furrowed his brow in concern, and said with disbelief, "And you have not been able to catch the fellow, or at least discover his identity?"

The admiral shook his head. "It is a little more complicated than that I am afraid. The affair must be handled with some delicacy. We are certain this man is just a hireling. We have followed him to an apartment at number four Downing Lane, where he identifies himself as a Mister Raven, but this name proved to be an alias."

The admiral met Ambrose's eyes. "The danger will not disappear with his capture. You must see that only when we have his employer will the ladies be safe—and then we too will have our answers."

A moment of silence followed these revelations. Ambrose felt his stomach twist into a knot at the danger Katherine was being exposed to. His first instinct was to track and attack the man who had been following her, the man who was most likely to be responsible for the break-in at her shop. The idea of immediate action and vengeance was a satisfying one, but clearly it would be the most ineffective. The admiral had taken pains to see that he understood this aspect of the problem.

He realized the admiral was focused upon him as though waiting for some indication he comprehended the situation.

He nodded slowly. "I understand. I will provide the

ladies with what protection I can. Furthermore, I will keep you informed of any headway I make in the situation."

The admiral rose to his feet. "It is time I took my leave. I am afraid there is much to do at my office."

Ambrose noticed the approach of Theo with another gentleman. "Thank you for meeting me, Admiral Hews. And thank you for the information."

Admiral Hews extended his hand. "And thank you for your service. We will be losing a fine officer in you, sir. Best of luck with your future, young man." He turned to Theo and nodded in the direction of his acquaintance. "I am afraid I must rush off. Take no offence. My duties await me."

He hurried away.

Theo smiled, his eyes following the admiral to the exit. "Rather a serious breakfast companion for a lieutenant. I hope I have not interfered in your plans, my man."

"Not at all. We had just finished our conversation."

"Ah, good." He turned to his companion. "Edmund, Viscount of Serves, may I present to you my friend, Ambrose St. Claire. Shall we have a seat, gentleman? I see that Jenkins here is eager to serve us."

Indeed, Jenkins took their orders as they made themselves comfortable in the plush leather seats.

The viscount shook Ambrose's hand. "I have heard a great deal about you, St. Claire. In fact, I recruited Pembroke here to give me an introduction."

The viscount looked him over as though assessing a future employee.

Ambrose noted he looked much like his son, Jeremy, with the same pale skin and dark blond hair. Yet in the viscount the features were hardened, and his face was longer, with deep frown lines etched into his cheeks. Like

Jeremy, his clothes were perfectly tailored, but conservative and elegantly formal. There was an air of solemnity about him; he did not appear to be a man inclined to humor. He carried himself like a gentleman entitled and accustomed to the accolades and privileges of his title and position in society.

"I find that hard to believe," Ambrose said. "I keep a rather low profile here in town. In fact, it has only been a few months since I returned from service abroad."

The viscount smiled thinly. "So I have been told. As it happens, I fear I must take an interest in you, sir. I hear you are often in the company of my niece, Miss Katherine Blythe. She is also my ward."

Theo interjected, "I too have met the young woman. Miss Katherine is a jewel. You must be immensely proud of her, my Lord."

"Yes. She is a lovely woman. Sadly, events have not gone well for her." The viscount shook his head. "She has not been received well in the social world. She has a broken engagement in her past. Not her fault of course, but society can be most unforgiving."

He looked at Ambrose. "It was broken after a year's engagement. Most unfortunate, a horrible scandal." He paused and seemed to evaluate the impact of his revelations before continuing. "It did, of course, leave the polite world wondering just what could have been the cause of it all. She is quite notorious I am afraid."

Ambrose raised his eyebrows. "I am sure those stories are safely in the past. People are like children who lose interest quickly in their toys. What was once much in their minds is easily displaced with new curiosities. You may put your mind at ease, sir. That gossip has long been forgotten."

The viscount gave a long-suffering sigh. "The poor dear

has little to recommend her. Her father was a wastrel and her inheritance, The Meadows, has been a drain on resources rather than a boon." The lines on his face seemed to deepen as he continued. "I fear she is long on the shelf. My only hope is that my dutiful son Jeremy might take her off my hands."

Theo saved Ambrose from replying by bursting into laughter. "You must be joking, sir! I have met the woman. She is a diamond of the first water. If you are in search of a suitor look no more. I am at your service."

The viscount scowled at Theo in annoyance. Ignoring his offer, he addressed Ambrose. "I am sure as a second son, you will consider your options carefully." He gave Ambrose a hard look before standing. "And now I must leave you gentleman. I see my companion the Duke of Bedford has arrived."

Ambrose and Theo watched the viscount depart in stunned disbelief.

Theo turned to Ambrose. "What was that? The man demands an introduction. I was sure he would sing the Lady Katherine's praises in hopes of making a match. But this? It was like he was determined to dissuade you. Poor Katherine. I wonder how many suitors he has sent running with his sad tales of woe."

"Most bizarre. It is strange indeed. No wonder she has had such a challenge in holding her suitors. That was daunting." Ambrose watched the man from across the room. "Either he is a dull creature, or he has motives of his own."

"My guess is the latter. Enough of him. You must tell me why I found you here with the esteemed admiral." Theo looked at him curiously.

Ambrose filled him in on his decision to resign his

commission and the disturbing conversation about Katherine's predicament that followed. And though he knew the news of his marital plans for Katherine would be received with much hilarity, he informed him of those as well.

At this point, he needed all the assistance he could get.

Chapter Twelve

It was a late breakfast, more of a brunch for the ladies gathered around the table. Kate was thankful for Clarissa's excited chatter. It seemed to her that for Clarissa at least, last night had been a magical evening. It had apparently been a resounding success, with Jeremy acting the perfect escort. Kate let the renditions wash over her.

"You seem quiet this morning, Katherine. Is your head still bothering you?" asked Lady Carstairs, looking at her carefully. "Can I get you something for it?"

Kate found she could not meet her eyes. She was sure the events of last night were written on her face. "No. I am fine. I am just thinking about my day."

To her relief, Milly bustled into the room. "A gentleman caller for you, Miss Katherine. A bit early for visiting in my mind. Afternoon tea is the time for callers. It is barely lunch." She frowned. "Lord Jeremy. He has asked for a private word."

A clatter from across the table drew everyone's attention. Clarissa dropped her fork onto her plate. She stared with an expression of shock at Milly. "For Kate? Are you sure? A private word?"

Milly gave another snort. "He has asked for Miss Katherine." She shot Clarissa a dark scowl, before turning back to Kate. "Now then, shall I send him to the library or leave him standing in the hall?"

The question fell upon a silent table.

Lady Carstairs was the first to recover. "Send him to the library, Milly. Tell him Miss Katherine will be in shortly." She looked at Kate and added softly, "Do you wish me to attend with you, Katey?"

Kate leaned back in her chair and closed her eyes. Dealing with Jeremy this morning, of all mornings, was not a scenario she could cope with today. She sighed. "No. I think I will have to handle this myself, thank you, Aunty."

Clarissa emitted a strangled sob. "Not my Jeremy. Surely, he cannot be making this request after last night. A private word can only mean one thing. It must be a mistake."

She covered her face in her napkin.

Kate rose and walked up behind Clarissa. "It will all be well, not to worry, Clarissa."

She patted her absently, looking over her shoulders at Lady Carstairs, who watched her intently. She was in no mood to comfort her friend.

She repeated her assurance listlessly, "All will be well."

Lady Carstairs stood. "There is no rush, Katherine. No need to make any decisions today should you be asked. Keep that in mind."

"Let us hope he has come to discuss some issue with The Meadows." Kate tossed her napkin on the table and, straightening her shoulders, headed for the library.

Jeremy rushed to greet her as she entered the room. He

had dressed in his usual flare, in fawn-colored jacket and trousers, with a bright pink waistcoat that sparkled with his signature gold threads. Kate saw that he had mastered the cascade neck cloth, for his head was held stiffly erect above a waterfall of white silk, secured with a diamond tie clip.

Grasping her hands, he said, "I have such news for you. I am sure you will be overwhelmed. Come, we must sit down."

Kate allowed herself to be led over to the davenport. He settled beside her.

He cleared his throat. "Now, then, as you know it has always been my wish, and indeed my family's wish that we marry, Katherine—"

"Oh, please, Jeremy, not today." Kate felt her stomach turn with disappointment.

Jeremy ignored her objections. "As you know it has always been assumed the two us would marry—"

"No. No, Jeremy it has not. Please, please. Let us just leave this. I have no interest in a marriage." She tried to pull her hands from his, but he held them firmly.

There was no stopping him. He went on as though he had not heard her objections. "I realize you have been made to wait. I am here to tell you that, at long last, I have decided to come up to scratch."

He nodded sagely.

"Jeremy—" Kate tried once more to pry her hands from his to stand, but he hung on to her, forcing her to remain in her seat. She felt a wave of annoyance.

He pressed on. "I know this must be exciting for you. I can only imagine you thought this day would never come. And after all, at twenty-four years of age, you had to have assumed your prospects were rather hopeless. But here I am. You may be relieved of your worries at last."

He graced her with a wide smile.

Kate finally managed to free her hands and stood. "I assure you I am far from relieved. Jeremy, you must know that I—"

Jeremy stood with her and interrupted, "I have spoken to Father. Though you are not the match I had hoped for, after all your father was a mere Baron, the arrangement is adequate. He assures me that despite the financial problems of the past, The Meadows will provide a substantial dowery for you. Indeed, with my income, we will do rather well. You must be pleased to know that father supports the match."

He arched his back, expanding his chest with pride. "And just think of it, Kate! Despite your dismal prospects, you can now see yourself a future viscountess." He leaned back on his heels and though it seemed an impossible task with his tightly strung neck cloth, managed to raise his chin a notch.

Kate had had enough. It was too much. "My dismal prospects? How dare you." She took a deep breath and attempted to continue more calmly, "I will not marry you, Jeremy. You must see that we do not suit."

Jeremy's mouth dropped. "Not suit! What can you mean? I came here today with the best possible news for you. I have asked you to be my bride—"

Kate interrupted, "But you have not asked me, Jeremy. Not at all."

Jeremy smirked. "So that is the problem. You expected me to get down on one knee. I have obviously offended your romantic sensibilities."

He made as if to get down to his knees.

Kate grasped his arm. "No. Do not. I will not marry you, Jeremy. No matter how the offer is put." She continued to hold his arm and repeated herself, this time more slowly and with firm emphasis, "I will not marry you."

She held his gaze and allowed her words to sink in.

A dull red stain inched up his face as the realization of her rejection took root. At first, he seemed to deflate before her eyes. Then his eyes glittered with anger as he began to absorb her rejection. He shook off her arm.

"You are making a grave error, Katherine." He walked to the door and, opening it, turned back to Katherine. "You can be assured I will be speaking to my father the viscount about this. He is after all your guardian."

Kate crossed her arms, and replied, "Joint-guardian. And not for long, for as you pointed out, I am fast reaching the age of majority. The matter is closed."

"We shall see." With that, Jeremy stalked through the foyer and pulled open the door.

On the step, posies in hand stood Ambrose. Jeremy brushed past him, red-faced and muttering, and headed for his carriage.

Chapter Thirteen

Kate saw Ambrose at the door but found she could not face him just yet. Letting Milly greet him she whirled around and hurried back into the parlor for a moment's respite.

Aunt Elizabeth hustled into the room behind her, followed by a wide-eyed Clarrisa.

"Am I right in assuming Jeremy's proposal was not successful?" she asked.

"You are right. And I dare say he was not pleased."

"Oh!" Clarrisa could not contain her smile. "I... I am certain you have made the right choice, Katey. But are you sure? He is a fine catch."

Despite her question, she was unmistakably thrilled with Kate's decision and could not resist clapping her hands together gleefully.

Milly appeared at the door looking annoyed. "Lord Ambrose is still waiting at the door. Shall I send him on his way? Hardly finished lunch. Gentleman callers at this time of day—"

Lady Carstairs interrupted, "Perfect. We could use a

little distraction. Bring him to the library. We will have our tea there, with a little dessert, Milly, if you could. Those jellied biscuits would be fine."

Milly snorted her displeasure but turned to escort in their guest.

Kate felt her cheeks grow warm as Ambrose entered the room. She realized again how handsome he was. His black hair and olive skin set off his startling blue eyes. He was impeccable as always, dressed in a deep brown morning suit, with hessians pulled over matching trousers.

He held out a bouquet of violets to Kate. "For you, my dear."

She found that she was momentarily frozen in place. She could only look at him with her mouth slightly agape. She had been anticipating his arrival today with apprehension. Now that he was here, she had no idea how to proceed.

Aunt Elizabeth came to the rescue, reaching for the bouquet. "Why, how lovely." Turning to Clarissa she said, "Perhaps you could put these in water, Clarissa."

She handed her the flowers before taking Ambrose by the arm and leading him to the settee. "You must join us for tea."

"Tea. Yes, well...perhaps later." Ambrose turned back to look at Kate who was slowly regaining her composure. "I wonder if I might first have a private word with Katherine."

"A private word? Today?" Lady Carstairs was now the one to find herself speechless.

Kate walked towards them. "Ambrose, I think it might be better if—"

"Yes," Ambrose replied more firmly, ignoring her interruption, "I have an important matter to discuss."

He straightened his shoulders and gave Kate a determined look.

"I am not sure that today is the best of days," Lady Carstairs said. "Maybe tomorrow would be more suitable. Or next week? I am just not sure that now is the time..."

She turned to Kate helplessly. "Katherine?"

Kate sighed and replied to her while eyeing Ambrose with a look of irritation, "It will be fine, Aunt Elizabeth, if you could give us a few minutes."

Lady Carstairs reluctantly went to the door. "All right, my dear. I will get Milly to hold off a while with the tea."

With a final concerned look at Katherine, and a pitying glance at Ambrose she left, closing the door behind her.

Feeling exasperated, Kate turned to Ambrose. "This had better not be some hare-brained proposal after last night's debacle because if it is, let me just say a resounding no right now."

"Katherine, you cannot mean that." Ambrose went to her and raised her hand to his lips. "It would be my fondest wish if you would consent to be my wife. I realize—"

"Oh, heavens it is." Kate shook off his hand and went to her desk. She folded up the oversized pattern book she had been working on earlier in the morning and tucked it into her satchel. "I will not hear another word about it."

Ambrose faced her from across the desk. "But Katherine, we must talk. I understand last night was a bit of a disappointment. But you must see that—"

"A disappointment. Yes, it was a disappointment." She rested both hands on the desktop and leaned towards him. "I have longed to have an adventure. From all the talk of love making I had hoped for a transcendental experience. Everything I read, or heard, made an affair sound exhilarating and exciting. The whole experience was a complete letdown. It turns out the thrills of an affair are much exaggerated."

"As to last night, you have my apologies. But you are wrong, there are thrills to making love. Though I admit last night was a rather tawdry affair." He furrowed his brow and turned to her with a grimace. "Things might have been different had I known you were..."

He paused. "This is not where I saw this conversation going. Katherine, you must see that marriage is our only option. You were an innocent, and it is my responsibility to make matters right. It is my duty."

"I will not be married out of some misdirected sense of honor." She straightened up and glared at him. "And I am not an innocent girl. I will be twenty-five in two weeks. Can you say with honesty that you would be making this proposal if not for last night?"

Ambrose looked at her with a wounded expression. "That is not fair. Of course not."

"Ah ha! There you have it." Katherine gathered up her satchel and came out from behind her desk. "And now this conversation is closed. I am afraid I must get to work. I have plenty to do today at the shop."

She headed for the door. She turned and faced him with her hand on the doorknob. "I cannot believe I had two proposals this morning. First from Jeremy who had the audacity to tell me I must marry him out of desperation and be relieved that he offered some pathetic last chance at marriage, and now you. You, with your talk of duty! Well, may I just inform you," she said, raising her voice, "I am not interested or obliged to marry either of you!"

Ambrose's eyes widened with outrage, "Jeremy proposed to you? Surely you would not consider that fop. Katherine, you must—"

"I think now is not the time to tell me what I am obligated to do." Katherine felt her face burn with frustration and anger. "This may come as a surprise to you, but I am not interested in a marriage. I wanted an affair, some excitement and adventure. But it seems there is nothing to be found in that direction either."

"Katherine we must talk. There are other matters we need to discuss."

"Not today. I find I am through with talking for today." With that, she swung open the door.

Clarissa tumbled into the room, landing in a heap at her feet.

Kate looked down at her, surprised. It was apparent she had been listening a little too closely at the door. She could not stifle a bitter laugh as she stepped neatly over her.

She looked back at Ambrose. "I will leave you to assist her, Ambrose."

Ambrose stood, helplessly trapped in the library by the sprawled Clarissa. "Katherine, wait. We need to talk."

Katherine was determined to leave as quickly as possible. She grabbed her cloak and bonnet from the rack at the entry and headed out the door, putting them on as she went.

She was almost at the end of the block when she turned to see Ambrose running towards her. Of all the nerve, she thought, as she rounded the corner. She quickened her step.

Lifting her skirts, she tried to run, but the heavy material became tangled in her legs. She turned back to check her distance from Ambrose and ploughed headlong into a man.

"Ugh. So sorry. I did not see you there." She lurched back.

Looking up, she saw the fellow had his face covered in a black mask. Too late she realized she was in danger. She spun around and attempted to get away, but he grabbed her by the shoulders from behind. Kate was only able to let out a single scream before his hand covered her mouth. He dragged her along, veering off the street into a narrow alley. The sweet odor of pipe tobacco overwhelmed her. A ring on his finger bit into her lip. His other arm gripped her across the chest, holding her tight.

"Keep your trap closed." He growled into her ear; his covered head held close as he pinioned her from behind.

Kate continued to struggle. She twisted her body, jamming at him with all her strength. She connected a solid blow to his midsection with her elbow and heard him grunt.

He tightened his hold.

"Stop it, you wild cat. You'll not be hurt if you hand over your bag." He put his head close to hers again. He said quietly in a lilting voice, "Calm down. It's the bag I'm after, and when I get it, you will be on your way unhurt. If you behave yourself, missy."

Ambrose interrupted them; his voice was soft and calm. "Be still, Katherine. Let him take the satchel."

Kate stopped struggling. She was weak with relief. Ambrose had found them. Her eyes met his. He stood immobile at the alley entrance only a few feet away, his open hands spread out from his sides, showing his lack of weapons.

"Let him take the thing, Katherine. All will be well," he said in easy tones, as if gentling a wild horse. He had not moved from the entrance to the alley, except to hold his arms a little further from his body.

"Listen to the man." The scoundrel's hand left her mouth. He began to pull the strap from her shoulder.

"No!" Kate held her satchel with both arms tightly

against her body as the strap was ripped from her shoulder. "My patterns. You will not get them."

"Kate, for the love of god, give the man your bag."

Kate glared at him. "I will not!"

The man gave the strap a hard yank, pulling her along for a few steps before she was forced to release it or be dragged down the alley.

"Ambrose! My patterns." Kate watched the thief run to the end of the alley and out of sight. "Ambrose. Do not just leave him run off with my patterns!"

She hiked up her skirts and began to run after him.

"Wait, Katherine." Ambrose sped after her and grasped her arm. "Wait. Let him go."

"No. We must follow him," she said, trying to free herself from his hold. She sagged in defeat. "Hours of work. Gone."

She felt hot tears trail down her face as she realized the thief was beyond their reach. All was lost. She cast Ambrose an accusatory glare. He had been of no help at all. Indeed, she might have been better off if he had not appeared in the alley.

He pulled her gently into his arms. "It is okay, my dear. Everything is all right."

Kate rested her head on his shoulders, comforted by the warmth and strength of his arms.

Remembering her patterns, she pulled back and smacked him hard on the chest. "How could you have just let him leave? He was not even armed. We could easily have wrestled him down."

She pummeled him with both hands on the chest in frustration.

Ambrose grabbed her wrists and held them firmly. "Stop. It is good, Katherine. He is gone and you are safe."

Nothing was going as Kate had hoped it would. All her hopes for adventure and romance were squashed. First the disappointing interlude in the carriage, then a morning of half-hearted proposals, and now this. It was too much.

Kate laid her head back on Ambrose's shoulders and sobbed.

Ambrose held her gently, until the sobs subsided. When she slowly leaned back out of his arms, he wordlessly held out his handkerchief for her.

Kate blew her nose and mopped her cheeks before handing it back. "Why, Ambrose? Why just let him rob me?"

"I wanted him to get the bag. It was important that he get away cleanly with that blasted satchel. I told you earlier that we had to have a talk."

"I think you better explain."

Ambrose took her arm. "We will talk as we walk. We need to get out of this alley." He paused as they reached the street. "Now, then, do you wish to return home or proceed to your shop?"

"To work. I spent hours copying that pattern book and now I must begin again." She gave him a disgruntled look. "Some villain has my work. I fail to see what possible explanation you can give."

Ambrose gave a long sigh. "I always knew about the salon, and your work. I know about your friends and acquaintances and even your financial situation."

Kate looked at him with confusion. She was about to speak when Ambrose continued. "I will explain all. But you must first promise me you will listen without interrupting."

"Ambrose, what are you saying?"

"You must promise to hear me out before you comment." He stopped walking and turned to her. "Let me finish the entire tale before you jump to conclusions. No interruptions. Promise me."

His earnest expression only served to make Kate more apprehensive. "I promise."

Ambrose sighed in relief, took her arm, and continued down the street. He took a moment to gather his thoughts and then began to speak.

Kate listened silently. Ambrose recited the whole sordid affair from its beginnings in the village of Hernes to their recent confrontation in the alley. They had reached the back entrance of the shop before he had concluded his tale.

Kate unlocked the door and led him in.

"My office." She indicated a chair and said, "Perhaps you should sit down. I think this situation calls for a cup of tea. I certainly could use one. I will be right back."

As Kate prepared the tea, she contemplated the situation. She must remain calm. That Ambrose had met her under false pretenses was neither here nor there. She was sure his attraction for her was real.

She was furious with the loss of the patterns. But they were copies. She could do them again. Ambrose was convinced her safety depended on the robber getting the faked codebook.

And the codebook. She thought back to her meeting at the wharf with the smuggling captain. How bizarre that she had managed to say a password by mistake. 'The ides of March.' She frowned. But it had been March, and it had been a miserable blustering evening. The captain had made her repeat her words. Everything began to make sense. The break-ins, her horrible feeling that she was being followed, all of it fit together now. And Ambrose. He had tracked her down in London, not because he was attracted to her, but because he was after the codes.

She reasoned that his dedication to the admiral and to his country was to be commended despite the invasion of her privacy. With a shock she realized she did not want to give him up. She enjoyed her time with him. He had invaded her life; she had seen him daily since her trip to Hernes. Somehow, she had developed strong feelings for him.

In the aftermath of the robbery, she had forgotten his halfhearted proposal. Somehow that proposal was more infuriating than all the other events of this bizarre morning. She decided to set her frustration with his proposal aside for now and concentrate instead on the matter at hand.

Katherine took a deep breath and prepared to face Ambrose.

She entered her office with the tea tray. Ambrose rose to assist her. After pouring for them both, she settled herself behind her desk.

"Ambrose," she said, "about the break-ins at my home and office, was it the Home Office which ordered them?"

"No. Only the first one. The admiral had a man slip into your home to steal the notebook. The plan was that he not be noticed. Unfortunately, he was discovered by your man."

Kate sighed in relief. "That is good to know. I found the intrusions and the destruction of my office quite disturbing."

She could not suppress a shaky smile as Ambrose reached for the biscuits she had included on the tea tray. The events on the street had apparently not affected his appetite.

"I am sorry for that, Katherine. I am sure it has been most distressing for you. I think we can reasonably assume the man we encountered today was the culprit. I wonder…"

Ambrose paused to munch his biscuit. "Was there anything about the man on the street that you found familiar? Is there anything that might help identify him?"

"I am not sure. He wore the mask over his face." Katherine thought back to the incident in the alley.

Ambrose commented, "Anything we can remember might be of help to us. For instance, he certainly was not a regular footpad. He was dressed more like a gentleman than a street thug."

"Yes, you are right!" Katherine looked at him with enthusiasm. "But a country gentleman or perhaps a businessman. He wore short pants and stockings. Those are not the current fashion. Not at all what a London gentleman would wear."

"Ah, you are right. We have not seen short pants and hose in town for some time. There are only a few country gentlemen, and some of the merchant class seen in them." Ambrose flashed her a look of appreciation. "Excellent idea. That may help."

Katherine beamed beneath his praise. She concentrated on the moment the thief had pulled her into the alley.

"He smelled of pipe tobacco. A sweet blend." Kate replayed the scene again in her mind. "And he wore a ring. It bruised my lip. When I think about it, there was something about him that was familiar."

She concentrated once more. There was something she was missing.

"His voice! Yes. He called me, missy!" She looked at Ambrose with excitement. "There is only one man who has ever called me missy. I wonder..."

Ambrose watched her. "Katherine, what are you thinking?"

Kate took a long sip of her tea. "How old would you say he was? I thought that he was definitely not a young man—too thick." She leaned back in her chair, taking another drink of her tea. "But he also was not old. He did after all, run down the street. Would you say he was about forty, Ambrose?"

Kate's excitement was growing. "It all fits. He even smokes a pipe. And the accent. He had a bit of a Scottish brogue. But I do not want to be too hasty."

Ambrose was becoming impatient. "Who, Kate? Do you know him?"

"I cannot be completely sure," she answered slowly, "but he may be someone I know. He resembles our overseer at The Meadows, Mr. McClury. It seems outrageous and I am by no means positive, but the more I sort through the incident the more possible it becomes."

"That is marvelous, Katherine. I will have to bring this information to the admiral immediately." He rose to his feet.

Kate went to him. "Remember, it is only a theory, Ambrose. I am not entirely certain."

"It is something. The admiral will check it out." Ambrose stepped towards her. He reached out and touched her bruised lip. "I am sorry for this."

He leaned in close to her and brushed his lips across hers. "My offer from this morning still stands. I want you for my wife, Katherine."

"Ambrose—"

Ambrose interrupted before she could object. "You must take a hansom home today. You may not walk. And do not leave your house tonight."

Kate was irritated. His arrogance knew no bounds. "Really, Ambrose, I think you are being a bit overbearing. I am not one of your men. It is hardly your place to issue orders."

Ambrose ignored her objections. "What are your plans for this week? Will you be attending any soirees?"

Kate debated not answering him but glancing at his determined face decided it might be best to give in. He would not be waylaid. Kate was given a brief insight into his role as a commander of troops. He was formidable.

She told him, "We have the Chesterfeld's ball tomorrow night, and we will be attending the Earl of Hargrove's masquerade the next night."

He nodded. "I will be at your house at eight with the coach tomorrow night. And I suppose I can find a mask for the Hargrove's." He reached over and smoothed her furrowed brow, then rested his hands on her shoulders. Looking at her intensely, he said, "Do not be irritated, Kate. I cannot allow anything to happen to you. Promise me you will be careful, at least until we are absolutely sure you are safe."

"I promise."

Ambrose seemed satisfied.

"There is one more thing." He reached to her bruised lip again, touching it carefully then running his fingers down the curve of her chin. Holding her face cupped in his hand, he continued, "I regret the most your disappointing initiation into the world of love. I promise I will see to that little problem as soon as possible."

Kate felt her cheeks turning pink. She could think of no reply. She watched him walk to the door and open it. He paused with his hand on the knob.

Turning back, he gave her a boyish grin. "It seems I will have a busy couple of days looking after my future bride."

He quickly slipped through the door, closing it behind him before she could reply.

Chapter Fourteen

Kate examined her fresh copies of the patterns with pride. She had spent all of yesterday afternoon and evening working. This morning she had attached swatches of cloth to the designs as possibilities for her clients. She leaned back in her chair and smiled with satisfaction. Another few days and she would have recovered what she had lost to the footpad.

Madame Bouvier stood at her open office door. "Mr. Bentley Brown is here to see you. He insists. I have tried to remove him, but he refuses to take no for an answer."

Bentley Brown pushed past her into the room.

Madame bristled. "Mon Dieu. You cannot come back here, monsieur."

"It will be fine, Madame. I will speak to him."

Madame hesitated. "If you need assistance, Roland is here packing our material order. He will have no problem removing this man."

She glared at Mr. Brown.

"Thank you. Tell Roland I will call for him if it is needed."

Madame gave Mr. Brown another warning look before leaving. She purposely opened the door wide before heading back down the hall.

Once again, Kate did not rise from her desk to greet him. "What is it you have to say to me, Mr. Brown? Whatever it is, make it quick. I have a great deal of work to do."

Bentley Brown walked to the desk. "Good day, Mrs. Sevile," He smirked. "Or should I call you Lady Katherine Blythe?"

He grinned at her, rocking proudly back and forth on his heels, waiting for her response.

Katherine looked at him and said nothing. She swallowed the initial panic that his words had wrought. Looking at him as he stood in her office, proud of his discovery, she felt a rage wash over her. How dare this slime of a man threaten her. She waited for his next words.

"Now that is a little secret you do not want anyone to know, do you? Imagine the talk. Lady Katherine involved in trade. The lovely young miss pretending to be a widow so she can hawk her wares around town. A shopkeeper! I cannot see many ladies sitting down to tea with the likes of you. Can you my dear?" It seemed impossible that he could smile more broadly, but he did. "I bet you are ready to deal with me now, aren't you?"

He laughed, smoothing back a tendril of greasy hair that had fallen over his eye. Kate watched fascinated as he used both hands to smooth back his hair, revealing a forehead covered in pimples. She shuddered.

"A young woman like you, looking for a husband," he said with a chuckle, "would not be too pleased to have that information bandied about, now, would she?"

Kate willed her voice to remain calm. "Just what is it you want?"

"I am thinking you could work for me, Lady Blythe. We can start with those new French patterns and then after that who knows?" He laughed again, obviously enjoying this moment.

"I will never work for you!" Kate felt a rush of anger. How dare he? This little weasel of a man! She concentrated on keeping her voice more controlled before she replied. Curling her lips into a smirk, she said, "You have miscalculated. I am not interested in a husband. Furthermore, my place in society has little interest to me. Fire away. Perhaps your gossip will be good for business."

Bentley Brown looked at her with his mouth agape. He seemed to regain his composure and leered.

"But you will be ruined." He adjusted the grimy cuffs of his tan jacket downward as he planned his next words. "Come now, Mrs. Sevile, or pardon me, Lady Blythe, what is a little work in exchange for all that peace of mind?"

He leaned forward, and said conspiratorially, "Only think of what your new gentleman, the one you have been riding about the park with, will think of you."

Kate realized he must have caught sight of her with Ambrose on one of their morning rides and then hatched his plan. She thought about Ambrose and his reaction or non-reaction, to the discovery that she was involved in trade. Just yesterday he had taken tea in this very office.

The memory gave her confidence. "You have picked the wrong victim, Bentley Brown. You see, I have already experienced the social ruin you speak of and survived it. Your threat does not scare me. In fact, it is laughable." Kate leaned back in her chair and took in his shocked expression with satisfaction. "It seems you are as miserable as a blackmailer as you are a businessman. Now if you do not mind, I have work to do."

"I know your guardian is the Count of Serves." He raised his voice in desperation. "I wonder what he would have to say?"

Kate laughed aloud. "The Viscount will be my guardian for two more weeks. After that, he will have no say in my affairs." Kate stood. "Now I believe it is time for you to leave, or do I need to call Roland to help me remove you?"

Bentley Brown leaned forward as though to threaten her. He glared at her with his hands fisted in frustration. A quiver of fear tingled up her spine as she waited for his response. Kate wondered if she did indeed need to call for Roland. But Bentley seemed to think better of it. He turned and left without a word.

Kate sat and thought about what had just occurred. That Bentley Brown had resorted to blackmail was not a surprise to her. He was a scoundrel. His desperation indicated that his business must be floundering. What surprised her was her reaction to his threats. She realized her words were not bravado at all.

If Mr. Brown made good on his threats, she would weather the storm. If the scandal was too much for Ambrose, then so be it. She would soon learn if her Ambrose could accept her as she was.

Chapter Fifteen

The evening was everything Kate had hoped for. She found herself whirled around the dance floor by many admirers. Theo had graciously taken her for the first dance. Having the attention of an Earl seemed to pique the interest of the other gentleman of the town. She had then immediately stood for a country dance with Ambrose. After that, it seemed as though she struggled to catch her breath as man after man requested a dance.

Ambrose handed her a glass of champagne as she returned to the sidelines at last. "For you, my dear. I thought you might take a moment."

"Thank you, Ambrose. This is perfect."

An elderly gentleman, accompanied by a younger man approached. "Ah, Mr. St, Claire, you must introduce me to your lady."

Ambrose immediately obliged. "Admiral Hews, may I present Lady Katherine Blythe."

The admiral smiled and took her hand. "It is indeed a pleasure to meet you at last." He looked her up and down.

"Ah, but you are lovely. I have heard only good things about you. Such a pleasure, my dear."

The admiral leaned in and said quietly, "My men are looking into your Mr. McClury, a good piece of work that. I commend you and St. Claire, here, on a job well done. You can be assured that all this nonsense will end soon."

The admiral stepped to the side and indicated his companion. "And this is my friend and fellow employee, Sergeant Joseph Ames."

The sergeant was a very tall, very serious looking young man. Kate smiled in greeting.

"A pleasure to meet you, ma'am." The sergeant gave his bow. He seemed preoccupied. "If you would excuse me, I see someone I must catch a word with. So sorry to rush off."

He gave another short bow and disappeared into the crowd.

Lady Carstairs approached.

The admiral smiled widely. "And the Lady Carstairs." He took her hand and raised it to his lips. "So honored to meet you once again. I have not danced in many a year, but I find I cannot miss the opportunity to dance with the most beautiful woman at the ball. I wonder, would you honor me with this waltz?"

To Kate's surprise, her aunt blushed a light pink.

"I would," Lady Carstairs replied.

Kate and Ambrose watched the couple as they glided across the room.

"Now that is interesting," Kate mused.

Across the room, Jeremy waltzed with Clarrisa. She tossed back her head and let out a peel of laughter, while Jeremy gazed at her with an indulgent grin.

Kate smiled to herself. They made a rather fashionable couple.

Kate decided to take the opportunity to visit the retiring room. She touched Ambrose's arm and handed him her glass. "Would you excuse me? I will be just a minute."

The lady's room was down a hall just past a curtained alcove.

Upon returning to the main salon, she stood next to the alcove and searched for her party. The ball had become a crush. More and more guests had arrived. She could not seem to catch a glimpse of Ambrose and Lady Carstairs. A low murmur coming from behind the curtain interrupted her perusal. She glanced down and saw two pairs of boots extending from beneath the curtains.

She was about to move on when the drapes were pulled back. She faced a disgruntled looking Sergeant Ames and his companion, an unfamiliar older gentleman, who had the look of a country squire. The sergeant said, "Eavesdropping, were you?"

He looked down at her, his grave face twisted into sharp disapproving lines.

"No, no." Kate shook her head, flustered with the accusation. "I was just looking for my party. I... I am terribly sorry."

The sergeant did not reply but shot her a suspicious look.

"So sorry. I had no idea you were there." She blushed a bright pink. "Truly I heard nothing."

When he did not respond, she continued awkwardly, "I will just move along."

It was with some relief that she found Ambrose standing alone along the edge of the dance floor.

He reached for her hands. "It has become a little crowded for me I am afraid. Perhaps it is time you and I took a turn in the gardens. There is something I hoped I could show you."

"Excellent idea."

Kate and Ambrose slipped through the patio door and out into the grounds. To her surprise, Ambrose took her hand and led her around the corner of the house.

Kate could not suppress a giggle as he pulled her into the stables. He yanked the heavy door closed behind them, secured the latch, and reached for the lantern. If anyone else was out on the grounds, they would not be disturbed here.

Ambrose lit the lantern, illuminating the stables in a soft amber light. A horse gave a muffled acknowledgement from one of the stalls.

Ambrose led her to the first stall. "Chesterfeld has some of the best horse flesh in town," he said, reaching to stroke the nose of a curious mare who had reached over her gate to greet them. "I have tried on several occasions to purchase one of his Arabians, but he is uninterested in selling."

They walked further down the aisles, stopping to admire the horses along the way.

They reached an open area near the rear of the stables where a mound of hay was kept. Ambrose hooked the lantern to the side of a stall.

He reached for her and said softly, "It is true that there is much beauty in these stables. And I have in my arms the most beautiful prize of all." He pulled her close and kissed her gently. "I must confess I have ulterior motives for bringing you here tonight."

He leaned down and kissed her again. An explosion of heat reverberated through her as he deepened the kiss, holding her tight against his body.

"Tell me you like my kisses, Kate," he murmured against his lips.

"I love your kisses, Ambrose," Kate responded breathlessly. She slid her arms into his jacket and ran her hands up and down his back, feeling the strength of him as his muscles contracted with her touch. "Oh, Ambrose."

She breathed deeply, taking in his male scent.

She could feel his hot breath as he planted moist kisses along her neck. He paused and, pulling back from her, waited until she opened her eyes.

"Let me make love to you, Katherine." He looked at her earnestly, his blue eyes black in the soft light. He kissed her again. This time their lips met with desperation. Their teeth banged together as his tongue explored her mouth. His held her close to his body. She could feel his bulging sex against her belly as he rotated his hips.

She moaned as he trailed kisses down her throat. His hands grasped her hips, then slid up the soft silk of her gown to cup her breasts.

She gasped. "Yes. Oh yes, Ambrose."

Ambrose leaned back and shuffled out of his jacket. He spread his coat out on the bed of hay. Reaching into his pocket, he pulled out a handkerchief and set it out next to it.

He reached out to her. "Come, Katherine."

Katherine knelt on the coat. He gently turned her and laid her down, his eyes never leaving hers as he joined her on their makeshift bed.

"My beautiful, Katherine," he whispered as he placed warm kisses in a trail from her hairline to her mouth where he lingered before moving slowly to her throat and down to her breasts.

Katherine wiggled out of her sleeves, allowing him to

pull her silk dress to her belly, exposing her small breasts to the soft amber light.

Ambrose took each nipple into his mouth before blowing on it. Her nipples hardened and tingled with his attentions. He leaned back and looked at his handiwork before falling upon her and suckling her breasts passionately. He groaned. His hand moved up her leg, pushing her silk dress up as he reached her thighs.

His fingers touched the soft lips between her thighs. He ran his fingers slowly across her, feeling her damp response. Kate felt a deep rumbling in his chest. He rested his head against her breasts, kissing and sucking as he stoked her. He reared up again, this time lifting her hips. In one abrupt movement, he pushed her gown past her waist, exposing her completely to his touch. He shifted his body lower on hers, while he continued to stroke her. He cupped her using his palm to rub her swollen nub.

Kate moaned. She ached with a familiar desire. "Oh, Ambrose. Oh, my."

Her words faded away as her body arched to welcome his touch. She opened her legs wide, unable to resist her desperate need. Ambrose moved between her legs and lowered his head to run his tongue along her.

"Ambrose, what are you...Oh, my god." Kate lost herself to his intimate touch. She could only moan as he found and suckled her most sensitive parts. Her stomach clenched. Her body was no longer hers to control as she writhed with the agony and pleasure of his touch. His mouth worked her tender parts, his teeth and tongue alternately massaging her. She began to whimper with a strange desperation. She let out a shriek as the world exploded in racking release.

She lay back, panting, and grasped his head, her fingers

entwined in his hair, as wave after wave washed over her. She trembled as Ambrose licked her, his tongue caressing her with long slow strokes, allowing her to regain her breath.

She let her hands fall to her sides as Ambrose rose and, fumbling with his trousers, took his organ into his hand to rub the tip of it gently along her wetness.

"My Katherine. You are so ready for me," he breathed.

She felt him slowly push into her body. "Ambrose...perhaps we could leave it here. I don't think we quite fit...I cannot see this situation working."

"No, my dear. It will work fine. Trust me with this."

She tensed, waiting for the stab of pain. This time, she felt nothing but a pleasurable tightness as he entered her. He arched above her, filling her completely. She could feel him pulse inside her. He began to move slowly. Kate opened her eyes. He was watching her intently as he began to move rhythmically into her body. After a minute or two she was able to relax and concentrate on the strange new feelings.

To her surprise, she wanted more of him. She raised her legs, spreading them wide, then wrapping them around his back. She reached for his shoulders, pulling him to her as she found and moved with his rhythm. Ambrose let out a long groan and increased his pace.

She felt an irresistible yearning to take as much of him as she could. She began to meet his thrusts with her own. Her body clenched him and pulled him deeper inside her. She was lost to everything except the feel of him. His rhythm increased as he began pounding his body into hers.

The shrill sound of a horse whinnying wildly nearby filled her ears as Ambrose reared back with a groan. He arched his body over hers. For a second time, she felt her world explode as Ambrose grabbed her hips, pulled them tightly against him, and pumped into her. She held him close when he collapsed against her. They laid together wet with perspiration, panting as they recovered their breath.

After a few minutes, Ambrose shifted to her side. She was unable to open her eyes just yet as she enjoyed the lethargy of the moment. A scent of dry hay combined with the smell of their love making filled the air. She became aware of the restless stomping and snorting of the horses, who had been awakened and sensed their actions. Ambrose rose to his knees beside her.

She slowly opened her eyes. He was looking at her intensely. He gave her a lazy questioning smile.

She returned it, which made him chuckle.

"You must tell me if making love was a disappointment for you this time." He reached down and brushed the hair from her face. He smiled again, and using her words said, "For me it was a transcendental experience."

He grinned.

"Oh, Ambrose. It was marvelous. It is even more exciting than I had ever expected. Somehow, I never imagined it could be so...so..." She was at a loss for words.

He reached for his handkerchief and gently wiped her body, closing her legs carefully and attempting to readjust her dress, before helping her to her feet.

Reality returned. Kate began to put herself together. She adjusted her dress, lifting it back up to cover her breasts. Her legs trembled. Ambrose reached out to steady her. She realized that her hair had come completely down. Her chestnut locks fell to her waist, with bits of straw amongst the tresses. Her gown was crumpled and in total disarray.

She looked with panic at Ambrose who had shook out

his coat and was slipping it on. "Ambrose, what on earth am I going to do? I cannot return to the ball like this! Oh no!"

Ambrose set his hands on her shoulders to steady her. "Not to worry. I will escort you directly to the carriage. No one will see you and all will be well."

He leaned forward to kiss her lightly on the lips.

She pulled back from him. "But what about Aunt Elizabeth and Clarissa? They cannot be left here at the ball. Oh, dear."

"All will be well. You will see. I will head back into the ball after I have you settled into the coach and find Theo. He will be most happy to report to Lady Carstairs that I have taken you home with a headache and offer his services as an escort."

Kate was again reminded of his ability to take charge. This time she was relieved that he had the situation well in hand. He brushed off his sleeves and deftly retied his cravat. Kate scowled as he ran his fingers through his hair. It was unfair that he seemed perfectly put together while she was a disaster.

He looked at her disgruntled face and laughed again.

"You are a mess." He plucked several pieces of straw from her hair and twisted her tangled gown back into place. "It is a good look for you."

He pulled her towards him, and smiling, he kissed her once more.

Minutes later, Ambrose stood at the back of Chesterfield's grand hall and scanned the crowd for Theo. Fortunately, he found him sipping champagne near the entry.

Ambrose walked over. "Just the man I need to see," he began. "I have a favor to ask you."

"Hmm, what could that be, I wonder?" Theo looked Ambrose up and down, his gaze resting on his shoulder with amusement before he met his eyes.

"It seems Katherine has developed a headache. I have offered to run her home. I wonder if you might inform Lady Carstairs and offer her and Miss Clarissa a lift to their residence?" Ambrose looked at him hopefully.

Theo laughed loudly. A few gentlemen turned toward them to see the source of his amusement.

"A bit of hay fever perhaps?" He reached over and picked a piece of straw from Ambrose's coat. He brushed another off his shoulder. He laughed again.

Ambrose felt his face become warm.

"Not to worry, my man," Theo said with a chuckle, "but you owe me one." He strolled away glancing back at Ambrose to grin and wink at him before making his way to the company of Lady Carstairs.

Ambrose was untroubled by Theo's glee. His mind was filled with thoughts of Katherine. In his estimation the evening had gone rather well. He grinned with satisfaction. He was sure he had made some progress in influencing Kate's decision to take him as a husband. He was determined to make her his wife. But first he would have to be sure she was no longer a target. Despite the theft of her satchel on the street, he felt uneasy. Keeping her safe was his priority.

Chapter Sixteen

Ambrose stood in the foyer of Kate's home looking around the room with dismay. The house was filled with flowers. He shifted the bouquet of red roses he had purchased for Kate to his left hand as he stood uncomfortably by the door.

Clarissa flitted around the hall bubbling with excitement. "Why look! There is even one for you, Lady Carstairs." She indicated the big bouquet of yellow roses in the foyer. She read the card aloud. "Old friends are the dearest friends. How lovely. Now who could that be?"

She twinkled at Lady Carstairs.

Lady Carstairs waved away Clarissa's remark and gestured to Ambrose. "Do join us for tea. Katherine is upstairs but she will be down soon."

"Thank you, ma'am. I believe I will."

The door rang. Milly came muttering from the kitchen. "Constant traffic this morning."

Clarissa scrambled forward. "I will get it," she hollered.

Lady Carstairs graced Clarissa with an indulgent smile

before turning to Milly. "My dear, could you please put these lovely flowers in a vase for our young man."

Ambrose handed his bouquet to Milly who muttered her disapproval. "Can't see where I am to find another vase," she said as she waddled from the room.

Lady Carstairs took Ambrose by the arm and led him from the cluttered foyer to the parlor. It was with some relief that he settled into his chair.

Clarissa burst into the room waving a letter. "It is for me!" She grinned and ripped it open. "Oh. It is Jeremy." She beamed as she read. "He reminds us of our commitment to attend the Hargrave masquerade tonight. He wants to know our costumes so he can have the first dance."

Clarissa flashed a wide smile. "How perfectly marvelous! I believe I shall write him a note immediately."

She turned and hurried from the room eager to attend to her correspondence.

Lady Carstairs smiled apologetically. "I am afraid our Clarissa is a little excited this morning. You must forgive her rudeness. I assure you it is completely unintentional."

"I have taken no offence ma'am."

Once they were settled, and tea had been poured, Lady Carstairs addressed him. "I am glad we have this time together today. I have been meaning to have a chat with you." She looked across at Ambrose who shifted uncomfortably in his chair. "I shall get directly to the point. I believe relations between my niece and you have become rather intimate. I wish to know your intentions."

Ambrose felt his cheeks flush. For a moment he even wished Clarissa had remained in the room. He cleared his throat. "I have once proposed to Katherine, as you know. She refused." He looked Lady Carstairs in the eyes. "I still intend to make Katherine my wife."

"You are aware that she was engaged before. I am afraid the situation did not turn out well. I do not intend to sit back while she has her heart broken a second time." Lady Carstairs took a sip of her tea, watching him over her teacup. "I want you to know Katherine has confided to me all the unfortunate events surrounding the codebook. I know all. While I am concerned about her physical safety, and certainly the incident on the street yesterday is distressing, I find myself equally concerned for her emotional wellbeing."

Lady Katherine set down her cup and pressed on. "Katherine likes to present herself as a mature woman with much experience. You of all people must know that is not the case."

Ambrose cheeks burned again. "I am determined to make her mine." He stumbled, before continuing. "I can assure you my relationship with Katherine is entirely separate from my responsibility to the admiral. I have resigned my commission. I want to you to know that my interest in Katherine has nothing to do with my work for the state."

He looked her directly in the eyes. "My feelings and intentions are my own."

He was at a loss. His military training had not equipped him to deal with a formidable Lady Carstairs, who was determined to protect her niece. He knew he must get this right. Unsure what her concerns might be, he decided to tell Lady Carstairs about his career plans, hoping to convince her of the viability of the match.

"While I am not independently wealthy, I... I do have prospects." He found himself stuttering and cleared his throat. "Breeding horses is my goal. I have started a herd. I see a future for us that..."

Ambrose's eyes caught a movement from the doorway. Kate stood at the entry with his bouquet of red roses. She sent him a wide smile of greeting as she glided into the room, setting the vase on the corner of her desk. "Good morning, Ambrose." She propped his card carefully against the base of the vase. "Thank you for the lovely flowers. I am going to keep them right here where I can enjoy them."

Ambrose had risen as she walked into the room, not at all displeased with the timely interruption. Now he too smiled a greeting as she approached.

"Katherine." He took her hand and kissed it.

Kate felt her cheeks flush as she recalled his kisses from last night. "Good morning. I had not expected to see you here so soon."

"It is a pleasure to see you as always. Did you sleep well, my dear?" he asked with a twinkle in his eyes.

"Quite well, thank you." She grinned back at him.

Ambrose waited until she had settled on the sofa, and her tea had been poured.

"I am afraid I have some rather startling news. Please accept my apologies for disrupting your day. I had breakfast with Admiral Hews this morning." He reached for a biscuit and contemplated how to continue. He decided that directness was his best course. "It seems our suspect Mr. McClury was murdered last night."

Kate gasped. "Are you certain?"

"Do you mean the man who accosted Kate?" Lady Carstairs asked. "But how terrible."

"Yes. He was found in the early hours of the morning. He was shot in his rooms at Downing Lane. The neighbors heard the blast and came to investigate but the assassin had already left the scene. The watch and the Home Office have no suspects at this time," Ambrose said, "though both will be investigating, I am sure."

"But what can this mean? Why would he be killed?" questioned Lady Carstairs.

"The Admiral believes whoever hired him to rob Kate was concerned that she might be able to identify him. And rightly so," he added. "We had hoped to trace the man who hired McClury by following him to his source. But now, it seems, those plans are dashed."

Ambrose reached for another biscuit. "The admiral is quite disappointed. Whoever murdered the man was able to get into McClury's apartment undetected."

Lady Carstairs leaned forward. "Does this mean the threat to Katherine is over? Surely now that the villain has the codebook the danger past."

Ambrose sighed. "The admiral is concerned with the number of connections to Katherine. McClury was, after all, your overseer. He is convinced that whoever is behind this ordeal is somehow connected to Katherine." He looked at Katherine and cleared his throat. "The admiral and I are curious to know how you came to say our password, the ides of March, at the docks."

Kate looked at him with wide eyes. "What! The ides of March? I hardly remember what I said at the docks. But it was March, and a storm was approaching." Kate scowled at him. "What a ridiculous password."

"Yes. Well. I admit we may have stumbled when suggesting that one." Ambrose sipped his tea and set the cup carefully back on its saucer. "The point is, whoever it is that has been after the codes, has just proven themselves more dangerous. They are willing to kill to keep their secrets. We must take this as a warning. Admiral Hews has agreed to keep his man on surveillance of your home and I will continue to escort Katherine when it is needed."

Lady Carstairs commented, "I cannot imagine a contact of ours involved in espionage. Kate and I have lived quietly these past few years. It seems unlikely."

"This situation becomes more and more distressing. And here I thought my only worries were Bentley Brown," Kate mused.

"Who is Bentley Brown?" Ambrose asked, his curiosity evident.

"Oh, it is a long story." She sighed, "Are you sure you want to hear it?"

"Of course, I want to hear it." Ambrose leaned forward. "I have never heard of a man named Bentley Brown."

Kate wrinkled her nose. "Well, he is not much of a man."

Lady Carstairs interjected, "Quite right, my dear. I must say I was outraged when Kate confided in me."

"You see, when we first attained the patterns, I was concerned that someone would attempt to take them from us before we had a chance to copy them and present them to our clients." Kate paused and took a sip of tea.

Lady Carstairs added, "The patterns are valuable in the fashion industry. Every Lady in town would jump at the chance to wear a gown fashioned for the Empress Josephine. It was quite a coupe to get the patterns, and, I must say, a boon to business." She smiled at Kate. "The modistes in town are extremely competitive. It is the start of the season. There are fortunes to be made outfitting ladies in their gowns."

"Bentley Brown owns a competing shop," Kate said. "He heard of the new gowns when we first released them and wanted some of the works for his own. I refused. He was not deterred. Just yesterday he threatened to expose me to society as a tradeswoman if I did not consent to handing over the patterns."

She snorted. "And worse, he demanded that I work for him. I refused of course."

"Let us not forget that he also threatened to inform Lord Serves, your guardian." Lady Carstairs nodded with a scowl.

"Co-guardian," Kate amended, "and yes, the man is a complete scoundrel, a blackmailer."

Ambrose's shoulders had squared to a military stiffness as he listened to the tale. "You must keep me informed, Katherine. I cannot protect you if I am not apprized with all the facts."

"I am informing you." She gave him a disgruntled look.

"I will speak to this Bentley Brown. Do you know his address?" Ambrose asked.

"Heavens no. His shop is just two blocks down from ours. It is the Le Chateau. Though you may not find him there. He leaves much of the management to his modiste. The man is a failure as a businessman."

"I shall try to track him down. Threatening women is not an action I tolerate well. He is dishonorable fellow for sure, but he may not be our man. I cannot think of what his connection could be." Ambrose looked at Katherine. "Were you around Mr. McClury? Could you perhaps have over-heard something?"

"No. I did not even really know the man. I met him only a few times. Uncle Edmund has handled anything to do with The Meadows and Mr. McClury." Katherine laughed. "But just last night I was accused of eavesdropping. Sergeant Ames found me standing outside an alcove where he was apparently having a private discussion. I heard nothing and I must say I was disconcerted to be suspected of it."

"Hmm. Sergeant Ames. And being perceived as knowing a secret in this case might be as dangerous as actually knowing something you should not." Ambrose looked at Katherine and shook his head. "That was unfortunate. You must be more careful, Katherine. Ames is a strange fellow."

Ambrose sipped his tea and considered the sergeant. "If he is a double agent, there will be much trouble in the Home Security Office. He certainly is close to the admiral and would be privy to many of his secrets. He could be an operative. And it is interesting too that shortly after the conversation in the alcove, McClury was killed." Ambrose sighed. "But again, it is unlikely. I am sure the admiral, who is most astute, will have checked him out."

Ambrose set down his teacup and stood. Morning visits were restricted by the laws of etiquette to fifteen minutes. He had long overstayed his welcome.

"Thank you, ladies, for a lovely tea. I hope I have not distressed you too much. I will do my best to discover what all of this means."

"And thank you, Ambrose, for the lovely flowers. They are most beautiful."

"You are most welcome. I shall be here at eight to take you to the Hargrove soiree. Until then, you must remember my orders to take every precaution."

Kate rose, took his arm, and walked him to the entrance. At the door, he scanned the room over her shoulders to ensure they were alone, then with a grin, leaned in to plant a kiss upon her lips.

Kate laughed. "Very sneaky, Ambrose."

He put his hands on her shoulders and attempted to pull

her into his arms. Kate held him back with a hand upon his chest.

"Oh no, you don't," she said with a laugh.

"I am just making sure you have not forgotten last night." He smiled.

"I will never forget last night. And now it is time you left." She opened the door and nudged him forward.

"Until tonight." Ambrose trotted down the stairs as Kate closed the door. She leaned against it for a minute. Ambrose was indeed the stuff of dreams. He had a boyish countenance at times which was incongruent with military background. Every moment she spent with him told her he was the man for her. The events of last night had only made clear what she had begun to suspect. She was in love.

The smile died on her face as she realized she would be heartbroken when her time with him was over. She could not marry him for all the wrong reasons. If she were to marry, now at this late date, it would only be to a man that loved her. She was not willing to accept anything less.

Clarissa skipped into the foyer. "Katey! I have just sent a letter off to Jeremy. I hope you do not mind. I told him our costumes. He requested to have a dance and wanted to recognize me. Oh, it will be a grand time." Clarissa could not smile wider. She grabbed Kate's arm. "Why so glum? Come upstairs with me. Let's try on our costumes!"

Kate allowed herself to be led to the stairs. "Yes, I think a little distraction will be good for me."

Kate had a shepherdess costume. It had sat in the back of the closet since last season, ordered for a ball she had not attended. Its layers of petticoats and rows of ruffles in alternating shades of pink were extravagantly overdone. It was cut low, exposing an unseemly amount of cleavage. It came with a staff encased in ribbon and a fuchsia half mask. Clarissa's costume was a Cleopatra ensemble, in white and gold, complete with a black square cut wig and black mask.

The ladies stood side by side gazing at their reflections in Kate's full-length mirror.

Clarissa frowned at her appearance. "This costume is too simple." Her bottom lip protruded as she took in Kate's exaggerated flounces and wide skirt. "And this wig. It is really too bad. I have to hide my beautiful blonde curls, while you can show your plain brown hair."

Clarissa backed away from the mirror and sat dejected on Kate's bed. "I don't know what Mama was thinking, putting together this unflattering costume."

"It will be all right, Clarissa. We can spruce it up a little with a choker, perhaps change the half mask to gold. And the skirts are lovely; they flow—"

Clarissa interrupted, "I want yours. It suits me much better." She looked at Kate with pleading eyes. "Only think of how beautiful my hair will look in ringlets with matching ribbons. My hair is my best quality."

She pulled off the wig and fluffed out her blonde curls, moving to the mirror once more to admire the results.

"Clarissa, I—"

"Please, Katey. Please, please. Only think of what a charming picture I could be. And pink suits me. I am perfect for that costume." Clarissa eyed Kate's outfit long-ingly. "It is wasted on you."

Kate felt a flood of annoyance as she looked at Claris-sa's pouting face, with the bottom lip extended and her head tilted in a childish gesture of appeal. Though she agreed that the Cleopatra costume suited her better—she actually preferred the simple elegant lines of the Cleopatra outfit, to the flamboyant monstrosity of the shepherdess costume—she debated refusing Clarissa just to satisfy her growing frustration with her.

With a sigh, Kate decided the scene that would ensue was not worth the momentary satisfaction. "Fine, Clarissa. You may have my costume. We will switch."

Clarissa let out a squeal of excitement. "Oh yes!" She clapped her hands together. "It will be a perfect evening. Jeremy will be thrilled with me in this costume. Masquerades are my absolute favorites!

Chapter Seventeen

Across town, the Count of Serves and his son Jeremy were also discussing the Hargrove ball.

"Have you determined the costume Katherine will wear tonight, as I instructed?" The count sat at his desk and eyed Jeremy with a scowl of distaste. His son was dressed in his usual flamboyant style. His bright orange and gold waistcoat practically hurt the eyes. His neckcloth was an elaborate mess held together with a diamond clip. His son knew how to spend a fortune but had no idea how one was attained.

"Clarissa has sent me a note. Katherine will be wearing a Bo peep costume." Jeremy replied. "She is to be a shepherdess."

The Count of Serves scowled at Jeremy. He could leave nothing to chance. Each detail must be carefully explained. Jeremy was sure to foul it up if left to his own devices.

The count gave a long-suffering sigh. How he had sired this imbecilic son was beyond him. Jeremy never failed to disappoint.

"Father, why?" Jeremy whined. "I fail to see why I must

marry Katherine. I proposed as you as asked. I even offered to get on one knee. Me, a future viscount! And she turned me down."

"I know," the count replied with a sneer. "It boggles the mind. How you could be so incompetent that even a spinster with few options would turn you down is beyond me. But you have bungled it as usual and now we must force her hand."

The count shook his head sadly. The frown lines in his face deepened. "I should have demanded you ask her earlier when she was more pliable, but you wanted a few years of freedom." He gave Jeremy a hard stare. "I granted you that, for all the good it did."

"Father, I do not want her. I fail to see why I cannot marry a woman worthy of me, someone who at least admires me, a countess maybe or—"

"You fool! Do you understand at all what is at stake?" Serves sprang to his feet, his chair crashing to the floor.

Jeremy flinched, but the count ignored the noise.

He raised his voice. "Where do you think the money for that fancy diamond clip you are sporting comes from? If you presume it is from our estates, you are wrong."

"But father, I do not think she even likes me. Surely—"

The count felt hot rage flush his cheeks. "Like you? Like you! Who in god's name do you expect to like you? I do not even like you! And why worry about it? You marry her and you find a piece of fluff to *like you* if that is what you need."

Realizing he had lost his temper, the count took a long breath. He slowly turned and picked up his chair, seating himself once more.

"Sit down, Jeremy. I will explain this situation to you one more time." He repeated in a dangerously soft voice, "Sit down."

Jeremy pulled the chair back a safe distance from the desk. "Father, I understand The Meadows are profitable for us but surely there is another way."

"No. The Meadows makes an income which we thankfully have had at our disposal, but it is the free trade, the smuggling, which provides the lion's share of this family's wealth. The wharf, the dock workers, and our connections have run smoothly from The Meadows for many years. My father received those lands from his second wife. They should have been mine instead of going to her mongrel of a son, my useless half-brother." The viscount scowled at the memory. "But that is neither here nor there. We cannot lose access to them now."

"But father. I have heard all this before. I think you are obsessed with The Meadows. We have an estate, Father. What of it? We make a decent income from it."

"Our estate does not have the potential of The Meadows. I have done much to keep the property in my control. I will not lose it now." The count considered telling his son all he had done to maintain control of Katherine's estate, starting when her father was alive. His fool of a half-brother, John, had insisted that The Meadows be turned into some kind of horse farm. John had had no interest in the smuggling trade. He had instead ignored it and did not profit from it. It was an intolerable waste.

When a fortune could be made trading in gold, John had refused to participate. He had even forbidden the trade of gold through his port, calling it a betrayal to the country. For the viscount, it was an insult. An insult which was costing him his rightful inheritance, his fortune. The trade in gold was still at a premium. Napoleon was willing to buy English gold at a price which gave him a tidy profit. The viscount was determined to get his share.

He looked across the desk at his son. Jeremy was not the son he had hoped for. He understood little beyond the niceties of town life. He could be trusted with nothing; he would confide in him nothing.

"Let us go over this again. You will send a footman with a message for your Little Bo Peep to meet you in Hargrove's upstairs library. You will accost her. Ravish her forcefully if you must. Do not let her leave until I arrive with the Earl, her suitor St. Claire, and whoever else I can assemble. She must be in a state of complete disarray, thoroughly compromised." The count leaned back in his chair and waited for his son to confirm his understanding of the plan. He was pleased with his idea to include St. Claire in the charade. He could put an abrupt end to that threat.

"When we enter the room, you will assure Hargrove, St. Claire, and whoever else that Kate is your fiancé. You will say you intend to marry her." The Viscount twisted his lips into his thin smile. "She will be trapped. There will be no avoiding the marriage after that little scene."

He chuckled. "Furthermore, we can expect the marriage will occur without delay. Another problem will be solved."

Jeremy frowned. "Really, Father, must I?" Jeremy's face had colored a bright red. He visibly shuddered. "There must be another way."

Serves leaned forward and held his son's gaze. "You have failed at the other ways. The time has run out. She will be twenty-five and we will have lost all chance. For god's sake, we could lose The Meadows!" He raised his voice and said, enunciating each word clearly, "You will do your duty."

Chapter Eighteen

The ballroom at the Hargrove mansion was one of the finest in London. Tonight, its lofty ceilings glittered with thousands of lit chandeliers. Footman in gold livery wandered the room with trays of champagne. The guests took to the floor for a country dance; men and women across from each other as the minuet signaled the beginning of the set. Ladies wore full costumes in an array of colors. As the minuet played, the dancers swirled, stepping in unison through the intricate synchronized maneuvers of the dance.

Kate stood this dance with Theo, who like many of the men at the costume ball wore the mandatory mask, but little else in the way of costume. Each time they met in the center to touch hands and spin, he smiled most charmingly.

"Ambrose is fortunate to have had the first opportunity to meet you. To think I lost such a prize in Hernes to the flip of a coin."

Theo's expression was such an exaggerated portrayal of forlorn that Kate laughed.

"I am not sure being the prize of a coin flip flatters me." She smiled as she executed the turn. "Tell me, Theo, how is it that with all of your charms you have not been snatched up?"

The dance separated them once more before he could answer.

When they came together again, Theo responded, "The girls have given me a merry chase. Only when I meet someone as lovely as you, will I slow down."

Kate smiled. "Oh, Theo you are outrageous. If my heart was not already taken, I might have entered that race."

Theo's face became serious as they completed the turn. Kate realized with a jolt what she had inadvertently shared. Her cheeks burned as she tried to think of a way to cover her misstep.

When they came to the center for the final time, Theo looked down at her distressed face. "Your secret is safe with me, Cleopatra." He took her arm to lead her back to Ambrose who watched them from across the floor. "This race I will watch from the sidelines, nursing my broken heart." He put his free hand on his chest with an exaggerated expression of pain.

It was impossible not to laugh as Theo leaned into her with his wounded expression.

"If your heart is taken, and I have heard no engagement announcement, I can only assume my poor friend Ambrose has bungled his proposal." Theo gave a long-suffering sigh as they circled the dance floor. "You must be patient with my friend. I fear he is better in the battlefield than the ballroom."

He led her to where her party waited and placed her hand on Ambrose's arm. "Your queen, Mark Anthony."

Theo gave his friend a little bow.

Ambrose rolled his eyes, while pulling Kate close to him. "Some days, Theo, it is fortunate you are my best friend."

Theo laughed. Before he could reply, the band began the opening strains of the Viennese Waltz. There was a pause from the guests, then an audible murmur as the Earl and Lady Hargrove opened the dance. The waltz had not been accepted yet at Almacks or many of the other clubs in London. It was only beginning to be played at the town's parties. It was still considered risqué for an unmarried woman to participate.

Ambrose bowed over Kate's hand. "May I have this dance?"

He raised his eyebrows as if challenging her to accept.

"Most definitely," Kate responded, taking his hands eagerly.

He led her out to the dance floor, joining a smattering of other couples.

Her stomach did a little flip as Ambrose held her hips snuggly to his. It was apparent at once why the dance was so controversial. As the music swelled, Ambrose glided her expertly around the room. His warm hand rested on her lower back while the world spun around her. Their bodies moved as one. She began to feel a dizzying sensation and remembered the words of her dancing instructor: "Keep your head slightly raised and look to the left to avoid vertigo."

Kate found herself watching the endless chandeliers spinning above her. "Oh, Ambrose. I feel as though we are floating beneath the stars."

She stole a glance at him. He was smiling down at her.

"I am holding my starlight here in my arms."

Kate returned her head to the required position and

allowed herself to become lost in the dance. The beautiful sounds of the waltz, and the feel of Ambrose's body held close to hers were intoxicating. His unique scent, mixed with a spicy cologne filled her senses. Together she and Ambrose flowed effortlessly across the room, whirling and spinning. Too soon the music faded to a stop. Kate promised herself she would remember this magical dance forever.

Ambrose took her hand and escorted her back to where Lady Carstairs and Clarissa watched her from the perimeter.

He bowed over her hand then kissed it, before releasing her. "Thank you, my beautiful Cleopatra."

Before Kate could respond, Clarissa let out her signature squeal of excitement. "Katey! I could hardly believe that it was you. How scandalous!" She gasped. "I am so jealous."

The footman approached and performed a little bow before Clarissa. "A note for the shepherdess."

He handed Clarissa a small missive tied with a pink ribbon.

"Oh!" Clarissa giggled. "What could it be?"

Clarissa eagerly removed the ribbon and unrolled the message. It was a handwritten note.

Katherine, meet me in the upstairs library on a matter of importance. Tell no one. The life of your new suitor may depend upon it. Jeremy.

Clarissa's face fell.

"What is it, my dear?" asked Lady Carstairs.

Clarissa slowly looked up.

"How disappointing. Just a note from my new friend Lady Isabella asking to meet her in the ladies' withdrawing room." She tucked the note into her reticule and adjusted her mask. "I suppose I must. Please excuse me."

Lady Carstairs watched Clarissa depart. "That is odd. Do we know a Lady Isabella? What could she be up to?" Lady Carstairs continued to frown suspiciously as she followed Clarissa's progress across the room to the staircase.

"I am sure it is just young ladies wanting to share the latest gossip. Clarissa thrives on it," Kate answered.

"Can I get my favorite ladies some refreshments? Punch or champagne?" Ambrose asked.

Lady Carstairs smiled. "I am feeling a little decadent. I think this occasion could do with champagne. What do you say, Katherine?"

"That would be lovely." Kate settled herself in a seat next to her aunt, as Ambrose departed in search of a footman. "I do need to take a few minutes off my feet. I believe I have danced every set since arriving. Is it not strange how popular I have become this season? I wonder what is different?"

Lady Carstairs chuckled. "My dear, there is nothing more attractive than a happy self-assured young woman and that is what you have become."

"I think it helps that I seem to have the attentions of the Earl and Ambrose," Kate said.

"That too," Lady Carstairs agreed.

The ladies silently watched the country dance being performed. It was some time before Ambrose returned with their drinks. Like many of the men at the party, he had given up on his mask, which was pulled off his eyes and rested on his on top of his head.

"I am so sorry. It has become an awful crush. Finding a footman was impossible. I had to make my way to the cardroom to find these." He handed each of the ladies a flute.

Lady Carstairs smiled as she accepted her glass. "Quite all right. We have been enjoying the break. Thank you, young man."

The ladies sipped their drinks.

"What could be taking Miss Clarissa so long?" Lady Carstairs inquired with some concern. "It has been some time since she left."

"I am sure she will make her way back soon enough. Perhaps Lady Isabelle has introduced her around," Kate said, peering around the ballroom, searching for a glimpse of the elaborately ruffled pink ensemble.

Lord Hargrove and a set of companions, the Count of Serves and Duke of Bedford, approached. Like Ambrose, they had retired their masks.

"There you are, St. Claire. Thought we would never find you. My friends and I," he said, and gestured to Bedford and Count Serves, "have a debate you must settle. I have purchased a painting of a sea battle. I believe it is the Battle of Trafalgar but Serves insists it is a West Indies skirmish. You, a navy man, can decide this for us."

"Well, I..." Ambrose looked helplessly at Katherine.

"Bring the ladies. It is a painting worth seeing." The Earl of Hargrove interjected.

Lady Carstairs turned to Katherine.

"You run along, my dear." She said to Hargrove, "I must stay and wait for one of my charges."

"Ah, but you may find her on the way. It would be unfortunate for you to miss this sight," the Count of Serves added with a thin smile which did little to alleviate the deep frown lines on his long pale face.

"No, it is quite all right," Lady Carstairs replied. "I am afraid I am lost on the topic of sea battles or paintings for that matter but thank you your grace."

She returned his thin smile with one of her own.

"Well, then, come along, St. Claire and Cleopatra." The Earl led the way to the stairs. Looking back over his shoulder at Ambrose as they began to ascend, he laughed, "I have a hefty prize wagered on this, St. Claire. Make sure you get it right."

"I will do my best, sir." Ambrose turned to Katherine and winked.

At the landing in front of the library, Lord Hargrove paused. "You will find that whatever the battle, this painting is quite the spectacle. It dominates the room."

He waited until everyone had gathered at the double doors of his library. In a grand gesture, he flung them both wide, watching their faces to catch their response to his prize.

His audience stood, open mouthed with shock. On the divan facing the door, a couple appeared to be in the middle of an intimate encounter. All that could be seen was a pale bare arse bobbing amidst a sea of pink petticoats and ruffles.

"My God!" Lord Hargrove roared. "What in the name of heaven goes on here?"

The gentleman rolled to the floor, then scrambled to his feet attempting to pull his trousers up from around his ankles.

Kate gasped with shock when she realized his identity. "Jeremy!"

She put her hand to her mouth.

A screech came from beneath the pile of pink petticoats. A wave of horror washed over Kate as she realized who may well emerge from the tangle.

Clarissa flipped back the skirts of her gown. She looked

at the crowd in the doorway, then covered her face with her hands and began to wail.

Lord Hargrove roared into the chaos. "How dare you treat my home as a whore house! I will have you horse whipped! See if I don't!"

From beside her, Kate heard the Count of Serves yell into the chaos, "What? Clarissa Dumont? What the hell?"

The count spun around and glared at Kate. She could feel his anger and shock as his eyes bored into hers through her mask. Kate could only look at him open-mouthed. She lifted her arms to indicate her confusion. The gesture released her from her frozen stance in the entry. She realized the volume of Clarissa's howls had increased as the Earl of Hargrove continued to bellow his tirade. Whatever Clarissa had done, she was in dire need of some support now.

Rushing into the room, she sat at Clarissa's side. She pulled her against her shoulder and tugged up the bodice of her gown, covering her exposed breasts. The sobbing continued as did the yelling, now from both the Count of Serves and Hargrove.

A small crowd had gathered at the door to see what the commotion was about. Kate realized with a sinking heart that this event would not be easily explained, nor would it be quietly covered up. Within minutes, everyone at the ball and indeed everyone in society would hear of it.

Kate held Clarissa's head close and whispered in her ear. "Did he force you, Clarissa?"

"Noo," she sobbed. "But he said he loved me."

Kate looked up to see Jeremy, trousers up at last, attempting to offer a stuttering apology.

"I... I am m ...much embarrassed. The Lady is my...my

finance." He swung his head back and forth as though searching for an ally. "I intend to marry her."

Lord Serves surged forward with a guttural cry and slugged him in the face. Jeremy sprawled to the floor, knocking over a small card table on his way down. Serves lunged forward and kicked the downed Jeremy squarely in the stomach. "You incompetent bastard!"

Ambrose grabbed the viscount by his shoulders, pulling him back, before he could land another blow. The volume of Clarissa's wails increased.

"My word," the Duke of Bedford muttered, "this is a scene I will not soon forget."

"Enough!" The Earl of Hargrove thundered. "Stop that noisy sniveling girl. Just what were you thinking?"

Clarissa lifted her hands from her tear-streaked face.

"I was an innocent—he said he loved me." She pointed to Jeremy who had staggered to his feet. Clarissa sobbed and buried her face on Kate's shoulder once more.

"This mess will be cleaned up and I am the man to see to it." Hargrove scowled at Jeremy who was rubbing his bruised cheek as he painfully rose from the floor.

Kate felt a rush of pity for the young lovers. Jeremy looked like a small boy. His face was bright red. He was completely disheveled; his lime green waistcoat hung open, with his shirt tails dangling out below. He shifted back and forth on his feet. Clarissa had buried her head once more in her shoulder, crying quietly now.

Lord Hargrove looked at Jeremy and narrowed his eyes. "There will be a wedding and in no short order, by god." He looked defiantly around the room as though expecting someone to disagree. "Tomorrow. By special license. And to be sure it is all done up nice and tidy, and the young scoundrel does not think to back off, we will have it right here in my hall. Five o'clock."

He glowered at Jeremy. "Are we in agreement, you young pup?"

Jeremy glanced at his father whose usually pale face was dark with rage. He squared his shoulders and faced Lord Hargrove.

"I will be here." he said quietly.

The room was silent. Clarissa had not made a sound since the pronouncement but held her head still against Kate's shoulder.

The Count of Serves pushed Ambrose's hands from his shoulders. He shot his son an expression of disgust and left the room without a word.

Kate cleared her throat and addressed Ambrose. "I wonder if you could collect Lady Carstairs and fetch our cloaks?" When Ambrose nodded, she turned to Lord Hargrove. "I think it might be best if we left through your rear entrance."

She indicated Clarissa with her eyes.

"Yes. Yes. I will arrange it." He looked down at Clarissa's huddled form. "Five o'clock, girl, and see that you are on time."

Their exit from the Hargrove ball was much less auspicious than their entry. However, they managed to slip through the servant's quarters and kitchens with only a few snickering maids as an audience.

The carriage ride home was a silent one. Clarissa was apparently no longer distraught, but sat quietly, lost in thought. Lady Carstairs was rigidly staring straight ahead. Kate and Ambrose occasionally looked at each other wide-eyed but could think of nothing to say.

Chapter Nineteen

Kate walked into the breakfast room to find her aunt already seated and sipping a cup of tea. She looked as though she had had a sleepless night.

Lady Carstairs rubbed her hand across her forehead. "Is our house guest up?"

"I believe she is on her way down," Kate answered as she filled her plate at the sideboard. "I suppose we shall have to brace ourselves for a scene. She is likely to be most upset."

Kate had just settled when Clarissa burst into the room. She flashed a letter and smiled widely.

"A letter from Jeremy! So exciting!" She ripped open the letter and perused the contents. "Oh, oh, oh! Jeremy has planned for us to leave directly after the wedding! He wants to know if a visit to my family would be appropriate."

Clarissa held the letter to her chest. "He is so thoughtful. Such a gentleman."

Clarissa looked from Kate to Lady Clarrisa as if expecting to hear approval.

Lady Carstairs cleared her throat. "Clarissa, are you genuinely happy with this marriage? Because if you are not, you need not go through with it. No matter what happened at the ball, no one can force you to marry if that is not your wish."

Clarissa sat completely still, her blue eyes wide. "I want it more than anything in the world. It is the perfect match for me—better than anything I could have hoped for. Besides, Jeremy loves me." For an instant, her face was uncharacteristically serious. "He has told me so and I believe him."

She turned to Kate, her eyes dancing with excitement once more. "It is perfect." She let out a little squeal. "Only think of it, Katey. I will be a viscountess!"

"Have you written your mother, Clarissa?" Lady Carstairs shifted uncomfortably in her seat. "I sent a missive off this morning to let her know about the events of last night."

"Oh, yes. I wrote her first thing this morning. She will be so proud of me. I am to be married!" Clarissa giggled happily. "Just think, I am to be wed this afternoon at the palace of the Earl of Hargrove. What a coupe! It is the most beautiful home in the city." She looked at Kate with an expression of pity. "It is really too bad. I do not think you will be able to attend. Very exclusive, you know."

Clarissa set her letter next to her plate, rubbing it affectionately, and turned her attention to the sideboard and her breakfast.

Kate looked at Lady Carstairs and raised her arms in a gesture of disbelief. Clarissa was thrilled with the prospect of her marriage. There was nothing left to be done except to celebrate her success.

"Clarissa, if you are happy with this situation, then I am happy for you."

Clarissa sat down with her plate. She looked at Kate and allowed her bottom lip to protrude slightly in a pout.

"I know this must be hard for you, Katey. After all, I have made an excellent match while you must stand by and watch. It is really too bad." She reached across the table and grasped Kate's hand. "Do not lose heart, my dearest Katherine. I am sure something will come your way. You do have Ambrose. Who knows? Maybe he will come up to scratch if you play your cards right."

Clarissa released her hand, then patted it reassuringly. "Of course, you cannot expect to be a viscountess like me, but it would at least be a marriage."

Kate pulled her hand back. "Yes, well. There is that of course." She swallowed with difficulty the words she longed to say. "I am happy and relieved to see you so pleased this morning."

The ladies continued to eat their breakfast in a strained silence. Only Clarissa attacked her plate with relish, apparently unaware of the tension in the room.

Lady Carstairs burst into laughter. Kate looked at her in confusion.

Lady Carstairs waved her hand as if dismissing her interruption.

"It is nothing... I am just relieved the situation is resolved. I believe I am overtired. I had a little difficulty sleeping last night." She arranged her face carefully into a more stoic position. "Well, then, Clarrisa, you must pack and prepare for your honeymoon trip."

"Yes, I must." Clarrisa flashed a beaming smile. "Just think, Katey. One of your best friends will be a viscountess. I will be a fine connection for you. Oh... Lady Clarissa! I shall be Lady Clarissa! I can hear it pronounced! My mother will be thrilled!"

Clarissa tossed her napkin on her plate. "I really must pack and prepare for today. What shall I wear?" Clarissa gave Kate a speculative glance. "I wonder if I might wear your blue silk? Would you agree? Oh, it would be perfect!"

Clarissa clapped her hands together and looked at Kate hopefully.

"Clarissa, you may pick whatever you wish from my wardrobe for your big day. I will make it a wedding gift."

"Thank you! Thank you! Oh, I am so excited!" She lifted her eyes upward. "And Jeremy is perfect for me. He is the man of my dreams."

Clarissa hugged herself.

Kate smiled at her. "I think you may be right. I am sure you will be happy together."

Clarissa hustled around the table and gave Kate a quick hug before rushing out of the room.

Kate and Lady Carstairs sat in silence.

Kate took a bite of her toast. "The more I think of this match, the more I approve. Clarissa is obviously thrilled, and Jeremy will get a young woman who is eternally grateful. Someone who will admire him. He needs that." She chewed her toast thoughtfully. "It is well done. Jeremy will have a well-bred young woman and though I am sure there is not much in the way of a dowery, Uncle Edmund and Jeremy can cope with that. Heaven knows Uncle Edmund is not in need of funds."

"Ah, yes. Your uncle. You and I must have a talk. Next week, you will turn twenty-five. It is time to take charge of your inheritance. From what I understand, you have lost your overseer. Have you any plans for his replacement?" Lady Carstairs sipped her tea, then set it carefully on the saucer, while she gave her niece a serious expression. "I realize you have relied on your uncle to manage the place. Perhaps now is the time to take the reins. Heaven knows you cannot do worse. You have not seen a profit from the estate in years."

"I had no choice but to rely on Uncle Edmund. As my guardian, he has had the right to make all of the decisions." Kate sighed. "And I must admit I have been disappointed and confused with my uncle's failure."

Kate thought about her years of frustration as she had listened to the grim reports on the status of her inheritance.

"As have I. It has been a mystery to me how a viable estate could suddenly become a financial burden after years of supporting your family in style. But until now we have not been in a position to understand the problems, nor make things right." Lady Carstairs compressed her lips into a fine line.

It was a look Kate was familiar with. Lady Carstairs was a businesswoman at heart. The situation with The Meadows had long been a problem for her. Their discussions and attempts to get a comprehensive report from Uncle Edmund had left her frustrated and annoyed.

"Perhaps it is time for a thorough audit," she said. "It is what we would do with our salon. We will soon see what the cause of the decline is."

Kate nodded. "I agree. It is time to take the situation in hand."

Lady Carstairs exhaled a long breath.

"Good. I am glad you agree." She paused for a moment, gathering her thoughts. "As you know, I have looked forward to the day you gain control over your inheritance for some time. That the Count of Serves refused to give you the accounts, despite your repeated requests for them, has long been an issue for me. I have my suspicions about your uncle—"

Kate interrupted, "I refuse to believe that uncle would be anything but candid with me about the estate. He and father were close, as you know."

Lady Carstairs waved away Kate's words. "Yes, yes, my dear. You never fail to defend him. But all of that aside, you have agreed it is time to for a review, a change in management." Lady Carstairs rose and refilled their teacups. "I have given this some thought. Your overseer was obviously a shady character and no loss to The Meadows. It is the perfect opportunity for making some investigations and some changes."

Kate nodded. "I see what you mean."

"Now then." Lady Carstairs settled herself in her seat. "I have taken the liberty of making some inquiries."

Lady Carstairs held up her hand when Kate opened her mouth to comment.

"Wait, my dear, hear me out. I have contacted my brother, your maternal uncle, Lord Mcpherson, from the North. He has long managed his estates and has done rather well for himself. I asked about an overseer and book master. He replied just yesterday."

She clasped her hands together in front of her and looked at Kate seriously. "He has found the perfect men to assist you. If you are interested in assessing your property, in determining its problems and setting them to rights, then your Uncle Niall has assured me these men are the fellows for the job."

She sat back and waited for Katherine to reply.

Kate contemplated the offer. She sighed. "I cannot help but think that Uncle Edmund might be offended."

Lady Carstairs said firmly, "It is business, my dear. Your

uncle knows that. When Edmund gave us his last report, he made it clear the estate was a burden for him. If The Meadows has been struggling as he says, it is your responsibility to determine the cause and to rectify it. This was your father's much-loved home, your inheritance."

Lady Carstairs leaned back. "You have many times confided to me your wish to someday return to the estate full time, to pursue your dream of breeding the new thoroughbred horses as you had planned with your father all those years ago. If you lose The Meadows, you lose it all."

"It cannot be as bad as that," Kate responded with concern.

"Oh, but it can. As a businesswoman, you know no enterprise can sustain loss after loss. According to your uncle, it has been several years since the place saw a profit. In the six years of his management, it has continued to decline. For the first few years, the place at least paid for itself, but last year, as you know, Edmund reported a loss." Lady Carstairs leaned forward to make her point. "The situation could be very dire indeed."

Kate frowned. "We do need a new overseer. And an audit at this time would make sense. If I am to take over the reins, then I want to know exactly what I am dealing with firsthand. Yes. Write to Uncle Niall. Tell him we will hire his men. The jobs can start immediately upon their arrival. The sooner the better." Kate set down her cup. "We have only a week before the estate transfers to my control. It will take that long for them to arrive and get settled in."

Kate smiled. "I must say, I am excited to begin. It has been too long since I took an active role in the operation of The Meadows."

"It is the right decision, Katherine. I have confidence in your ability. One hopes that in your time here with me you have learned a few things about managing your own affairs." Lady Carstairs took a sip of her tea. "Now then, I will send a message to Niall. Edmund, too, will have to be informed. I can send him a note to come to us at his convenience. And you, my dear, will be busy helping our house guest prepare for her wedding."

Lady Carstairs smiled. "I must say I am pleased to leave that job for you. I confess I have no idea of the etiquette or traditions involved in a situation such as this one."

She chuckled.

"Nor do I," Kate said with a sigh, setting aside her tea, "but I believe if anyone can pull this off with aplomb, it is Clarissa."

Things will all work out for the best Kate thought with a smile. Clarissa will be happily married. And the more she thought of The Meadows, the more convinced she was that Uncle Edmund would be much pleased with her plan to take over its management. She could not wait to give him the news.

Chapter Twenty

The next morning's breakfast was a quiet one. Kate enjoyed her tea while Lady Carstairs checked the morning post.

The breakfast room was her favorite in the house. A long dining table faced the bay windows which overlooked the back garden. A door next to the side table on the left led to the kitchen. As a result, the room was always filled with the warm smells of baking. Another open doorway led to the seldom used formal dining room and back parlor.

"It is pleasant to have our home back to ourselves," Kate said.

"It is." Lady Carstairs handed Kate a card. "Clarissa sent us a lovely note before departing from the Hargrove's yesterday. Very thoughtful of her."

Kate read the card. "It seems all went well, at least from her perspective." She sighed. "Clarissa suggests that there may be a reception once they have settled. She says they will be in Hernes for at least a week."

Lady Carstairs pursed her lips. "I should think they will stay out of town for the rest of the season. They are quite notorious. I am afraid the scene at the Hargrove's will be the talk of London for the next few weeks." Lady Carstairs helped herself to a scone and began applying jelly. "I shudder to think of the conversations over afternoon tea yesterday."

"Yes, but they are now a respectable married couple. The marriage will have solved everything," Kate replied.

Milly stood in the doorway with her hands on her hips. "Viscount Serves requests an audience. I told him we were not in the habit of receiving guests this early, but he insists."

"Ask him to join us in the breakfast room. And bring another place setting, Millie. Perhaps he will want breakfast." Lady Carstairs looked at Kate. "Do you want me to remain, my dear? I do believe this will be a business discussion."

"Please do, Aunty. I feel a little nervous about this discussion. I hope to accomplish it without offending Uncle Edmund," Kate replied.

Lady Carstairs reached across the table and patted her hand. "The time has come, my dear. Taking control of your inheritance is the right thing to do."

The viscount entered the room. He was impeccably dressed in soft gray jacket and trousers. His long face and deep frown lines gave him a mournful appearance.

"Good morning, ladies. I hope I am not inconveniencing you." He gave his short bow in greeting.

Lady Carstairs rose and indicated a chair. "Please sit down, my Lord. We were just having breakfast. Would you like to join us? Or perhaps just tea?"

"Thank you. Tea will be fine." The viscount settled in his seat as Lady Carstairs poured his tea. He brushed away her offering of cream and sugar. "I received your note. I am afraid I was rather busy yesterday but came as soon as I could."

"Please accept our congratulations on your son's wedding. I realize it was a bit rushed, but I am sure they will be very happy." Kate smiled.

"Ah, yes. Thank you, Katherine. You must know I had hoped to unite our families, but sadly it is not to be." The viscount's frown lines deepened. He looked more sorrowful than ever. "Now then, I understand from your note you wish to discuss The Meadows. I have given the matter a great deal of thought. I am aware you are reaching the age of majority. And I am sure you are concerned about the future. I am here to assure you that despite the ordeal of managing the place, I am willing to continue to work on your behalf." He nodded seriously.

"That is most gracious of you. I understand the estate has been a trial for you, Uncle Edmund. I want to thank you for all you have done for me." Kate cleared her throat and glanced at Lady Carstairs who nodded her encouragement. "But I have given the matter a great deal of thought as well. Lady Carstairs and I have discussed the situation at length. I have decided I cannot continue to burden you with this responsibility any longer."

The viscount turned pale. "Not burden me. But what does this mean?" He looked from one lady to the other. "Ah. I see."

Some of the color returned to his cheeks. "I believe I understand. You wish to sell. Well, now." He rubbed his chin thoughtfully and pressed his lips into a thin smile. "The place has depreciated over the last bit. You will not get the price you hope for. But I suppose I could produce the funds to give you something for the place."

"No, no. I have no intention of selling," Kate interjected. "I have decided to manage the place myself."

"What? What nonsense is this?" Lord Serves looked at Kate with horror. "You cannot be serious."

He turned to Lady Carstairs. "You must talk her out of this foolhardy plan at once. This is a ridiculous notion!"

"Actually," Lady Carstairs continued in a calm voice, "I agree with Katherine. I think it is high time she took matters into her own hands."

"But you cannot! She is too young, and a female. This is a disaster. It is too much to even contemplate." He glared at Lady Carstairs. "You realize that in encouraging her in this bizarre idea you are neglecting your duty. You of all people should be aware of your responsibility to Katherine, and to your departed sister as well. This is irresponsible of you, Elizabeth!"

"Oh, but you are wrong, Edmund." Lady Carstairs emphasized his first name as though to remind him of his lapse in using hers. "Katherine is old enough. Indeed, the law agrees. Furthermore, she is quite capable of managing her own affairs."

Lord Serves sneered at Katherine. "You do not have the least idea of how to go about this."

Kate's cheeks burned with indignation. She took a deep breath. "I believe I do. I helped father for many years. Unbeknownst to you, I have also managed a business here in town. I think I will be able to handle The Meadows."

Lord Serves snorted. "I am aware of the clothing shop."

Kate looked at him with wide eyes.

"Do you honestly think that paltry business can compare to an operation like The Meadows?" He picked up his tea, then appeared to think better of it and returned it to its saucer with a clang. "No. I cannot allow this. You will stop these fantasies immediately. Tomorrow I will send my man of affairs over and you will sign a contract stating that The Meadows will remain in my control."

He gave his most intimidating glare first to Kate and then to Lady Carstairs.

Kate returned his scowl.

"No, you will not. And if you do, I will not sign it." She squared her shoulders and raised her chin a notch. "I had hoped to not injure your feelings this morning, but you have made that impossible."

She took a deep breath and continued more calmly, "While I am thankful for all you have done, I am entitled to make my own decisions. I would remind you that under your management my inheritance continues to depreciate. Indeed, I would be hard pressed to do worse, for if your reports are accurate, I am on the verge of losing it anyway. You yourself stated the place has been a burden to you. It should be a relief to have it off your hands."

"Well, as to that, it has been a hard couple of years. Your father left the place near bankruptcy. I have worked tirelessly on your behalf."

The viscount continued in a soft fatherly voice. "Come now, Katherine, I am your father's only brother. You know I only want the best for you. You must see that the estate is too much for you. You have your life here in town. You do not need the headache. And if I genuinely thought you had any idea of how to manage the estate, I would be happy to let you take the reins."

"I have already begun the process." Katherine glanced at Lady Carstairs who smiled her encouragement. "I have hired a new overseer and an accountant. They will arrive as soon as next week to assess the property. I intend to discover its problems and find a path to prosperity in the future."

The viscount's mouth dropped. "You have what? You cannot have! Do you mean that without the slightest indication to me you have gone forward with this ridiculous plan? Thank goodness I came by this morning. This is outrageous!" He stood and placed both hands on the table. He leaned forward and stared intently at Kate. "You will sign those contracts, Katherine. I will allow no alternatives."

"No." Katherine glared at him. She stood and braced her arms on the table in an exact replica of his intimidating stance. "And no amount of bullying will change my mind."

"After all I have done for you, you dare to tell me this!"

Lady Carstairs spoke up. "She has hired new management for the place. Her uncle, my brother Lord Mcpherson, is sending us two trustworthy employees to help put the place to rights." She too leaned forward from her seated position, to emphasize her point, unimpressed with his attempts to intimidate. "He assures me they are the absolute best and will leave no stone unturned."

Lady Carstairs leaned back once more and grinned triumphantly. "They will be enroute to The Meadows as we speak. You can rest assured the place will be in good hands."

Kate relaxed her stance, sitting once more and released a long sigh. "Your guardianship is over, uncle. It is done. The process of transferring management has already begun. I would think you must feel at least some comfort in relieving yourself of this burden."

Kate attempted to catch his gaze which was now cast down. He pulled his arms off the table and let them hang limply by his side. He seemed to have deflated before their eyes.

Kate attempted to console him. "Once again, I would like to thank you for your service to me. But it is over. I will

give my best effort in restoring the place to its former prof-
itability."

He slowly sank down into his chair. Kate had hoped
perhaps he would now be reassured, but his frown lines had
only deepened. His long pale face seemed to extend even
further.

For a moment, there was silence. Kate and Lady
Carstairs looked at him, waiting for his reply. Raising his
eyes at last, he reached forward to pick up his teacup. His
hand began to tremble. Tea splashed from the sides of his
cup, which he set down quickly.

He took a breath and let out a long sigh. His gaze travelled from one lady to the other.

"I understand you have proceeded with this choice
without consulting me. You will come to a bad end. It is
most unfortunate." His face transformed into a mask of
polite indifference. The count seemed to have lost the
sadness and anger of his initial reactions. In its place was a
cool and distant demeanor. "I have done what I could to
dissuade you. I am afraid you have chosen your own
destructive course."

He rose from the table, shaking his head sadly. "You are
much like your father, Katherine. And like him, you will
come to a bad end. I can at least be certain I have done
everything in my power to protect you from his fate. But you
have determined your course. A pity."

With a last steely glare at Katherine, he turned and
strode from the room.

Kate stared at the open doorway her uncle had exited.

"That did not go well. I fear I have insulted the man."
She sipped her tea. She was disconcerted by the extreme
reaction of the viscount. "I wonder what he meant by

protecting me from my father's fate. Does he think I will take a tumble from a horse?"

"I believe he was speaking of bankruptcy, my dear. Set those concerns aside. As you said, it will be hard to do worse." Lady Carstairs pushed aside her breakfast plate. "Edmund will come to accept your decision. He has no choice. Now, then, what are your plans for today?"

With an effort, Kate shook off her feelings of unease about her uncle.

"Ambrose will be arriving to take me for my morning ride. Then, this afternoon I hope to visit the shops. I need a few items. Clarissa has gone through all of my gloves." Kate chuckled. "It will be a pleasure to enjoy my own wardrobe once more."

Kate rose to go up to change into her riding clothes. She added from the doorway, "You are welcome to join me this afternoon. Or if you need anything I can pick it up for you."

"No, my dear. With all this talk of business this morning I feel the urge to look through the salon's books. I am anticipating a tidy profit from this season's orders." She smiled at Kate. "Enjoy your day, Katherine."

When Katherine came downstairs, she was pleased to see Ambrose waiting in the foyer. He wore a dark gray riding suit, with white cuffs and neckcloth. His vest coat was a lighter shade of dove gray. The jacket was stretched tightly across his broad shoulders.

Kate smiled. "When I am with you, I know I am accompanied by the handsomest man in town."

Ambrose laughed as he helped her adjust her cloak. "I am the one who is supposed to shower you in compliments. We must get these roles straight."

They entered the park. It was a crisp spring day. Here

and there, droplets of dew caught the light and twinkled their greeting to the morning sun. No one was about. Trees lined the perimeter of the park, with thick shrub bushes blocking all vestiges of the busy city life beyond. The place had been designed with bluffs of thick willows and tall oaks. The land was not flat but had gentle rolling hills, its valleys dotted with ponds inhabited by ducks of several varieties. Flowers grew in wild tangles in the random plots along the tree lines in an English country garden style. At this time of day in the deserted park, it was easy for Kate to imagine they were alone in the countryside.

Starling began to prance and pull at her reins in anticipation of a run.

"Shall we have a gallop? I fear I can hold this beauty back no longer."

"There is no one on the carriage run," Ambrose said. "Let's gallop them to the pond."

They gave the horses their lead, taking them around the park along the lanes. Galloping with Ambrose was exhilarating. Riding was what she had most missed when she had moved to town. She would be forever grateful to him for giving her this gift of morning rides.

Kate glanced at Ambrose. He sat his horse perfectly. He turned to her and smiled, and for a moment as the horses raced down the path, they shared their mutual joy. Once the horses were satisfied with their run, they slowed to a trot and eventually a walk. Ambrose veered off the track and led them into the green expanse of lawns.

"I assume the wedding went off without too much trouble yesterday," he said into the quiet.

"Yes. Clarissa was quite thrilled with her wonderful prospects." Kate grinned. "One cannot help but to marvel at her. She absolutely and shamelessly indulged in bragging about her accomplishments. I suppose all's well that ends well."

Ambrose smiled. "I am glad to hear it. I admit I was relieved to be rid of my competition, the ever-present Jeremy, in such a final way." He looked at her more seriously. "Have you given any more thought to my proposal?"

Kate felt the joy of the morning drain from her. "Do you think I am like Clarissa then?" She could feel her cheeks flame with anger. "Do you think I could celebrate a proposal forced upon you?"

"Katherine, our situation is nothing like theirs. It is not the same at all."

"It is exactly the same! It only lacks the crowds poor Clarissa had to endure!" Kate spurred her horse forward. It was time to trot toward the exit. She could hear no more about it.

Ambrose attempted to keep pace with her. "Our marriage would not have to be a rushed affair. We could make our announcement and choose our date. Whatever you decide would do. No one need know our reasons for the marriage,"

Her face remained stoic.

"It is totally different, Katherine."

Kate turned to him in anger. "No, it is not. What happened with Clarissa was a ridiculous fiasco. I am not interested in repeating her choices. I want more." She raised her chin. "That you should think I am the same creature as Clarissa, relishing my success at snagging a husband no matter how it was accomplished, is beyond endurance. You insult me when you suggest what you offer is good enough. Do you think I too should be thankful for these lukewarm proposals?"

"It is not a lukewarm proposal. And it is I who would

be thankful if you were to accept. I cannot dishonor you and just walk away." Ambrose cleared his throat. His face had begun to flush lightly. "I think we would do well together. I want you for my wife. I don't know what else I can say."

He looked at her helplessly.

"I have told you I will not be married to appease your misguided sense of honor and I meant it." Tears stung her eyes. How she yearned to hear her Ambrose give her a real proposal. To declare his love for her and his desire to spend the rest of his life with her. To have him spout these words of duty was a bitter reminder that he may never return her love. She squeezed her eyelids tight to fight back her tears. "I wish to go home now."

Ambrose reluctantly turned his horse towards the gate. "Katherine, I—"

"Do not. Not another word."

The remainder of the ride was spent in strained silence. It was with some relief that they reached the gate to her home. Ambrose helped her down from Starling with care.

He walked her to the door. "There is one more thing. I want to remind you that I still expect you to take all precautions for your safety. You are not to walk to the shop. Call a hansom. You are to go nowhere without me accompanying you."

Kate turned to him in absolute astonishment. How dare he issue orders at a time like this? She gave him a sarcastic smile "I am afraid you have mistaken me for one of your former troops. I do not take commands well."

Ambrose pressed his lips tightly together as he escorted her to the door. "Katherine, you must promise me you will follow my instructions. If you do not, I will be forced to stay here at your door indefinitely."

Kate looked at his determined face and realized at once that he was serious.

She expelled a full breath. "Alright, yes. I will try to take every precaution."

Ambrose nodded, satisfied. "I will be at your service. I have given both you and Lady Carstairs my address. Should you decide on going out or if anything untoward should occur, I expect you to send me a message immediately."

"Aye, Aye, captain," Kate replied as she slipped through the door.

She had no intention of following his commands. The danger had passed. She had sacrificed a week of work to the bloody codebook and that was enough.

Chapter Twenty-One

Kate decided that today she would visit Pall Mall to do her shopping. She had not visited the shopping district since January eighth, when the street had celebrated being the first in the world to sport gas lights. Since then, Harding, Howell, and Co. had opened one of the first ever department stores. It was based on the new trend towards warehouse shopping but was designed to serve the needs of the upper classes. Katherine had heard rave reviews about both its comforts and the variety of stock it contained. Besides, her favorite bookstore, Dodsley's, was also in the neighborhood. She hoped to pick up a few novels while she was in the area.

She felt a certain satisfaction in disobeying Ambrose's orders this afternoon. He'd had no business issuing them. She had used a hansom cab and that was the extent of her precautions. Ambrose was out of line in curbing her activities. It was difficult to hold her own against the man. She was determined to withstand him.

The wide streets were relatively quiet this afternoon.

Occasionally, a coach lumbered through the soft mud of the thoroughfare, while the faster hansom cabs buzzed back and forth collecting and depositing shoppers and sightseers.

She wandered about. The sidewalks were wide and bricked. It was a rare luxury in the city of London. She had purchased a lace handkerchief and several pairs of white gloves. She decided to peruse Dodsley's that was opposite the leather works. The shop was further down the street where the road narrowed considerably. Here, entrepreneurs were allowed to hawk their wares from carts dotted along the curbs.

On a whim, Kate stopped at a flower cart which was manned by a young lad.

"What beautiful flowers." She admired the display of violets which covered the entire cart in brilliant shades of purple.

"Beautiful flowers for a beautiful lady." The young man held out a small fist of posies.

Kate laughed. "I will purchase one. How much, my boy?"

"For someone as lovely as you, my lady," he said, holding out his flowers and executing a perfect bow, "only two shillings."

"You are a charmer. And for that I shall buy two." Kate dug in her reticule and handed the lad her coins. "One I shall carry with me and one I will leave for you to give to the young lady of your choice."

The boy blushed. "Thank you, your Grace."

He bowed once more.

"Well done." Kate shook her head at him and chuckled.

He gave her a cheeky wink.

Kate balanced her purchases as she progressed carefully across the muddy street. A curricle turned the corner and came towards her. Katherine watched in horror as the driver, perched on its tall seats, whipped his horses to a gallop. The horses lunged towards her. Kate stood frozen for a precious moment. She could see the coachman continue to wildly whip his team.

She heard a shout from the side of the street. Someone rammed into her back. The momentum flung the two of them across the path of the coach towards the opposite curb. They hit the street and rolled to safety. Kate's eyes widened in terror as the wheel of the curricle passed inches from her face.

Kate sat up gingerly. The coach sped off into the distance.

"Crazy sot." The flower boy pulled away from her and rose to his feet. He reached down and assisted her upright. "Are you all right, ma'am?"

Kate stood, swaying unsteadily. She opened her mouth to answer but could only stare helplessly. Her skirt and jacket were covered in mud. Her cheek ached, where she must have caught an elbow. She had lost her bonnet, and her hair had tumbled around her shoulders. She looked about her trying to find it.

The flower boy followed her gaze. He gathered her parcels and reticule which were strewn about in the mud. He forced them into her hands.

"You best take a step back onto the walk, my lady." He nudged her back a step. "Nasty business. Can't imagine what got into the man. He looked to hit you and that's for sure."

The boy continued to mutter as he stepped back into the street to pluck her hat from the muck. He looked at it with disgust. A band of black stained its flattened top where the wheels of the coach had crushed it. Its underside was a thick layer of muck. The lad banged the hat against his sodden pants to knock off any larger pieces of grime and handed it to her with an apologetic look.

Kate regained her voice. "Th... Thank you," she stuttered. "Thank you so much. I believe you have saved my life."

She shuddered. In her mind she could still see a black-cloaked coachman viciously slashing at his horses. He wore a cowled hood, but she could swear she had seen him glare at her from beneath its folds. She took several deep breaths to calm herself.

A group of ladies in the wide skirts and brocaded jackets of the working middle class rounded the corner and walked by her, gawking curiously.

The oldest of the group turned back, shaking her head, and gave her a pitying glance. "Tut, tut. One must take care crossing the streets my dear."

The comment shook Kate out of her reverie.

"That driver did not swerve an inch to miss you. I'd say you have nasty enemies, ma'am. He came at you like he wanted to hit you for sure." The boy peered intently into her face. "It looks to be like you will be sporting quite a bruise on that cheek. It is puffy and all red-like."

Kate began to attempt to put herself together. She touched her cheek lightly. It stung, but it was a minor injury considering what could have happened had the young man not come to her aid. A vision of the iron wheel squeezing into the mud right before her eyes flitted across her mind.

She pushed the memory aside.

She shook out her skirts the best she could and began to work on her hair. A greasy braid would be all she could manage. Her hands trembled only slightly as she began to braid her hair.

Kate took a deep cleansing breath and contemplated the young man at her side, while her fingers worked her thick chestnut hair back into some semblance of normalcy. He shifted back and forth from one foot to the other, peeking up at her, then looking back to his abandoned cart. It was clear that he was at a loss, not sure what he should do.

Kate smiled at him. "You have been my hero today. You are my knight in shining armor."

The boy gave her a sheepish grin, his face flushed with pride.

"I shudder to think of what could have happened without your quick actions. Can I pay you?"

The boy looked insulted. "Oh no, my lady. I will take naught for the trouble. Any gentleman would have done the same."

Kate looked at the boy's cart which sat across the street. A haggard donkey was attached to its hitch, its head low to the ground as it munched an old feed bag. "What is your name, young man?"

"It is William, ma'am. But my friends call me Willy."

"Well, William, I have decided that violets are my favorite flower." She considered for a moment. "What happens, my boy, when you sell all your flowers?"

The young man chuckled. "That is not likely. It only happened once and that was the night we lit the lamps. We had the crowds here on that night for sure."

"Did you get the night to yourself then?"

"I did! My da was right pleased too!" He grinned at her.

"Good. It is decided then. I will take every violet you have." Kate reached into her reticule and jotted down her address. "Bring your cart to this address. I will have informed my housemaid that you will be arriving. She will be told to purchase every single violet on your cart."

Kate grinned as she thought of Milly's reaction.

The flower boy flashed a wide toothy grin. "All of them?"

"Every blooming one." Kate smiled at her pun.

"I cannot wait to see my old da's face. Hooray!" He looked at Kate seriously. "You won't be changing your mind, will you?"

"I will not."

A hansom cab turned the corner up the street and meandered slowly towards them. Kate flagged it down. Once settled on its seats Kate sighed, thankful to be on her way back to the safety of her home. The coach lurched forward. She looked back, leaning out the narrow window. The old donkey was bumping happily along behind her. The flower boy raised his hand and gave her a brisk wave.

Kate leaned back on the seat and shuddered with the memory of her near miss. And the unpleasantness was not yet over. Ambrose would be sure to hear of it. He was unlikely to react kindly to her disregarding his orders.

Chapter Twenty-Two

Ambrose arrived early the next morning to take Kate for a morning ride. His eyes widened as Milly let him into the foyer. The room was a purple blush. Every surface was covered in violets. Even the stairs had bowls of violets at the corner of each step.

He felt a rush of annoyance. Would he have another suitor to deal with?

"The ladies are still at breakfast. It is early." Milly put her hands on her hips and eyed him from his head to his boot tops as though assessing his worth. She nodded slowly and even graced him with a hint of a smile. Ambrose gave her a tentative smile in return.

"Ah... would it be possible to see Katherine? I believe she expects me—"

"I will tell her you are here." Milly muttered to herself and headed past the stairs to the breakfast room. She turned back. "You might as well come along with me."

Ambrose raised his brows in surprise. Milly had never let him past the foyer without a great deal of fuss and bother. And certainly, he had not previously been admitted without first having been announced and approved.

"I believe you are warming up to me Milly." Ambrose chuckled as he stepped carefully around a massive bowl of violets.

"I will bring you a place setting. The food is on the sideboard." It was the only concession Millie would make.

"Lord St. Claire, a pleasure to see you this morning." Lady Carstairs rose to greet him. "Do sit down and enjoy some breakfast with us."

"Thank you. An excellent idea." Ambrose took a plate and began to heap it with scrambled eggs and bacon from the sideboard as Milly laid out a setting directly across from Katherine. "And thank you, Milly."

Milly responded with a grunt as she filled his teacup.

Ambrose sat down and took in the array of scones and buns placed intermittently between the bowls of violets on the table. He selected two rolls and generously spread them with jelly.

"Good morning, Katherine." He looked at her curiously. She had kept her head down. Usually, he could expect at least her wide smile in greeting. He crouched low over his plate attempting to peer into her face.

Kate slowly raised her head. A purple bruise marked her left cheek. Ambrose stared at her with his mouth slightly open.

"Good morning, Ambrose." She smiled shyly.

Ambrose smiled back, hiding his unease. Everything was wrong. Lady Carstairs, who normally was the perfect hostess, was silent. Milly had brought him in without ado. The house was full of violets. And worst of all, Kate was sporting a bruise on her cheek and a reticent attitude. He decided to eat his meal while he considered the situation.

He ate heartily despite the uncomfortable silence. Outside of Lady Carstairs once offering him a selection of fruit, there had been no table talk. Katherine had kept her head down while nibbling a piece of toast.

He was not sure what was amiss, but he was determined to find out. He decided that he would tackle the situation head on. When he finished his meal, he set his napkin on his plate and sipped his tea.

He looked from Lady Carstairs to his downcast Katherine. "Well, now, I know something untoward has occurred and I would appreciate an explanation."

Lady Carstairs cleared her throat.

"Yes, there has been a problem." She glanced at Kate who shook her head. Lady Carstairs was not deterred. "Katherine had an incident on the Pall Mall yesterday afternoon. Katherine and her rescuer, a flower boy, both agree that a curricle attempted to purposely run her down. It was a narrow escape. Katherine wants no fuss. I disagree."

Katherine glowered at her aunt. "No harm was done. I am quite all right."

"Katherine, someone has purposely made an attempt on your life. It is a serious matter. Ambrose deserves to know, because if nothing else I want you protected." Lady Carstairs pressed her lips and looked at Ambrose.

"Why were you on the Pall Mall Katherine? I remember specifically asking you to stay put unless accompanied by me," Ambrose asked in a soft dangerous voice.

Kate did not meet his gaze. "I hired a hansom as you directed. I took every precaution."

Ambrose squared his shoulders. His stomach clenched. "Are you truly all right, Katherine? Do you have other injuries?"

"I have the bruise on my cheek. Outside of a few bumps and scrapes, I came away from the ordeal unscathed."

Ambrose took a cleansing breath, closing his eyes. His first instinct was to holler his frustration with her. She had disobeyed his direct orders. He reluctantly chose to save that for another time. There was no point in lecturing her now that the deed was done. He needed to hear the facts and come up with an immediate plan to keep her safe. He swore softly under his breath. Somehow, he must find out what was occurring and why. To keep her safe, he had to understand the threat.

"Katherine, I want you to describe the incident completely and thoroughly."

Kate gave the details of yesterday's events as best she could. Ambrose listened carefully.

"Do you think you can tell us something about your attacker?" Ambrose asked.

"Last time I could give you information, describe the man, but this time there is nothing. I know only that he wore a hooded cloak. And that he viciously whipped his horses." Kate shuddered.

Ambrose thought about the attack. "What confounds me is the fact that the villains who had wanted the codes have them. Why would Katherine be targeted? It makes no sense. There must be something else. Something we are missing."

"Could there be another party after the codes?" Lady Carstairs asked.

"Perhaps. But this man wanted to kill her. Why? If someone were after the codes, removing Katherine would not be to their advantage." Ambrose thought for a minute. "There is Sergeant Ames and his assumption that Katherine overheard something of importance, but I cannot see the admiral having a man close to him who was not secure. Do you have other enemies, Katherine? Have there been other conflicts?"

"Well, there is Bentley Brown. He has threatened to blackmail me. But to kill me? I cannot imagine what good it would do him. Revenge might be his motive, but that would be extreme, even for him."

"It does not seem feasible, but I will check him out," Ambrose said. "Is there anyone else? Anyone you have had even the slightest conflict with? Perhaps a customer?"

"My customers are females, though I suppose that is neither here nor there. But I would hope that we please most of our clients. Certainly, none of our ladies would resort to this over a disappointing double row of ruffles." Kate attempted to smile.

"Do you have a customer with a sizable bill? Or have you had a dispute with anyone?" Ambrose asked.

"No. We are very careful managing credit. We have had a few problems in the past, but they have been resolved." Kate shook her head. "I just cannot think of anyone who might want to kill me."

Lady Carstairs replied, "There is Uncle Edmund. Just yesterday morning we had a nasty confrontation about Katherine's estate. Katherine comes into her inheritance next week. The viscount was hesitant about letting her control her property."

Kate interrupted. "It was not Uncle Edmund. This coachman was much too small to be the viscount. He was a slender figure, all hunched over in his cowl."

"That is something. We know he is a smaller framed man." Ambrose contemplated his options. There were thousands of 'small-framed men' in London.

Lady Carstairs shifted on her chair. "I wonder if you

may be dismissing your uncle too quickly Kate. He was livid when he left our home yesterday. And he certainly could have hired someone to do the job," she said.

"No Aunt Elizabeth. Uncle Edmund may have been angry, but he would never do such a thing." She looked at Ambrose. "Uncle Edmund was awfully close to his brother, my father. He is family."

"I will visit the admiral and request his assistance once more."

Ambrose leaned back in his chair and debated what was to be done. His priority was to protect Katherine. For now, it was the key factor. He knew nothing helpful about the motives of Katherine's attacker just yet.

"I will hire a bow street runner. He will be given the task of protecting you, Katherine."

"Is that really necessary, Ambrose?" Katherine asked.

"Yes, it is." Ambrose looked at Lady Carstairs. "I know this may be an imposition to you, Lady Carstairs, but I am going to ask that you keep this man in your house. I want Katherine protected twenty-four hours a day."

"Really, Ambrose, that is too much." Katherine said.

"No, it is not," Lady Carstairs said. "I think we must take every precaution until we discover what this nonsense is about."

"And this time, Katherine, you will follow my orders." Ambrose leaned forward and met her gaze to emphasize his point. "You will go nowhere, absolutely nowhere, without an escort. Either your man, or I, or both of us, will be with you wherever you decide to go. Is that clear, Katherine?"

Ambrose did not wish to leave anything to chance.

"Ambrose, you cannot be serious. Surely you are overreacting." Kate looked from Lady Carstairs to Ambrose.

"If you must go to your salon, you will take an escort—

in a hansom cab. Do you understand?" Ambrose glared at her.

"All right. I will do it," Katherine responded.

"And I will see that she does." Lady Carstairs gave Katherine a firm glance.

"Now then, what were your plans for today?"

"I had hoped to go for a ride with you this morning. After lunch I must go to work. Mrs. Merriweather has been promised a score of designs, variations of the Empress gowns, from which to select a dress or two for her eldest daughter. She will be in tomorrow. I have no choice but to finish them today."

"Must you go into the salon?" Ambrose asked. "Perhaps we could have your materials delivered here."

Kate laughed and shook her head. "You would have to haul cart loads of silks. I need to match up swatches of materials as samples to the patterns."

Ambrose scowled. "I will take you for your ride. Between my footman and I, we should be able to keep you safe." He glared at her. "I get the feeling that if you are too closed in, you will disobey me."

"Well, that is certainly a warm invitation." Kate chuckled.

Ambrose scowled at her. "You must take this more seriously, Katherine."

"But what if we are wrong? What if the incident yesterday was just a random madman, intent on scaring folks? I find it hard to imagine that someone wants me dead. It is inconceivable," Kate said. "It just does not seem real to me."

Ambrose gave her a look, then decided to ignore her queries. "After my ride, I will speak to the admiral. He may be able to help us. All of this began with the code book.

There must be some connection. Then I will hire a bow street runner." He leaned forward and pointed to her with a stern expression. "And you, my dear, will go nowhere until the runner arrives to escort you. I want your promise."

Kate sighed. Ambrose glared at her waiting for her response.

"There is no need to be continually repeating your orders. I promise. I promise." Kate said.

The ride in the park was grim indeed. Ambrose kept her on his left and directed the footman to ride at her right. He spent his time watching the perimeters of the laneway, alert for any unusual characters. It was not a relaxing or enjoyable excursion. Thankfully, the park was quiet this morning. Only once did they meet a party of riders and they appeared to be harmless, a man and a boy of about ten years. Ambrose looked at Katherine several times, but she remained quiet, concentrating on Starling. He hoped that she was not too disappointed with their outing.

When they arrived safely back at her residence, he helped her dismount. He could not resist pulling her close as she slid from the saddle. The smell of her was intoxicating. His body responded to her nearness. He could not resist pressing her body against his and tucking his head into the curvature of her neck.

"Ah, Katherine," he whispered in her ear. "The worst of it is there will be little opportunity to be alone."

She rested her hands on his shoulders, gently pushing him away. She kissed him lightly before stepping back and out of his reach. She gave him her most charming smile.

"I will wait for you or the runner before leaving for the salon. Thank you for the ride, Ambrose. It is always the best part of my day." She added cheekily, "even today," before skipping up the steps and through her door.

Ambrose joined his footman and assisted him in attaching a lead rope to Starling. The vision of Kate's bright brown eyes and wide smile remained clear in his mind. She was his woman. He would find some way to protect her.

Once mounted, he sorted through the events of the morning. He would have a job protecting Katherine if he could not find the source of her threat. She was too headstrong to remain confined for long.

Chapter Twenty-Three

Time ticked slowly by. Kate checked her broached watch again. It was almost three; teatime had come and gone. She tapped her foot. She had gone over the books for the shop, checked the orders and supplies, and still there was no word from Ambrose. For the last half an hour, she had arranged and rearranged her desk. If she did not get into the salon soon, she would be working late indeed.

"I cannot imagine what has taken him so long."

Lady Carstairs watched her with concern. At last, the knocker sounded.

"Ah, there is the door, Katherine." Lady Carstairs jumped up and hurried to the foyer.

Kate picked up her cloak and bonnet and followed.

A rugged faced gentleman stood at the door with his bowler hat in his hand. He was an imposing figure in old-fashioned short pants and hose. He stood well over six feet with a wide girth. His jacket and waist coat were a conservative charcoal gray and were stretched tight across his massive shoulders. They looked as though they were at least one size too small. He had red hair and handlebar side-burns which covered his face from cheek to chin. He had the look of a Viking, squeezed into nineteenth century apparel.

"Ma'am." He executed an awkward bow in Lady Carstairs' direction, then repeated the movement for Katherine. "Lord St. Claire sent me. I am here for Lady Katherine. Ben Olsen's the name."

"Pleased to meet you, Mr. Olsen. I am Lady Carstairs, and this is my niece, your charge, Lady Katherine."

"Honored, ma'am." He gave another short bow. "I want you ladies to go about your business. I will try to be as discrete as possible. I just need to know the whereabouts of Miss Katherine at all times."

"Perfect," Kate said. "I am glad you have arrived. I will need to go to work immediately."

Lady Carstairs said, "Katherine! I believe we should let the man get settled in. Milly can show him his room."

"No, ma'am. I can find my way around later. I am ready to escort you, Miss Katherine." He nodded. "I have a hansom waiting on the street, ma'am."

"Lovely. Let us be off then." Katherine turned to Lady Carstairs. "I will be a few hours, Aunt Elizabeth, not to worry."

Kate pulled her bonnet onto her head. Mr. Olsen opened the door, and they were off.

The shop was hectic. There were several gowns due to go out at five. As a result, the seamstresses were rushed with the finishing touches. Ladies could order a gown, and for an extra fee, have it completed within a day or two. The shop girls often worked most of the night, especially during the season. With the increased demand due to the new French patterns, the salon had additional orders to fill.

At first, Kate had been a little disconcerted to have the huge bodyguard lurking behind her. He had stood at the alley entrance to her office for some time before she had been able to convince him to take a chair and sit down. But as the afternoon progressed, she began to see how handy he could be.

Each time Kate finished a design, she would begin to match up her patterns with samples of material that she thought might best suit the dress design and the Merri-weather girl. Sometimes it was helpful to see a length of cloth and attempt to picture the flow of the gown. Mr. Olsen graciously helped her with hauling several bolts of cloth into the office. When the ladies working the shop discovered that a smile was all that was needed to get assistance with the heavy bolts of cloth, they were quick to take advantage. Kate decided that Mr. Olsen might be a positive addition to her staff.

After several hours of work, Kate paused for a moment and stretched.

She looked over her shoulder at Mr. Olsen. "I think it is time for a little break. Would you care for a cup of tea? I will be making one. We have at least an hour before I am finished here."

"I could. I could at that," he replied. "I can go make it up if you tell me where I can find the fixings."

Kate rose to her feet. "No, no, I need to walk around a bit. You stay here." She smiled. "Guard the door."

She chuckled as she went to set the tea on. Having a bodyguard seemed a ridiculous notion to her. The poor man had sat there for hours.

The hallway was dark. She noticed that the salon was silent. All the ladies must have gone home for the night. The doors to the dressing rooms lay open, their interiors dark and silent. A lamp had been left on in the show room. The mannequins looked oddly alive in its soft orange glow. Their shadows stretched across the floor in eerie caricatures of the human form.

The coal stove in the corner of the showroom was cold. It was too late for tea. Time had passed quickly while she had concentrated on her work.

She turned back to her office. She sighed. If they wanted tea, and perhaps a bun, they would have to fetch it from Salvadore's down the street. Mr. Salvadore served up a few refreshments at his general store. If they hurried, they might be able to purchase some.

"Mr. Olsen, I wonder if you might fetch us some tea and a bun. From Salvadore's," Kate said as she walked into the room. "It seems the kitchen is closed here."

Mr. Olsen shifted uncomfortably in his chair.

"It will only take a moment and it is just down the street." She gave him a smile. "I will be perfectly safe here. You can go out the back and I will lock up after you leave."

"Well, if you lock up right and tight until I return. Don't be opening the door until I am back."

"Excellent. Two teas and a treat. Whatever he has."

Mr. Olsen rose. "I want to hear the bolt slide in place when I leave."

Kate followed him to the door. "Of course."

Kate closed the door after he left and slid the bolt in place.

With a sinking feeling, Kate realized that she had not given Mr. Olsen the schillings for their refreshments. How completely thoughtless of her. He may not have the money for the teas. Almost immediately, the door rattled. Someone rapped.

"Ah, he is back."

She hurried to the door and swung it open.

Bentley Brown stood in the doorway. Kate attempted to shut the door in his face. He stuck his foot in the jam and pushed. Kate was thrown back.

Bentley Brown entered her office and locked the door behind him. He looked more disheveled than usual. His light brown suit looked like it had not been laundered since the last time she had seen him. His eyes were wide and lit with a dangerous gleam.

He leaned against the door with an odd sneer on his face. "Mrs. Sevile. So glad to see that you are working late."

He giggled. It was a strange, disconcerted sound.

"Just what is it that you want?" Kate's stomach clenched. She rubbed her damp hands on the sides of her skirt. Backing away from him, she stepped behind her desk. At least from there she felt more in control of the situation. There was no reason for Mr. Brown to be in her office unless he meant to do her harm. She knew with a sickening certainty that she was in a life-threatening situation. Her heart pounded in her chest.

"I noticed your friend left." He giggled again, a high-pitched unwholesome sound that jangled her nerves. "I figure he is a bodyguard, and you are just a little too cheap to pay for the entire day."

He sneered. "Always the businesswoman. This time it will cost you."

"What are you doing here?" Kate tried to keep the panic from her voice.

He walked around to the entry into the shop and peered into the darkened hallway before he pulled the door closed. "My employer wants a little job done. I am just the man to do it. Finally, a job I can enjoy."

He wiped his greasy hair back from his face and grinned. His teeth were too big for his mouth and yellowed.

Kate stood frozen behind her desk. Her thoughts raced through her head. He meant to kill her. Screaming would not help. Her only hope was to stall him until Mr. Olsen returned.

She searched for something to say. "It was you who tried to run me down yesterday."

"It was a close one. I almost had you. You escaped from me that time, but now I have you. You are trapped." He laughed. "The boss wants it to look like an accident. I think we will have a little fire tonight. And with a fire—who knows how it started? Maybe the manager took up smoking a pipe. Mrs. Sevile, a secret smoker."

He chuckled at his little joke.

He moved toward her until he was directly in front of her with only the desk separating them. Kate backed up until she felt the wall pressed against her back. She watched with dread as he pulled a handkerchief and a jar from his jacket pocket. He poured a clear liquid onto the cloth and set the bottle on the desk. The sweet sickening smell of chloroform wafted into the room.

Kate edged towards the alley door. Her mouth felt dry. She desperately tried to think of something to say to distract him, to delay him.

"Yes, dangerously flammable, these silks." He pushed a bolt of silk off her desk to the floor where it landed with a resounding smack, while keeping his eyes trained on her. "They burn nice and easy."

He cackled. He started to move around the desk towards her. Unfortunately, he had chosen to come at her from the side of the desk closest to the back door. Her route to the back door was blocked.

"I have the patterns," Kate blurted out. "I could give them to you."

He raised his head and let out a shout of laughter. "Too late, my dear."

He lunged around the desk towards her. Kate scrambled around the desk and charged towards the back door. She reached it and fumbled with the lock.

She felt his arms wrap around her from the back. The chloroform cloth slammed against her face. The world blurred as she slid slowly to the floor.

Chapter Twenty-Four

Ambrose was satisfied with his day's work. He had hired a runner for Kate. The man seemed capable enough. He was sturdy and would be armed. He had sent him in a hansom to deliver Kate to her salon.

He had also managed to track down the lad, young William, who sold violets on the Pall Mall. That had not proved to be too difficult. Salesman purchased the rights to work an area. There could be only one flower cart on that particular corner.

William had been a solid source of information. He had described the curricle as one of the types which was often rented by the young whips around town. It was a high seater, a rare mode of transportation, drawn by two horses on its single axle. The vehicles were fast and mobile. It would have been the perfect weapon to run down an unsuspecting pedestrian.

But there were several livery stables in the immediate area; if Ambrose widened his search, there would be many more. It would be impossible to find the one stable that had hired out this coach working alone. Yet curricles were not as common as the other coaches and the list of possibilities once gathered might be small. There was the potential with this information to find the identity of Katherine's attacker but there were just too many stables for Ambrose to check on his own. Ambrose was optimistic of at least narrowing his list of suspects if he could get some assistance.

The Home Office was his best option for the help he needed. They had the manpower he required. He was convinced time was of the essence. Before investigating further, he decided to meet with the admiral. The resources of the Home Office would make a difference in his investigation. But this assistance was by no means guaranteed. While Ambrose knew the admiral would sympathize with his cause, he also knew he would only apply the state's resources if he concluded it was in the interest of the Home Office to do so.

Admiral Hews sat behind his desk. He leaned back in his chair and rested his hands on his belly in his usual stance, while he listened carefully to Ambrose describe yesterday's incident and the measures Ambrose had taken. He ended with a request for men to help with his search for the curricle.

There was a pause when Ambrose had finished his report of the affair. Ambrose glanced at Ames who stood in his usual position at the door. He could swear the man had the hint of a sneer on his face. Ambrose shifted uncomfortably in his chair.

At last, the admiral sat back up and reached for a paper and quill. He rolled the quill back and forth across his palm. "Interesting. And until the affair with the codebook, there have been no shenanigans involving your Lady Katherine?"

"Nothing. The ladies have lived rather quietly. Even their forays into the polite world are limited."

The Admiral nodded. "Yes. I recall the reports. We have been extremely interested in tracking the movements of the unfortunate Mr. McClury. We are convinced he was a hireling. The most obvious connection is the one with Katherine's guardian, the Viscount of Serves. It appears the two men met often. While the necessity of those meetings might be clear, given that he was the overseer at The Meadows, the lack of other connections has made us suspicious."

"Katherine insisted that the coachman was not the Viscount."

"Hmm." The Admiral began writing a note on his papers. "I am uncomfortable with these latest events. We have an interest in solving this little riddle. I will draft an order. You will have your personnel."

Ambrose sighed with relief. "Thank you, sir."

"I will be directing my men to begin questioning livery stables on the perimeter of London. It seems likely to me that the villains would try for a modicum of anonymity. You, sir, may begin with the stables closest to Pall Mall. We might be able to search a few before they are closed up for the night." The admiral stood, indicating the meeting was completed.

Sergeant Ames swung the door wide. As Ambrose stood, the admiral rang a little bell on the edge of his desk. A clerk entered his office.

Ambrose bowed. "Thank you again, sir."

With a nod to the stoic Sergeant Ames, he left the office.

He made little headway in his search. The first stables did not rent curricles. The second had several for rent but had not sent any out yesterday. On his third attempt he found a stable that both rented curricles and had leased one out for the afternoon. The gentleman that had rented the vehicle was the nineteen-year-old son of Lord Arran. He was obviously a young pup down for a few days from school. Not a likely suspect but Ambrose took down his name and particulars anyway.

It was closing time for most of the stables. Ambrose concluded that he had accomplished what he could for the day. He had thought of Katherine intermittently throughout the afternoon, however, for the last few minutes he could not shake a nagging desire to check up on her.

He looked out the window of his hired hansom. The streets were familiar. He was approaching the location of Katherine's shop. On a whim, he stood and flipped back the roof's trap door. He hollered out the location to her shop as his next stop. He could not shake his persistent feeling of urgency. He decided to ask the coachman to quicken his pace.

The coach came to a stop in front of the building. Ambrose hopped from the vehicle and gave his instructions to the driver to wait. He surveyed the salon. Like the other establishments, it had closed its doors for the evening. The blinds were discretely drawn, and its doors were locked. He pounded on the door but received no response. Deciding that Kate was unlikely to hear him if she was in her office, he chose to try the back.

The streets were quiet but for the occasional employee heading home after a day's work. As he approached the alley, Ambrose spotted a familiar figure lumbering toward him carrying a parcel and a tea can. His mouth opened with astonishment when he recognized the bow street runner he had hired.

"What are you doing out here, man?" He clutched at the man's shoulder. "Where is Katherine?"

The runner reddened. "She sent me on this errand to buy tea.."

Ambrose looked at him with disgust and the runner quickly added, "She is locked up nice and tight in her office."

Ambrose felt a disturbing premonition. He began running to the back entrance before Mr. Olsen had finished his explanation. His feeling of dread increased as he raced to the back door. He pulled at the door handle expecting to find it locked, but it sprang open.

Thick smoke billowed from the room.

"Katherine!" Ambrose's eyes stung. He forced them open and peered into the haze. A smoldering pile of silks near her desk ignited into renewed flames when the blast of oxygen from the alley rushed into the room.

The room was small, and the smoke cleared quickly. Katherine lay in a heap on the floor near the door. Ambrose scooped her up in one brisk move and carried her to the safety of the alley.

He plopped down with her on his lap. She was not moving. Her eyes were closed as though she slept. Ambrose lost all reason. He began shaking her. Her body flopped lifelessly.

"Katherine! Katherine! Open your eyes, Katherine!"

Olsen grabbed his shoulders and stopped the onslaught.

"No," he said firmly. "Check for a pulse, my lord."

The runner's words pulled Ambrose from his hysteria.

He fought his panic as he felt her neck, frantically searching for a pulse. To his relief he was able to feel a strong rhythmic beat. He kept his hand pressed against it to reassure himself that she was alive. He nodded at Olsen.

"She lives," he said. "It must be the smoke."

Ambrose began surveying her for other injuries. He

leaned in close to her to check her breathing. Chloroform filled his nostrils. He realized at once that she had been drugged. A cold sweat rushed over his body. Someone had tried to murder her. She may have other injuries. He ran his hands over her head but could find no trace of a wound. Her body likewise was unscathed.

He looked up with relief. Mr. Olsen was pulling bolts of cloth from the office and tossing them onto the cobble stones. Flames continued to shoot from the blackened husks. A small crowd had gathered at the entrance to alley.

A young man hurried to the scene to offer his assistance. He peered into the office door.

"It is all out there. Just these silks are aflame. If you could get us some water, the fire will be out," Mr. Olsen said.

"Water!" The young man yelled to the onlookers. "We need some water here."

Within minutes, a bevy of young men had poured buckets of water on the burning silks. Fire in London was a constant peril. With the city's tightly packed buildings and sometimes narrow streets, a fire was a fearful danger. Less than fifteen years ago, in 1794, a fire had swept through north central London, destroying homes and businesses. Four hundred and fifty buildings had burned to the ground. It had been the worst disaster since the burning of London in 1666. As a result, there was no shortage of help to douse out these flames.

Ambrose gently rubbed Katherine's cheek. There was still no response. He had to get her home and call a physician. He picked her up gingerly.

"I am taking Katherine home," he said to Mr. Olsen. "Finish up here. Get it cleaned up and locked up. You can meet me at the house later."

Ambrose carried her to the coach and settled her carefully on its seats before climbing in after her. As the coach began to move, she moaned. He lifted her and cushioned her head on his lap.

"Katherine," he murmured. "It is Ambrose. You are safe here with me."

He brushed a strand of hair from her cheek. Katherine began to cough. Her eyes opened briefly then closed again.

Ambrose felt a rush of relief. She would be all right. It was fortunate that whoever had started the fire was ignorant enough not to know that fire required oxygen as well as fuel. By closing her off in her office he had affectively smothered the flames.

She moaned again, opening her eyes a crack.

In moments, they were at her door. Katherine's eyes remained open, but she was dazed, and deathly pale. He slid her from the coach seat and began carrying her to the door.

"I am going to be sick," she moaned.

Ambrose shifted her so that she could vomit on to the step.

The door burst open. Milly appeared. She rushed down the stoop in time to hold back Katherine's hair. She wordlessly held her head while Katherine emptied her stomach.

"Bring her into the library, my lord. We can put her on the settee. I will fetch a bucket." Milly rushed to the kitchens. "Ned!"

When Ned appeared, she instructed, "Run to Doctor Mills. Tell him he must come at once. Lady Katherine is in need of him. Tell him it is urgent."

Milly rushed back to the library with the bucket and a bowl of cool water with cloths.

Lady Carstairs bustled into the room as Ambrose settled

Katherine on the chesterfield. Milly set the bucket beside it. She began to wipe Katherine's face which was covered in a sticky combination of vomit and soot.

"What has happened?" Lady Carstairs asked. "Has Kate been injured?"

She took the cloth from Milly and stroked Katherine's forehead with its coolness.

Kate's eyes had begun to clear. She coughed again, hard wracking coughs which shook her body.

"It is all right, dear," Lady Carstairs said. She reached down and loosened the ties at Kate's bodice, hoping to allow her to breathe more easily. "You are home now. All will be well. Just relax and try to breathe."

Lady Carstairs turned to Ambrose. "What in the world has gone on?"

Ambrose ran his hand through his hair.

"There was a fire at the shop." He held up his hand as Lady Carstairs gasped. "It is out now. Someone has tried to kill Katherine and almost succeeded. She was chloroformed and left to die. I stopped at the shop by chance."

Ambrose stood awkwardly while the ladies bathed and assisted Katherine. "I do not know how much smoke she inhaled. The office was thick with it."

He noticed with relief that Katherine had begun to regain some of her color.

The knocker sounded at the door.

"That will be the doctor." Milly started to rise to get the door.

"No, Milly, I will get it." Ambrose let the doctor in and stood back while he examined Katherine.

"Get this corset off her," the doctor said. "Even unin-jured, it is amazing she can breathe."

Lady Carstairs said, "Milly, bring down Katherine's nightie."

Milly rushed from the room.

Lady Carstairs looked at Ambrose. "You may wait outside the room, please."

Ambrose looked down at Katherine and caught her eye. She appeared quite lucid. He winked at her. He was relieved to see a trace of a smile on her face before he left the room.

After what seemed like forever, Milly came out into the foyer. She was followed by Doctor Mills.

"How is she, doctor?" Ambrose asked.

"She has had a narrow escape, that is certain. She must have been on the floor for the fire, where the smoke was thinner. She has suffered less from smoke inhalation than one might think." The doctor cleared his throat. "It is the chloroform that has affected her most of all. Luckily, the effects of the drug will wear off quickly now that she is awakened. You will find she is already back to herself. She will have a headache for a day or so and that is all."

"Thank you, doctor. That is a relief," Ambrose replied.

The doctor looked at Ambrose warily. His bushy eyebrows furrowed into an intimidating line. "I will be reporting this incident to the local rotation office. The injuries are clearly suspect."

"Yes, doctor. I would appreciate that. I too will be informing the runners," Ambrose said. "The sooner we can catch this culprit the better."

The doctor nodded, satisfied. "Well, I will be off then. She will have a headache as I said but there is not to do about it but to let the drug run its course. Be sure she gets no other drugs. No laudanum, just fluids and of course, rest."

Ambrose walked into the library. Katherine was propped up on the settee wrapped in a quilt. She looked quite fit as she sipped her tea. All signs of her ordeal had disappeared. She had been bathed and dressed in fresh bed clothes. Her hair had been brushed and woven into a thick chestnut braid that fell past her shoulders to her chest. Lady Carstairs too had relaxed into a chair and sat enjoying her tea. It was as if the episode had not occurred.

Ambrose smiled. He was relieved to see her so much recovered. "You ladies are looking lovely. And how is our patient?"

Kate smiled at him. "I admit to feeling much better." She wrinkled her nose. "But sadly, I have the most awful pounding head."

"Sit down, my Lord," Lady Carstairs said. "And have some tea with us. I admit I needed this."

She held up her cup.

Ambrose pulled a chair closer to Katherine. Lady Carstairs handed him a cup of tea. Milly bustled in with a plate of pastries. She offered Ambrose some before setting them down on the tea tray. Ambrose selected a couple and popped one whole into his mouth. The ladies smiled.

"Well, now, it has certainly been a hectic hour or two." Lady Carstairs looked at Kate. "Are you well enough to explain what happened, my dear? Or would you prefer to wait until tomorrow?"

Katherine cleared her throat. "I suppose I must get this over with. And yes, Aunty, I am feeling much recovered." She looked at Ambrose. "I am afraid I have blown it again. I fear you will be disappointed in me, Ambrose."

Ambrose grinned. "Well, then, tonight is definitely the time to give us the details—while you still have our sympathy."

Katherine sighed. She gave Ambrose an apologetic look. "I sent my bodyguard for refreshments."

"I am aware of that. I have a score to settle with that man."

"No, it was not his fault. I pleaded with him, you see. I promised to lock up after he left." Katherine took a deep breath. "Anyway, seconds after he left someone knocked at the door. I thought it to be Mr. Olsen and to my misfortune I opened it."

Ambrose leaned ahead and watched her carefully.

"It was Bentley Brown. I was unable to escape him. He told me I would burn to death; that the whole thing would look like a terrible accident." Kate shuddered.

Lady Carstairs said gently, "We can wait until tomorrow morning, Katherine, if this is too hard for you."

"No, no. I want to talk about it. I will never sleep until I get this off my chest." She took a sip of tea and set the cup back on its saucer. "He said that he had a boss. Someone who had hired him to kill me."

Her voice began to crack, "He said he was happy to do it."

"That slick scoundrel!" Lady Carstairs said.

"Did he give you the name of the person who hired him, Katherine?" Ambrose asked.

"No. I should have asked, I suppose. I tried my best to delay him with conversation, but it was difficult. He was not interested. He was able to drug me before I could escape. I was trapped, you see." Katherine put her hands over her face and stifled a sob.

"You can cry, Katherine," Ambrose said quietly. "It may help you feel better."

And she did. Katherine sobbed loudly into her hands. Ambrose moved over to the edge of the settee and pulled her into his arms. He held her tightly until the storm had passed. When she lifted her head, Ambrose handed her his handkerchief. She mopped her face, then blew her nose loudly.

"I am so sorry. It is the shock, I suppose. And the idea that someone could take pleasure from killing me."

"Yes. But rest easy, Katherine. We will find this man. He will be punished for his actions today." Ambrose reluctantly loosened his hold on her and sat back into his chair.

"Have some more tea, Katherine. It is an herbal. Milly says it will help settle your nerves." Lady Carstairs refilled her cup. "The doctor ordered plenty of fluids."

Kate sipped her tea. She seemed to have recovered.

"On the bright side, we know who accosted you this time." Ambrose smiled. "And this time I want to get to him before his boss does. I wonder if Bentley Brown knows his life is in danger?"

He looked at Katherine. "What do you think? Is he intelligent enough to know that having failed his master, his life is worthless?"

"I think he will discover soon enough that he has failed. Perhaps he already has. He knows he has been identified. He is a sniveling coward. He will run and hide." Katherine sighed and held her hand to her head.

"I think we have discussed this enough tonight. Katherine needs her rest," Lady Carstairs said. She looked at Ambrose. "I cannot thank you enough for all you have done today."

Katherine smiled. "Tonight, you will not have to warn me about leaving the house unattended. I can happily assure you I will be here, safely inside indefinitely."

"Goodnight, Katherine." Ambrose stood. He reached over, took her hand, and kissed it. "Sleep well."

Upon leaving the house, Ambrose was surprised to see the sun had set. Standing in the dark at the bottom of the stoop was Mr. Olsen.

As Ambrose approached, Mr. Olsen pulled his hat from his head. "My Lord, how fares Lady Katherine?"

"She will survive." Ambrose scowled at him. "No thanks to you. What were you thinking to leave her alone like that?"

"It was a grave mistake. I apologize." Olsen shuffled his feet. "I intend to stay here for the night. I will guard the house."

"Good. See that you do." Ambrose stared at him. He sighed. "I will send someone in the morning to relieve you."

Ambrose looked at the street and saw to his surprise that his cab still awaited him.

Mr. Olsen noted the direction of his gaze. "I made him wait, sir."

Ambrose nodded. "Thank you," he said and proceeded to the cab.

The night was not over for him. He would have to go the admiral and apprize him of the latest development. They could call off the search for a curricle. They were now looking for Bentley Brown.

From the admiral's residence, Ambrose would proceed to the nearest Rotation Office. He would need to hire a runner to relieve Mr. Olsen in the morning. He also wanted to give them a full report. The constables would also search for his man. If he offered a reward to those constables, the chances of them catching their man increased.

He was confident they would find Bentley Brown.

Chapter Twenty-Five

Katherine awoke the next morning to find her room filled with bright sunshine. She must have slept late indeed. She moved her head carefully from side to side. Last night, her head had felt as though it contained bricks. Even moving it had been a trial. To her relief, she felt nothing. The doctor had assured her that the effects would not be long lasting.

She was surprised to find that she was hungry and hurried with her morning routine. Once in the breakfast room, she realized it must be much later than she suspected. The side table had been cleared away.

Lady Carstairs came into the room. "There you are. How are you feeling, my dear?"

"It is odd. I was convinced that today would be a trial, but I am fit as ever."

Lady Carstairs smiled. "I am glad to hear it."

Kate looked at the bare sideboard. "Have I missed breakfast then?"

Lady Carstairs chuckled. "And lunch. It is early afternoon. I will see if Milly can fix you something while I myself take a little tea."

Her aunt returned a minute later with a parcel in her arms. "Milly will have something for you in a moment. You gave her quite a scare. She has been quiet and pleasant. It is a little disconcerting."

Kate laughed. "I am glad something positive has come from all of this."

Lady Carstairs set the parcel in front of her and settled into a chair.

Kate looked at the package curiously. "What is this?"

"Ambrose brought it. He was here for breakfast this morning. He was much concerned, poor man. I believe it is a gift. Open it." Lady Carstairs nudged the parcel closer to Kate.

It was wrapped in brown paper and tied with a ribbon. The bow was awkward and misshapen. Kate smiled.

She lifted the parcel. It was heavy. By its shape, it was obviously a book. She eagerly removed the bow and paper to reveal a leather-bound copy of The Illustrated Book of Horse Breeding and Practices.

"How marvelous!" She laughed. "How very sweet of him. This is perfect."

"What do you intend to do about your Lord St. Claire? He is quite taken with you," Lady Carstairs said.

Kate sighed. "I do not know. He has asked me to marry him again. But I cannot." She looked at Lady Carstairs, her voice sad and serious. "I want him to love me. I know it is a lot to ask. But I have held out this long without a marriage and know that I can be quite satisfied without one. This business with Clarissa has reinforced my determination to settle for nothing less. Is it too much to ask for?"

Lady Carstairs nodded. "I see." She leaned forward and

grasped Kate's hand. "I understand. You have been independent for many years. It would be difficult to give all that up without something in return. But you may be wrong about Lord St. Claire. I believe he cares deeply for you. He may not admit his love for you—even to himself. Some men find that hard."

Milly came in with a tray and arranged a place setting for Kate.

"I am glad to see you up and about. I have brought you a little soup and scones. Something easy on the belly. Are you feeling yourself then?" Her voice was uncharacteristically sweet. She eyed Kate suspiciously. "You look fit."

"I feel completely recovered, Milly. It is strange indeed. It is as though yesterday never happened."

"Well then, that is good to know." Milly put her hands on her hips and gave her a glare. "You had us all in a quandary here. I think it is time you quit gallivanting around town. Nothing good has come of it. London is full of scoundrels. Ladies should keep to the house, I always say. And I have the right of it—"

"Thank you, Milly," Lady Carstairs interrupted.

Milly grunted. "I have a letter here for you, just arrived."

She handed Lady Carstairs an envelope. She shot Katherine a dark scowl before leaving the room.

Kate watched Milly retreat to the kitchens. "Well, it is good to know that everything is back to normal."

She laughed. Her soup looked delicious. It was apparent that Milly had anticipated her needs. She began to eat.

Lady Carstairs ripped open the letter. She seemed engrossed in its contents. She looked up at Kate with an expression of shock.

"What is it?" Kate asked.

"Of all the nerve! You will not believe the audacity of that creature!" Lady Carstairs frowned.

"What? Tell me."

"It seems that Clarissa is planning a wedding party. You will not credit the venue." Lady Carstairs pressed her lips into a firm line and shook her head.

"A wedding party? That seems reasonable, Aunty. I can see that she would want one. Clarissa loves parties and to be the center of her own would be too much for her to resist. Sounds quite reasonable to me." Kate laughed. "At least she will not be wearing my clothes."

"Do not be too sure of that. She will be hosting this party at The Meadows," Lady Carstairs said with disgust.

"The Meadows! But how can she? That is my home!" Kate set down her spoon. "It cannot be possible."

Lady Carstairs handed the missive across the table to Kate. "It seems the viscount has suggested it. His reasoning is that it is easily accessible to Clarissa's family on such short notice. He has control over the estate for five more days. A last hurrah for him, I am sure."

Lady Carstairs was clearly annoyed.

"Can this be real? Am I to be paying for this event?" Kate felt her cheeks flush with anger as she scanned the letter. "I had better not. If the estate is as depleted as my uncle has said, then the last thing I can do is host an expensive party."

Kate rubbed her hand across her forehead. "Trust Clarissa to be an irritant even with this."

Lady Carstairs leaned back with a sigh. "And what is worse is that we are obligated to attend."

"Clarissa has added a note that we are to arrive early and help her with the preparations. It is too much." Katherine rolled her eyes. "But that we will do. Because the first thing I will make clear to the happy couple is that they will be flipping the bill for the expenses. That should cut down on any extravagance."

Katherine read further. "It seems they have already opened the house."

She shook her head in disbelief.

"The party is in two days. It means we will have to depart for the country tomorrow morning." Lady Carstairs sighed. "Are you up to it, Katherine? And there is all this other business. I do not know if it would be safe for you, given the circumstances."

"I cannot imagine a place anymore safe than a wedding with family. But I will talk to Ambrose and see what he thinks."

Chapter Twenty-Six

Ambrose decided that if he could not take Katherine out for her morning ride, he would do the next best thing. He would take her for a turn in his brother's coach. If she were not feeling well, it would be the perfect substitute. The seats were wide and comfortable. It was closed in and would be safe. For a coach it offered the smoothest possible ride.

He had ordered Katherine to remain in her house. Unfortunately, he did not think Katherine would be able to tolerate being confined for long. It was not safe for her to go out on her own. And though she had assured him she would not be leaving her home, he had little confidence in her ability to keep that promise. A carriage ride seemed an ideal solution.

He hoped she was well enough. He hoped too that she had enjoyed his gift of the book he had delivered this morning. He had wanted to purchase something for her that would be special. He grimaced when he thought of all she had gone through in the last few days. Any other Lady would have taken to her bed for a week in a fit of the vapors.

He had spent the morning first with the admiral, and then attempting to track down his prey. A visit to Le Chateau, Brown's business, had produced some results. Ambrose and an operative had been able to get the address of his residence. But it had been to no avail. A search of the place had only made it clear that Mr. Brown had left in a hurry. Drawers had been pulled out, and all was in disarray. They could find no correspondence, which was a disappointment, because it could have given them some leads as to his destination. Katherine had been right. He was a coward, and like a scared rabbit, he had gone to ground.

The admiral had set up a meeting with the magistrate. He hoped to have the constables search Bentley Brown's office at the Le Chateau. Perhaps then they could collect a few leads.

In the meantime, he had to see Katherine. He could not stop thinking about her. Twice in the night he had awoken in a cold sweat; the vision of Katherine's pale still face, as it had been after the fire, haunted him. This would be his second visit today. He must see her.

He had the coachman walk the horses. He banged the knocker at the door with some trepidation. Milly let him in.

She wore her usual frown, which was a relief to him after witnessing the uncharacteristic sweetness she had gifted him with this morning.

"Here to see Miss Katherine, I presume." She opened the door wide. "Well, come in then."

She left him standing in the foyer while she went to announce him.

Kate came flouncing into the room. He was relieved to

see that she looked bright and well. Her day dress was a soft yellow with white trim. It complimented her sparkling brown eyes and chestnut hair. She looked beautiful.

"Ambrose." She reached for him with both arms. "I love the book you got me! What a wonderful surprise!"

Ambrose took her hands in his, pulled her in close, and kissed her cheek. The scent of fresh air with a hint of lemons filled his senses.

He laughed. "You look wonderful. How are you feeling?"

"I am well, quite myself today." She gave him an impish grin. "I hope you too have recovered from yesterday. You were a bit peaked the last time I saw you."

Ambrose laughed, as much from relief as from her little joke. "I brought my brother's carriage around. I know it is not Starling, but I thought you might want a little outing just the same. I hoped we might do a turn or two around the park. Or explore the town. We could pick up an ice."

"Excellent. What a lovely idea." She looked serious for a moment. "And it will give me a chance to be brought up to date on the search for Bentley Brown. I want to know everything that is being done to find the man. I confess to feeling decidedly vengeful today."

They settled in the coach.

"Shall we go for an ice first?"

Katherine smiled. "Definitely. And you may give me an up-date on the way."

Ambrose told her the details of the search so far. She listened intently.

"Hmmm." Katherine looked thoughtful. "Who questioned the ladies at the shop? Because it seems to me to be the best place to find out more about the man."

"I was there with one of the admiral's men. We only spoke to the modiste, a French woman. She was able to give us his address but little else."

Katherine laughed merrily. "They are all French. It is good for business. I think you are speaking of Madame LaBois. She is a talented designer, but I am sure working for that man would be a trial. And not just for her, but for all the ladies who work there. A shop employs many women, especially during the season. I wonder if it would be worth another visit. I think I may be able to get a little more information from the ladies." She looked at Ambrose. "It is worth a try. And it can do no harm."

No one would know the workings of a dress shop more than Katherine, thought Ambrose. If anyone could glean more information from the Le Chateau, it would be her.

"All right. You can give it a try." The coach came to a stop. "But first we get our ice."

They had finished their ice by the time they reached the Le Chateau.

Ambrose said, "I will be coming in with you, Katherine. That man might be lurking there."

"It is unlikely." She took his hand as he helped her from the coach. "You may come, but you must promise to let me do the talking."

The inside of the shop sported several mannequins, dressed in the latest fashions. Ambrose watched Katherine examine the gowns with interest. The manager approached them.

"Bonjour, madame. How can I help you today?" The modiste had a thick French accent.

Katherine smiled. "I am pleased to meet you, madame. I am Mrs. Sevile," she said, and shook her hand, "from the LaFontane."

"Oh my. I heard of your misfortune." Madame LaBois examined her from top to bottom. "You look well. I was sorry to hear about your troubles, ma'am."

Ambrose noticed she had lost her French accent.

"How can I help you?" She glanced at Ambrose, recognizing him at once. "I told your man what I know this morning."

"I know and we were thankful to get his home address. But I was wondering whether Mr. Brown ever mentioned anyone he may be connected to. I thought perhaps he may have said something to your girls."

"I guess there is no harm in asking. I know he pestered the girls in the workroom. You can come on back if you like."

"Thank you. It may be most helpful." Katherine turned to Ambrose. "I will not be long."

She gave him a wink and followed Madame LaBois to the back room.

A few minutes later Katherine came back to the showroom with a wide smile on her face. Once in the carriage, she turned to him eagerly.

"I have two good pieces of information." She held up two fingers, grinning with her success.

"What did you learn?"

"First, he apparently spent a great deal of time at a hell hole near the docks called The Black Table. It is not much of a surprise that he was a gambling man. It certainly explains his desperation." Katherine was clearly pleased with her discovery. "Who knows? Maybe he will show up there to try his luck."

"That is excellent Katherine. We may find new leads at the Black Table. He may not show up there, but if he is a regular, then surely someone will know something about the man that can help us. And your second piece of evidence?"

Kate paused to relish her reveal. "He has a sister. And she lives only an hour from London, in Brighton. A spinster sister who runs a boarding house." Katherine was clearly excited about this discovery. "I think it would be the perfect place to run and hide, don't you?"

"You may be right. Katherine, that is marvelous. I will share this with the admiral. We should be able to find her. After all, there cannot be many Miss Browns who run a boarding house."

"It will be Mrs. Brown. No single woman would be allowed to run an establishment. Even I am the widow Mrs. Sevile, and I simply design."

"You are right. Mrs. Brown it is then."

"There was something else I wished to discuss with you. Clarissa is hosting a wedding reception," Katherine said with a grimace, "in my home at The Meadows. And may I add it was without consulting me. Very irritating."

She waved aside her annoyance. "But that is neither here nor there. She has invited Lady Carstairs and I. She would like us to leave tomorrow to help with the preparations as the event will be the following day."

Ambrose's initial reaction was to forbid the journey. Keeping Katherine close was key in his mind to keeping her safe.

"I feel obligated to attend. There will only be a few guests, and those are likely to be Clarissa's relatives and our mutual neighbors from the county. I thought if you were needed here in town to search for Bentley Brown, then I could take Mr. Olsen. I wondered too if getting out of town for a few days might be safer for me."

"There is that," Ambrose replied. "I admit that I had

considered sending you off to the country until the situation was resolved here in town."

Ambrose considered the dilemma. He knew she would be safer away from London at least until they found Bentley Brown. But the thought of her being far from his protection made his stomach clench. He realized with amazement that part of his reluctance was the selfish desire to keep her near him.

He sighed. "As much as it pains me to admit it, you may be more secure out of town. But we will send Mr. Olsen on the journey with you. The actual trip will be the most dangerous part. Once you are in your home, surrounded by family and friends, I am sure you will be sheltered from harm."

Ambrose reached across and took both her hands in his. "You know I will miss seeing you every day."

Leaning forward, he used her hands to pull her close. His head nuzzled close. He began to plant little kisses along her neck. He breathed deeply, taking in her scent. Katherine's nearness alone brought waves of desire.

Katherine groaned softly. His mouth had reached her lips. They came together with an urgency that surprised him. She yanked her hands from his and reached inside his coat to run her palms across his back. Somehow she got her hands beneath his shirt. Her nails scraped his bare torso. He kept his mouth to hers, kissing her wildly while he shrugged out of his jacket.

With one sharp tug, he pulled her dress past her shoulders to her waist. She freed her arms and reached for him. Her nipples stood erect and swollen. He cupped her breasts and sucked hard at each nipple. She moaned in response. Her hands gripped his shoulders. It was too much. His body ached and tingled. He needed to be inside her now. He could not wait.

He reared back and pushed her gown over her hips. His fingers found her. She was wet and ready for him.

"My god, Katherine." He rubbed her slick folds. "You are so beautiful."

She arched her back, wanting more. She spread her legs wide. Her feet rested on the seat behind him.

He could wait no longer. Using one hand to loosen his trousers, he plunged into her with one hard stroke. She gasped, and bracing her legs on the opposite bench, forced him deep inside. He began to drive into her. She found his rhythm and met each thrust with one of her own.

He was lost to everything but the feel of her. Her body gripped him. He increased his pace. Perspiration tickled his back. He slammed into her, relentless, demanding. He was swallowed by a frenzy of need. The world narrowed to only the feel of their bodies, wet and yearning.

Katherine began to whimper as her body tightened on him. Her hands gripped his shoulders hard, and she trembled against him. He heard a scream beginning in her throat and caught it by covering her mouth with his. Her body convulsed. He grabbed her hips and pumped his seed into her. He collapsed into her body, panting.

After a moment, he braced his arm on the seat beside her to free her from his weight. He used his other hand to push the chestnut curls from her face. She lay beneath him in a flurry of pale yellow, the ruffles of her gown now encompassing her chin. Her eyes were hooded and drowsy. A pink glow colored her cheeks and lips. She graced him with a lazy smile.

Ambrose realized he loved her with all his heart. She was his woman. He could never live without her. He knew it with complete certainty. Furthermore, he realized he had loved her from the start. He had wanted her from the moment she first laughed with him at The Running Boar.

He ran his finger down the delicate line of her chin. He touched her swollen lips. She raised her eyes to his. He leaned down and kissed her tenderly.

"Are you okay? Have I hurt you?" he whispered.

"Never. Oh, Ambrose, you make me feel so very good." She looked at him wide-eyed. "Is it always like this? I mean, between a man and a woman?"

She blushed slightly.

"No, Katherine, it is not. There is something between us. It is more than I have ever known." Ambrose struggled to find the right words. He touched her playfully on the tip of her nose and beamed, "We have a passion for each other, you and I."

He gently pulled away from her. Her disheveled appearance made him smile. Reaching for his jacket, he pulled a handkerchief from its pocket. She remained still while he wiped her carefully. It was not the time for declarations of love. Katherine had too much on her mind. There would be opportunities to convince her that she needed him too. Maybe someday she would return his feelings. He vowed that he would spend a lifetime trying to win her love.

He kissed her lightly on her thigh. "I hope I have given you something to remember me by, when you are out of town."

He looked up and grinned at her.

Katherine sat up, flipping down her dress. She pulled its bodice back over her breasts and slipped her arms into the short, puffed sleeves.

Looking up at him, she smiled cheekily. "You are very good at gifts, you know. First the book and now this."

Ambrose laughed. "There is something to be said about the joy of giving after all."

Ambrose watched as she adjusted her hair and settled her hat in place. He could not lose her now. Somehow, he would have to solve the riddle of her attacker. Bentley Brown had been hired. He would not rest until he found the man and discovered who that was.

Chapter Twenty-Seven

Early the next morning, the Suffex coach arrived at Katherine's door. It was escorted by Ambrose astride Thorn. He had ridden over to see the ladies safely off. They were excited to ride in style, none more than Millie.

"If we are to be gallivanting about the countryside, its best to do so in comfort," she said.

The journey would take about five hours. They could expect to reach The Meadows in time for lunch. Kate settled back on the plush seats. A smile played on her face as she remembered the time she and Ambrose had spent in this carriage. It was strange to consider her need for him. It had only been a few short weeks and yet she felt as if she was forever changed. Ambrose had said they had passion between them. She was glad of that. Her hand rubbed the velvet seats as she pictured the excitement and urgency of their last encounter.

"You must be thinking of your home. Do you miss life in the country as much as you once did?" Lady Carstairs asked.

Kate snapped out of her reverie. "Not as much. But I am happy to be going home." She sighed. "Someday, if I ever have my finances in order, I intend to stay home at The Meadows. I believe if I wished to, I could work on my designs from there."

"Yes, I believe you could, with seasonal visits to town to keep abreast of the fashions. And visit your aunt, who would sorely miss you." Lady Carstairs patted her hand. "It may be sooner than you think, if my brother is right and your new staff are able to put things to right."

"I do hope so."

"What will you do about Ambrose? The man is quite attached to you. You must see that, Katherine?"

Kate sighed. "I do not know. I admit that I cannot imagine a life without him."

Millie interjected, "Marry the man. Land sake's, girl, what are you waiting for? I say you jump at his offer before he changes his mind. You will not do any better. He is a perfectly good specimen of a man. And a lot more tolerable than any of the others I have seen about. I like the man. Besides…" Her lips turned up at the corners in a manipulative grin, and she leaned forward in a conspiratorial manner. "He knows his horses."

Lady Carstairs chuckled. "Well, now that is the truth. What could be finer than a man who knows his horses?"

She gave Kate a wink.

Katherine smiled. "There is that."

The rest of the journey was spent in relative silence except for the occasional snoring from the sleeping Millie. Lady Carstairs too had nodded off. Kate pulled back the curtain on the window and watched the rolling hills of Kent pass by. The fields were being plowed and seeded. Occasionally, they passed fenced in pastures where fat cattle, or herds of sheep grazed. It was a montage of pastoral views. She thought about her lands and wondered how they could not thrive amongst all this bounty.

She felt her stomach tighten as the land began to flatten out. They were nearing the coast and her home. At last, the coach slowed and turned into her lane. Mighty oaks protected the road, rising tall on each side and partially blocking the sun.

In the distance stood The Meadows.

Like always, her breath caught at the first glimpse of her home. It was not one of the huge stone houses of the moneyed aristocrats, and in comparison, would be deemed of modest size and stature. Yet in the surrounding countryside, nothing could compare to it.

It was graceful in its Queen Anne symmetry. The façade was of Flemish red brick, in soft light tones, with white vitrified leaders. The entrance and the story above it, jutted out from the building and featured an extended step. Four-tiered windows flanked either side of the double doors. On each wing, to the left and right of the entrance, the same windows appeared, a pair on each of the home's two stories. Above the entrance the second floor also had three four-tiered windows, which rose to meet the slate hipped roof. The roof itself had a pair of dormers on each side, providing light for the attic rooms.

The house sat high upon its cellar foundations, along which white framed windows could be seen peeking through the greenery. Though the house was technically only two stories, its cellars and attics were spacious and well lit, providing comfortable apartments for its staff and occasional guests.

Her father had renovated the house by adding to the back a series of service rooms. The one storied addition also in red brick could be seen extending past the house on each side. The overall effect was one of harmony and grace.

The coach lumbered around the front gardens and approached the house from its circular driveway. Katherine could hardly contain her excitement.

She did not wait for Mr. Olsen or Old Tom before opening the carriage door and scrambling to the ground. She left them to assist her aunt and Millie as she hurried up the stairs.

Mr. Churns, her long-time butler, met her at the top of the stairs, swinging the double doors wide. "Welcome home, my lady."

"Churns, how good to see you." Katherine stepped into her foyer.

The grand staircase dominated the entry. It curved elegantly to the second floor, opening to the balconies which overlooked the entry. To the left was the large parlor and to the right, an arched entry led to a smaller one they had named the family parlor.

Down the hall parallel to the stairs, the servants bustled about, going back and forth from the service rooms to the servant's stairs. Clarissa emerged from the family parlor.

"Katey! You are here at last. I have so much to tell you. The party will be perfect. So exciting!" Clarissa gave her a quick hug. "The musicians will arrive tomorrow, and we shall have dancing! And the food! It is all too much. Mother has been here to oversee it all and I am so thankful. She has just stepped out to pick up our orders from the village. But now that you and Lady Carstairs have arrived"—she peeked around her to smile at Aunt Elizabeth who had entered the hall— "all will be well."

Mrs. Churns, the housekeeper, cleared her throat to interrupt. "Perhaps, Miss Clarissa, it might be best if we allowed the ladies to get settled in. It has been a long journey." She turned to Katherine and Lady Carstairs. "Welcome home, Miss Katherine."

She nodded at her aunt. "Lady Carstairs. I will have your things brought to your rooms so that you can freshen up. I thought a little lunch and some tea might be in order."

Kate gave her a grateful smile. "Thank you, Mrs. Churns. That would be lovely. I believe we will take tea in the breakfast room."

Katherine started up the staircase with Clarissa skipping along beside her. "Mama insists that we have a course of fish at the wedding supper. But Jeremy apparently detests fish. Even salmon. Can you imagine?"

"No, I cannot."

"I do not know what is to be done. I suppose we could substitute something. Perhaps oysters. I am sure they would have some in the village. So lucky to be near the sea." Clarissa barely took a breath. "Oh, and I have decided to wear the blue gown that you gave me. After all, no one here tomorrow will have seen it. And Mama says that would be a waste. It is beautiful on me. It sets off my eyes perfectly. And Jeremy loves it. He called it the height of fashion."

She hugged herself with pleasure. "But I will have a new hat. It is gorgeous of course. It has peacock feathers that perfectly match. It is all quite extravagant."

They reached the top of the stairs.

Clarissa grabbed her arm and said, "And Mama says that I should ask you and Lady Carstairs to not wear blue—something gray or beige. She says it is especially important that the bride stands out. I agree. I would love to stand out."

Clarissa smiled widely.

"I am sure I can find something suitably dowdy."

"Oh, thank you. I knew you would understand."

Up in her room, Kate stood at the window. Her room overlooked the coach house and the stables of which her father had been so proud. The expanse of land behind it was lush and green this time of year.

She pushed open her window, rested her arms on its sill, and breathed the clean brisk air. She decided after lunch she would leave whatever preparations to others and go for a ride. It was exactly what she needed after this morning's trip.

Jeremy and Clarissa joined them for lunch. Kate had braced herself for a noisy experience. But thankfully, after she had made clear to the happy couple that the party's bills would be sent to Jeremy, they had eaten in relative peace. Clarissa sat with her bottom lip extended in a pout, while Jeremy picked at his food, his cheeks flushed with annoyance.

Lady Carstairs appeared unaffected by the tensions at the table. "I am glad you intend to go for a ride, my dear. If I were younger, I would join you."

"I am looking forward to seeing my horse, Perseus, today," Kate said. "I intend to take him to the North pasture. It looked wonderfully welcoming as we drove by earlier."

"Excellent. Do not be concerned about things here at the house. I am sure the staff have all the details well in hand."

"I would watch for badger holes," Jeremy added sullenly, "They have plagued the pastures this year."

Katherine looked up at Jeremy. Country life had not dampened his need for color. He wore no jacket, but his waistcoat was a flaming yellow.

"I will take care. Thank you for the warning." Kate gave

him a smile. "If it is too bad, I can always take the lane home. It is just off the field after all."

"If you take the road, I can escort you part of the way. I am going into the village," Jeremy said.

Kate appreciated his attempt to alleviate some of the tension with his offer. She smiled. "No. I am eager to get out into the pasture."

And for some time to myself, she added silently.

As she changed into her riding clothes, she could not help but feel excited about the interlude of freedom a ride would give to her. She would be on her land far from any danger, and safe from attack.

The uncomfortable memory of Mclury and his connection to The Meadows flitted across her mind. Could there be danger here? She shook off her feelings of apprehension. Far from everyone, on the familiar fields of her home, surely, she would be safe.

Chapter Twenty-Eight

The huge double doors of the stable had been swung wide. Sunlight beamed through the long aisle. Near the entry, the stalls on each side were empty and cleaned. Kate realized the stable lads must have moved most of the horses out to pasture to make room for the guests' horses. To the rear of the stable Kate was grateful to see her horse still standing in her stall. Perseus gave a soft whinny as a welcome when Kate approached.

She patted her downy nose. "Hello girl. You remember me. Good."

Perseus gave a snort.

From the stall next to hers, a high-pitched neigh was followed by a series of loud bangs. A black stallion bucked restlessly in his pen. He reared and smashed several double hoofed kicks into the rear of his stall.

"Whoa. You are a wild one," Kate said in a soothing voice.

Old Tom came up to her from the doors. "Stay back from that demon, Miss Katherine. He's not right in the 'ead. The count had him here. Tut, tut." Tom opened Perseus's stall and began leading her to the entry. "You'll need to saddle your mare away from that beast. There's something wrong with him. Been around horses all me life and I ain't never seen the likes of him. He has almost destroyed his stall. It's not safe at all. I will be puttin' up a rail or two on that pen. He is gonna kill someone, that boy."

As if to emphasize Tom's point, the stallion reared up and slammed into his front gate. A loud crack echoed through the stables.

Kate looked back at the stallion. His nostrils flared. He arched his neck, his eyes wild and angry. He gave a loud snort.

"He is a brute to be sure."

Tom helped her saddle up Perseus. In a few minutes, she was out on the pastures.

It was good to be out on the range. There was freedom in riding her horse. She was alone at last. It had been a long spring visit with Clarissa in London. And now with the party plans, Kate found her incessant babbling and self-centered machinations to be unbearable.

She smiled to herself, wondering if oysters were off the menu. Oysters were expensive. She was thankful for her experience working at the salon. One of the things it had taught her was how to have the hard, but necessary conversations. Lady Carstairs had shown her that stewing about a problem that could be resolved only led to resentment. It was better to have issues brought into the open and dealt with quickly, as painful as that process may be. Besides, Jeremy and his father, the viscount, could well afford the expense of an extravagant party; she could not.

Kate galloped across the home pasture. The brisk wind in her hair was exhilarating. It was one of those clear spring days that were so frequent at this time of the year. The sky was intensely blue, and the pasture was alive with new growth. Kate breathed deeply of the fresh country air. She was reminded of how much she had always loved life in the country.

It is past time I considered moving home.

Having spanned the home pasture, she picked her way carefully around the adjacent freshly seeded field. At the gate to the north field, a farmer and his wife loaded a seeder from a cart of grain. Their work horses rested in the shade, their heavy tails brushing the insects from their hides.

"Hello there," Kate greeted them cheerfully. "How goes the planting?"

The couple looked up from their work and smiled.

"Ah, and greetings to you, Mistress Kate," the man replied. "It is good to see you back."

He hefted a heavy sack of grain from the cart onto the hopper and paused. "The seeding goes well. Lots of moisture again this year. I was just saying to the wife that all looks well for another fine crop."

"Have you had good harvests then?" Kate asked.

The man smiled. "The best. It has been the land of plenty, wouldn't you say, Margie?"

He nudged his wife with his elbow.

"Oh aye." Margie smiled and ducked her head down shyly.

The farmer began cutting his sack of grain.

"I will leave you to your work then." Kate touched her hat in farewell and cantered into the pasture.

She grimaced as she rode. The farmer's words were more evidence that what Uncle Edmund had said about the productivity of The Meadows was untrue. The land the farmer planted was on her estate, leased from her. The rents would have been paid as a percentage of the crop. She began to suspect that something was very wrong with the accounts of her land.

Lady Carstairs believed Uncle Edmund had been less than forthcoming with her, but Kate had been hesitant to agree. Her uncle and her father had always been the best of friends. Even she remembered the evenings of fun and laughter when Uncle Edmund had come to visit. Poor Uncle Edmund had never been the same since her father's death.

She admitted she herself was partly to blame for the situation she found herself in. She had asked few questions, but rather had accepted whatever reports she had been given as truth. For the last several years, she had been so wrapped up in her career that she had spared little time on her estates. Even her visits had been rare and quick affairs.

But all that would now change. She was eager to take the reins. Already her new employees would be on their way. They would investigate. This time she would be paying attention to every detail they shared that concerned The Meadows.

She reached the tree line at the edge of the pasture about a hundred yards off the main road, which was sheltered from view by tall black poplars and thick shrubbery. She decided to walk her horse along in the shade heading to the lane. She would take the road home after all.

A shot rang out. It seemed to have come from the road ahead. Her horse began to dance about. A second shot whizzed past her face. Kate responded instinctively. She crouched low to the saddle and whirled her horse about. She and Perseus galloped off in the opposite direction. Her heart pounded. Her hands gripped the saddle horn. She dug her heels into Perseus's sides, urging him to faster speeds.

She waited in dread for the next shot. It did not come. The trees blurred as she raced past. She did not slow her horse until she had crested a hill and sped safely into a ravine. Only then did she pull up and bring Perseus to a halt.

She listened carefully. No one was pursuing her. There was no sound from the distant roadway. She could only hear the pounding of her own heart. She slid from the saddle and laid her head on Perseus's chest while she caught her breath. It took a few minutes for her to calm her panicked breathing.

Had someone tried to shoot her? Katherine shook her head in disbelief. She had trusted that she would be safe here in the country. That was untrue. Could Bentley Brown have followed her here? The thought had her shuddering.

The shot had come from the road. Katherine's stomach twisted as she recalled Jeremy's last words. He would be taking the road to town. Her mind revolted at the thought of Jeremy as a murderer. It was inconceivable. She crushed down that suspicion. But the fact of the matter was that she had been attacked here at her home. She had felt secure at The Meadows. She had relaxed, enjoying a respite from the tensions and fears of the last few days. But now that was over. Whoever was trying to kill her had followed her here.

Perhaps she should have had Mr. Olsen ride out with her. What he could have done under the circumstances was unclear.

Kate decided it would not have made a difference. But she determined that Mr. Olsen would be at her side for the rest of her stay. Ambrose would be livid when he discovered she had once again headed out on her own.

Whoever had taken a shot at her must have done so spontaneously. They had not followed her but intercepted her by chance. Had they been a little more patient she would have proceeded closer and well within range of the road. She had been lucky.

She decided to take the long way home. She would circle back, staying well away from any roadways.

As she cantered home, she thought about what could be done about the incident. There was little to consider. Whoever had taken the shots would be far away by now. She could see no point in raising a hue and cry about the business. It would accomplish nothing except to destroy Clarissa's party. But for Mr. Olsen, she would keep it to herself. There would be no more rides on this trip. She was now confined to the house.

Hot tears of frustration formed in her eyes. She prayed that Ambrose had found some information that could end this nightmare.

An image of Ambrose flashed across her mind. She wished wholeheartedly he had joined her on this trip. It had been less than a day. It was only late afternoon and yet it seemed a lifetime since she had watched him trot alongside their carriage early this morning. She ached for the comfort of his arms. The freedom she had enjoyed upon reaching her childhood home had evaporated. Danger surrounded her again.

Chapter Twenty-Nine

Ambrose escorted the ladies to the city limits. He sat upon Thorn and watched the coach disappear into distance with mixed feelings. He was sure Katherine would be safe now amongst her friends and family. She would have a much-needed reprieve from the dangers here in town. At the same time, watching her coach leave town left him feeling empty.

The admiral had sent his men to Brighton, an hour north of town. They would have left the city last night. With any luck they would have found the boarding house by now. He hoped that Katherine was right, that Brown had chosen his sister's lodgings as a place to hide.

In the meantime, he would check out the Black Table. As a gambling establishment it was on the low end of the scale in terms of clientele. The patrons would not be playing cards, but rather games of chance, like hazard. He felt the coins he had put in his jacket pocket. He was sure he could use them to entice someone to talk.

He entered the low-ceilinged gambling hall with trepidation. It took a moment for his eyes to adjust to the dim lighting. His nose was assaulted by the thick smell of stale alcohol and urine.

The front room of the establishment was laid out like a pub. There were a couple of heavy wooden tables facing a bar. A few dilapidated souls sat at their benches nursing their ale. The elderly man behind the bar spared him only a glance while he washed tin mugs. One patron was sprawled out near the fireplace.

It was early. He was not optimistic about his chances of finding many customers at play, never mind finding someone who knew Brown.

A roar came from an open doorway leading, he assumed, to the games room.

He strolled over to the backroom and leaned against the door frame, taking in the sight. He was surprised to see a score of customers gathered around the hazard table. Several more tables were in use for dice games.

Wandering from table to table attempting to get information was frustrating. The clientele resented his interruptions. Getting an annoyed frown as opposed to a suspicious glare was a success. He was definitely overdressed. His gentlemen's attire set him apart from the others.

Ambrose returned to the bar room feeling as though he had wasted his time at the Black Table.

The sound of the front door opening caught his attention. Sergeant Ames stood scanning the room. Ambrose hurried toward him. The two of them stepped outside into the light, closing the door behind them before speaking.

"Glad I found you," Ames said. "The Admiral wants you at the Home Office immediately."

"What is it? Have they found Bentley Brown?" Ambrose grasped Sergeant Ames' shoulder.

The sergeant looked down at Ambrose's hand with

disdain. He waited for him to remove it before replying. "They have. You are to come with me."

"Has the man talked? Were you able to get his employer?"

The sergeant shrugged. "The admiral will tell you what he wishes you to know."

It was clear that he would get no more information from Sergeant Ames. Ambrose would have to wait out the ride across town to get his news at the Home Office.

It was a long route. It was even longer with the stoic sergeant and his own curiosity to contend with.

At one point the sergeant steered his horse into a narrow lane. The hair on the back of Ambrose's neck began to tingle. This secluded side street would be the perfect place for an attack.

Ambrose's mind began to race. Bentley Brown had been hired. Could it possibly be Ames who was the villain? Ames had assumed Katherine was eavesdropping. What if he thought that she had overheard something of importance? And Mclury had been killed that very night.

It could be Sergeant Ames who was the spy. He would have known about the codebook. Indeed, he was one of the few people who would have known when it was arriving and its value. He was privy to most of the admiral's secrets. Perhaps he had hired Mclury, then had him killed when his identity had been discovered. And Ames would have been one of the first to know Mclury had been found out.

Ambrose shuddered. If Ames was the culprit, then eliminating Ambrose would be prudent. Katherine would be without protection and his next victim. His secrets would be safe.

Ambrose slowed his horse, ensuring the sergeant's back was to him and rested his hand lightly on his weapon at his side. Ames continued to lead them through the winding alley. The tall buildings on each side of them blocked the sun, leaving the narrow lane shrouded in shadows. The alley seemed to twist and turn endlessly. Ambrose concentrated on keeping his horse at a safe distance and his eyes focused on every move the sergeant made. All his military training was engaged in preparation for a surprise attack. Finally, a glow of bright light just ahead indicated that the lane would soon open into a welcoming street.

Ambrose stiffened. If Ames were indeed a villain, and this was a trap, now would be his last chance to make a move. The seconds crawled by. Ambrose flinched as a tin garbage can crashed into the street, rolling toward the horses who shied nervously. A tattered gray cat yowled and skittered behind a rotted step.

Ambrose could feel his pulse throbbing in his temples. They approached the entrance to the street.

The sergeant slowed his horse until Ambrose was almost at his side. He turned in his saddle facing Ambrose. His mouth twisted into a smile. "It's a short cut," he said as the two horses exited the alley into the bright sun of the busy thoroughfare. "It will have saved us several blocks."

Ambrose expelled a breath. He and the sergeant spurred their horses into a trot. Relief washed over him. He shook the tightness from his shoulders, taking several calming breaths. He was irritated with his leaps of logic. Obviously, his desperation to find Katherine's pursuer was getting to him.

In moments they reached the Home Office. As they climbed the broad stairs, Ambrose glanced at Sergeant Ames. Though his face was stoic, Ambrose was sure he discerned a glint of amusement in his eyes. The bastard was aware he had been spooked. He enjoyed it.

The admiral sat behind his desk when Ambrose was led into the room. Ames took up his usual spot by the door.

"Sit down, St. Claire," the admiral said. "We have some good news for you."

The admiral waited until Ambrose had settled rigidly in the chair before his desk. "We were able to locate the boarding house last night. And we have found our Mr. Brown. He was indeed in a room at his sister's home. My men took him at dawn."

Ambrose was impatient for him to continue. "Did he tell you who is behind all this?"

"He did. Apparently, Brown was eager to tell us all he knew." The admiral snorted with disgust. "Not the most loyal of fellows."

Ambrose opened his mouth to ask the obvious questions, but the admiral raised his hand to forestall him.

"Not yet, sir. I have a few questions for you first." He cleared his throat. "When I last talked to you, you were sending your Lady Katherine to a party at her estate. I believe it was a party in honor of the Viscount Serves' son and his bride. Is that correct?"

Ambrose furrowed his brow. "They left this morning, sir. Several hours ago."

"Ah." The admiral leaned forward and rested his hands on his desk. "Can we assume her uncle the viscount will attend?"

Beginning to feel uneasy, Ambrose shifted in his chair. Something was not right.

"Yes," he said slowly.

"We may have a problem. Katherine's uncle, the Viscount of Serves, is the man who has been behind the attempts on her life. It seems Bentley Brown had come to him with some sort of blackmail scheme and was hired to do the murder. I suspect Serves is also behind the attempts at the codebooks." The admiral grimaced. "If the viscount is with Katherine in Kent, then she will be in grave danger."

Ambrose jumped to his feet. His mind was whirling. He was determined to run to his horse and ride to The Meadows as fast as Thorn could take him.

"Wait," the admiral ordered. "I have two things to say that you must hear."

He paused until he was sure he had Ambrose's complete attention.

"First, before you go harrowing off, go home, get a second horse, your weapons, and a few supplies. You will need a fresh horse to complete the journey." He lowered his brow and continued in a soft voice. "And second, I want the viscount alive. I will be sending my men to follow you. We will need to question the man."

Chapter Thirty

Kate pulled one of the sliding barn doors open just enough to lead her horse through. Leaving it ajar, she led Perseus to her pen. The demon let out an angry bellow in greeting. Other than that, all was quiet.

The stables were normally lit with several lanterns hanging from hooks along the aisle. Most of those had been extinguished for the day. Those that remained lit had been turned down, casting the interior into long dark shadows, indicating that the work in the barns was done for the night. Kate realized that she was much later than she had planned. The journey around the far sides of the pastures had taken longer than she had anticipated.

She noticed that one of the formerly prepared pens was now occupied. A large roan was munching its oats. A guest must have arrived, and by the look of things, not too long ago.

Kate grimaced at the idea of entertaining tonight. She had hoped most of the guests would be from the neighboring countryside, who could come and go the same evening. The incident in the pasture had shaken her. She wanted nothing more than to retire to the comfort and safety of her room.

The demon in a stall just past hers, snorted at her as she walked up but was otherwise silent. She managed to pull off her saddle and hoist it up onto the rails of an open stall. Perseus would need a good brushing. Kate swung the gate open and hooked it to the empty stall beside her. She brought her horse into her pen, wrapped the reins into a loose knot on the side rail, and rubbed her down with the saddle blanket.

Looking after her own horse was a task her father had always insisted upon. She grabbed the curry brush and began to give Perseus the attention she needed.

She murmured to her as she worked, "You have been a good girl, Perseus. A fine lady—"

The demon snorted and rammed against his stall gate, signaling that someone had entered the barn. Kate looked up to see the viscount standing motionless in the aisle. Even in the dim light of the stables Kate could see an unholy glint in his eyes.

"Home at last. I have been waiting for you." He lifted his arm. An object glinted in his hand.

Kate's mouth dropped when she realized that it was a handgun. He followed her gaze.

"Yes, my lovely niece, it is indeed a gun. Most unfortunate." He nodded. His mournful face was illuminated, a pale glow in the lantern's soft light.

Kate stood frozen beside Perseus. The curry brush rested on the horse's flank, immobile. She tried to grasp the situation. Her mind raced. She was trapped again. Caged with Perseus, there would be no opportunity to escape but to hurl herself past the viscount. And he held a gun.

Her stomach rolled. She fought back the urge to scream.

She took several deep breaths to fight her rising panic. Her cheeks burned with a flush of anger. Her own uncle was behind the horror of the last few weeks.

Her fury gave her strength. "It was you who shot at me this afternoon in the pasture!"

He laughed. It was a bitter sound. "Yes, Katherine. I saw the perfect opportunity to eliminate you. A couple of quick shots and all my problems would have been solved. Sadly, my aim from the back of a horse with a pistol was not as accurate as I could have hoped." He sighed. "It would have been so perfect too. Not messy or complicated. Just a poacher mistaking you for his prey."

"And McClury? You killed him too?"

"McClury." The viscount snorted with disdain. "He had received word about you and those blasted codes at the docks. He was sure we could get them and turn them in to the Home Office for a pretty penny. But he managed to foul it up. Accosting you on the street was ridiculous. Of course, you would recognize him. Stupid man. He deserved to die."

"But why, uncle? Why have you targeted me?" Kate hoped that unlike Bentley Brown, the viscount would want to talk. Delaying him was her only option. She could at least hope that somehow, someone would interrupt his plans. For now, it was all she had. She edged around Perseus, hoping to keep the mare between her and the gun.

"The Meadows. It has always been The Meadows. It should have been mine." He sneered. "Your father inherited it as part of his mother's estate. He did not deserve it. He was losing a fortune in smuggling. God knows I tried to convince him to at least allow me to make our fortune, but he would not listen."

He looked at Katherine with a sorrowful expression. "I

had to kill John. Knocked him on the head and made it look like his horse had thrown him."

Katherine gasped.

He grunted. "He was always on a horse. It was inevitable that he should die upon one. No one questioned it."

"You killed my father? You killed your own brother?" Kate could not believe what she was hearing. Everything she had ever heard about the brothers was centered around their deep affection for each other. It was that which had kept her loyal to her uncle for so long.

"I had to. Don't you see? He would not listen. He stood between us and the kind of wealth we could only dream of."

Kate looked at him with disgust. This man, her uncle who she had always looked up to and depended on was a fiend, a murderer. "How could you? I thought you loved my father?"

"But I did love John. Everybody loved John. He was always so bloody happy, even as a boy. He was the only one who could make me truly laugh." The viscount gave her a desperate look. "I had to kill him. He left me no choice. Damn him! There was money to be made and lots of it. All he had to do was agree to allow me the right to move English gold through our wharfs. But no, he would not listen to reason. He brought it on himself!"

The demon in the stall next to them began to snort and bang restlessly against his pen. Kate cast a hopeful glance towards the door. A shadowy figure slipped silently into the stables. She turned back towards the viscount, hoping he had not followed her gaze. She was relieved to see that he had been distracted by the horse.

She shifted to the far side of the stall, resting her back against the rails separating her pen from the demon's, wanting the viscount to shift and turn towards her—away from the door. It worked. He turned his body just enough to block his view of the aisle.

"Do not think of escaping, Katherine. You have no way out." He shook his head. The frown lines deepened on his sad long face. "I am afraid it is time. I did try to protect you, Katherine. You should have married Jeremy. All of this could have been avoided."

Kate had to delay him. "What makes you think I left The Meadows to you? I could have changed my will and left it to my aunt."

That gave him pause. "But you couldn't have! I manage your affairs!" He stared at her, horrified, then visibly calmed. "Ah, you think to trick me with that. It will not work."

He took a step closer.

The demon snorted and kicked against the sides of his stall. The stallion was not comfortable with someone so close to his pen. Or perhaps it sensed the madness emanating from the viscount. The horse pushed his head far out into the aisle and raised it high in warning, its eyes wild.

Katherine caught a movement from the corner of her eye. It was Ambrose. Relief flooded her. She concentrated hard on not turning in his direction or showing any indication that she was aware of his presence.

She needn't have bothered. The demon held the Viscount's attention.

"Shut up," the viscount growled in its direction.

The horse responded by letting loose a shrill neigh.

Ambrose took the opportunity to fly at the viscount. The two of them hit the floor hard. The gun skittered from the viscount's hand and slid across the aisle. Kate scrambled after it but somehow managed to knock it into the next pen.

She reached between the rails, trying to snatch it but it was just out of her grasp.

The demon screamed his distress and slammed against his gate as the men wrestled directly beneath his stall.

Ambrose managed to pull himself up and connected a solid punch to the viscount's jaw. The demon let out a second scream and threw himself into the railing. A loud splintering crack echoed through the barn.

"Ambrose, the horse!" Kate hollered.

Ambrose flung himself backwards just as the gate came crashing into the aisle. He rolled to Kate's feet. The viscount had been unable to move in time. He was trapped beneath the planks.

The demon reared high into the air. Its nostrils flared and its eyes bulged fearfully. With a strange guttural sound from its throat, it came down onto the shattered gate in a splintering crash. The demon's front hooves pummeled the gate again and again. Finally, with a series of bucking strides and a loud neigh, it galloped down the aisle and out of the barn's narrow entry.

All was quiet. Ambrose stood and pulled Kate into his arms. He squeezed her tight. For long moments, he just held her. Finally, he drew back and said, "I was so scared that I would be too late. I love you so much, Katherine, that I cannot think of living without you."

Kate opened her mouth to reply but before she could find her words a groan issued from beneath the rubble that was once the stall gate.

"Oh god, the viscount."

Kate and Ambrose hurried over and began to lift the pieces of railing and splintered planks. The viscount lay with his head twisted at an obscene angle. His body was motionless. His eyes were open but were glazed and sightless. He was attempting to speak. Kate leaned in close to catch his words.

"John..." he whispered agonizingly soft. "John...I am so..."

He closed his eyes.

He took a rattling breath and opened his eyes once more. "I... miss you."

He closed his eyes for the last time.

Chapter Thirty-One

The news of her uncle's death caused an uproar at the house. Oddly enough, it was Jeremy who had taken charge. He had arranged for the body to be kept at the gate house. It would be transported back to his estates tomorrow, accompanied by Clarissa and himself. The proper authorities would be informed. His death would be ruled accidental. He had gone to supervise the arrangements.

Ambrose had convinced Kate that nothing was to be gained by confiding to Jeremy the circumstances surrounding the viscount's death. Jeremy was in mourning. If he knew nothing of his father's recent activities, then they would only cause unnecessary grief. The admiral would be told of this night's events. He would be disappointed in the viscount's death, but he would have to be satisfied he had at least found the culprit who had pursued the codes.

They sat quietly in the family parlor. Clarissa and her mother, Lady Carstairs, Ambrose, and herself. Kate considered it especially sad that though Jeremy was in mourning, the death of Uncle Edmund seemed to have had insignificant effect on anyone else.

"Does this mean I shall have no party?" Clarissa looked at the faces in the room with despair. "Oh no! Surely not?"

Lady Carstairs cleared her throat. "Your husband's father has died, Clarissa. There will be no wedding party. I think instead you might search your wardrobe for mourning dresses. It is what is expected now."

Clarissa gasped. "No. I must have my party. And surely, I will not be required to wear black? Not at my wedding reception?"

Kate looked at her with surprise. Clarissa could not possibly expect to proceed with wedding celebrations and parties given the circumstances. She decided she would allow someone else to make clear what would be required of her. There was an awkward silence in the room.

Finally, Mrs. Dumont accepted the responsibility and lifted herself awkwardly out of her chair. She walked towards Clarissa and patted her on the shoulder.

With a sigh, she said, "My dear, the party is off. At best there might be a funeral breakfast."

She was a buxom woman with a round stolid face.

She shook her head. "It is a pity. But there is nothing that can be done. On the bright side, you look wonderful in black. It sets off your fair skin." She hovered over Clarissa and pulled her in for a quick hug. "You will be on the road tomorrow. It is a sad way to start a marriage but there it is. And I will be heading home. Have a good trip tomorrow, my dear."

She gave her a final pat before turning to go.

"I will walk you out," Lady Carstairs rose and took her arm.

Clarissa's eyes filled with tears. "It is just so unfair. And it was all planned. There was to be dancing."

Kate did not know what to say. "I am sorry, Clarissa."

"Oh! I suppose I shall have to pack." She emitted a strangled sob and left the room.

Ambrose sat in a chair across the room. He appeared to be lost in thought. When Clarissa left the room, he rose and walked toward Kate. He took both of her hands in his.

"I know this is the worst possible timing. Theo would smack me. But it seems that I cannot wait another minute." Still holding her hands, he knelt in front of her. "Please be my wife. I promise to love you forever."

He looked in her eyes, then slowly lowered his head when she did not respond.

"Yes."

"Did you say yes?" He sprang to his feet. "Did you say yes?"

"Yes, yes, yes!"

Ambrose grabbed her by the waist, lifted her high into the air, and swung her about in a circle. They both began to laugh.

"Have I missed something?" Lady Carstairs stood beneath the arched entry with a quizzical expression.

Ambrose turned to her, his arm still clasped around Kate's waist. "Katherine has consented to be my wife."

"Congratulations to you both. I could not be happier." Lady Carstairs smiled from one to the other. "I guess we will have more wedding plans."

Ambrose groaned. "Wedding plans." He looked at Kate hopefully. "How do you feel about a tawdry rushed affair?"

Kate laughed. "Rushed maybe, tawdry never."

Epilogue

One year later

A spring shower left as quickly as it had arrived. The sun shone down on the pastures of The Meadows. Its rays found raindrops, on the blades of grass, and on the tips of leaves which caught the light and flashed. The air was crisp and fresh and as always, it had its base the salty tang of the sea.

Spring is a happy season. Nowhere did it bring more joy than at The Meadows. The pastures were full of play. The foals were arriving. They bucked and kicked their heels in the air, testing the boundaries of their physical capabilities. Often three or four would run together in wild racing games while their mothers grazed nearby, unconcerned.

This spring was a special one on the estate. There was to be a special birth. Everyone was counting down the days to the big event. Today was going to be the day. The labor had already started.

It was all the talk in the kitchens. The butler, Mr. Churns, leaned against the door frame and conversed with his wife and the kitchen staff.

"Does he plan to attend to the birth himself? I thought he might bring in an expert, even a doctor, someone with skills," Mrs. Churns said.

"He says he is more than capable. If there is no trouble, he should be able to manage it."

"I hope so." Mrs. Churns added, "But it might be a while. He just now sent a lad in to request a luncheon. He has asked for enough food for at least a half a dozen."

"He is allowing the lads in to watch the birth. I think a first-time mother might be a little skittish with that. But he insists that if they are quiet and stay well back all will be good."

Mrs. Churns snorted. "Well, we shall see how she takes it. By all accounts she is a calm little lady."

A stable lad burst into the kitchens, panting. "The baby is almost here. It's a coming!"

Betsy, the kitchen helper, set her carving knife down on the board next to the vegetables she had been chopping for the day's soup. "I think I will head down for a quick peek."

All was quiet in the barn. The stable lads hovered near the door. Kate stood by the pen. Her hand gripped the gate frame. Ambrose had let the other horses out to the pastures so that Starling would have the place to herself. She stood now in her open stall surrounded by fresh straw. Two little legs protruded from her. With each labor pain they were pushed forward and then slowly receded. On her last contraction, a little nose appeared.

Ambrose rubbed her belly and spoke in soft tones. "Almost here, my girl. Just a couple more hard pushes."

Starling arched her back, her body taunt and strained.

Ambrose grasped the little legs and pulled. Starling gave a painful grunt. The foal's nose reappeared. Slowly, a little head emerged, then a gush of birthing fluid. Starling's body relaxed. She began to shift restlessly.

Ambrose rubbed her once more. "One more push, Starling. You are almost there."

Starling tensed up again. This time the little one emerged completely and fell into a soft bed of straw.

Ambrose broke the birthing sack, helping to free the new foal. Using handfuls of straw, he rubbed the baby clean. The new foal began floundering about. Already she was looking to pull herself up on her wobbly legs. Starling turned. She held her head close to the little creature. She sniffed her curiously, then began to lick her new baby.

Ambrose shuffled backwards, to Kate's side. All was well. Starling could manage on her own now. He carefully closed the pen door. The two of them silently watched the little one find its balance and totter along beside Starling. Already it was searching for its first meal.

Ambrose took Katherine's hand and squeezed it. He looked down at her face, which was covered in fresh tears. He put his arms around her and pulled her in front of him, with her back pressed against him so she could watch the little miracle before them.

"You have your first thoroughbred, Ambrose. The first of many to be born and raised here at The Meadows." Kate smiled and leaned back against his chest.

Ambrose kissed the top of her head. "It is 'our' first. It is a girl, and she is a beauty."

He slid his hands down her body and rested them on her protruding belly. He whispered into her ear, "I hope we have a baby girl too. I want one just like her mama." He rubbed her belly gently. "I love you, Katherine. You are the best thing that ever happened to me."

"Oh, Ambrose, I will love you forever."

vinci-books.com/the-smuggler

She married for duty. She smuggles for freedom.

Lady Arabella has a secret. Posing as Captain Ara—a fearless
smuggling captain, running contraband along the wild Yorkshire
coast, her heroic exploits at sea have earned her the respect of her
crew and other captains alike. But when she accepts an arranged
marriage to a wealthy earl to save her beleaguered estate, Arabella
must balance her smuggling persona with her role of demure
young bride.

Turn the page for a free preview…

The Smuggler: Chapter One

Lady Osbourne glanced down at the fraudulent documents one more time and smiled. They were perfect. It would be difficult, even for an expert, to realize the forgery.

Setting down her teacup, she pushed a stray bit of her steel gray hair behind her ear and gave a satisfied sigh. "We have done it Adrienne, and nothing could be more suitable to me. My grandson Theodore will acquire a young lady for a bride who is worthy of him."

"But will he suspect?" Countess Myrell shifted forward and examined the documents one more time. Like Lady Osbourne, she was in her golden years, but there the similarities ended. Where Lady Osbourne was a buxom woman, with a personality as blunt as her solid body, the countess was tall and slender with an indolent air. "After all, he will never have heard of betrothal papers supposably written up all those years ago. Will he not wonder why an agreement like this one has never been mentioned? And even if he accepts these documents as real, he could find ways to avoid the arrangement."

"He could. Sadly, the world has changed. People are prone to take these contracts less seriously than in the past. A grave mistake in my mind." Lady Osbourne shook her head, causing her heavy jowls to tremble. She grasped an ornate cane at her side and gave it a little thump as if to emphasize her words. "But not to worry, Theo will never suspect me of fraud. If I say it is true, he will accept it. Besides, he is ready to wed. He has the responsibility of producing an heir. If he must find a wife, then why not Arabella?"

Lady Osbourne grinned conspiratorially and continued. "And of course, there is the trivial matter of money. He will gain a considerable fortune from my estate if he agrees. Theo is an astute businessman. He loves nothing more than managing money." She snorted. "And your Arabella, will she be a problem?"

The countess waved a languid hand dismissively and smiled. "My Arabella needs a husband. And she needs a marriage settlement to help her salvage Harwood Place. Since our Aran left on his tour, she has been quite dependent on me." She took a sip of her tea and considered the problem. "And like your Theo, if she must marry, then why not an earl? It is perfect for her."

Lady Osbourne thumped her cane sharply once more and ignoring the countess's wince, added, "Well then I see no need to delay. We will speak to our respective grandchildren." She shot the countess an assessing look. "You must be firm, Adrienne. Insist. With Aran gone, she is your ward. Therefore, you have the final say."

The countess lay back against the sofa cushions. "Do not worry, Amelia. I know how to handle my Arabella."

"Excellent. I will attempt to bring Theo to Harwood Place as soon as I can manage it. We have done an excellent piece of work this morning." She nodded, her heavy jowls quivering. "I doubt either of them will suspect the authenticity of the documents. Certainly, neither of them would consider their loving grandmothers capable of a forgery. Our families will be joined at last."

The countess gave a lazy smile as she helped herself to a dainty from the tea tray. "What is a little forgery if it brings about such a happy result? Besides, there is no one more suitable for the young earl than my Arabella. She is a paragon of womanly gentility."

"Move your arses!" Arabella yelled from the bulwark. "She is coming up fast! Rig up the foresail to the bowsprit. We will need all the speed we can muster to outrun her!"

"Aye aye, Cap'n Ara. We got her coming." Arnold and another sailor hustled to do her bidding.

Arabella hurried to the stern pulling her telescope from its loop at her belt to get a reading on the revenue cutter. Her first mate, Jem, joined her at the rail. She smiled when the lugger lurched forward as the foresail caught the breeze. The Bella was designed for speed, and she did not disappoint. She was gaff-rigged. The smooth lines of her carvel hull cut cleanly through the water. Even loaded with tubs of brandy as she was today, she was able to skim through the water.

Arabella kept the scope trained on the revenue cutter, feeling her stomach twist with dread as she took in the might of their pursuer. "This will be a damned hard run, Jem. Even the Bella will have a race against that monstrous cutter. That ship is fast enough to catch us."

As a smuggling captain who worked England's eastern

shores, Arabella was confident she was one of the best. Jem had trained her well. She and her twin Aran had been sailors since birth. Arabella had always been more skilled than her brother. Today she knew her skills would face the ultimate test.

"My god, Jem. She is seventy tons at least." Lowering the scope, she turned to her crew who were scrambling with the rigging, and hollered, "Hustle up, boys! Full sails! We're going to need all we can muster on this run!"

The sailors responded instantly. Canvas sails popped as they found the wind. The lugger cut through the waves.

Arabella watched her crew move with precision as they rigged out for full sails. As captain, she had always maintained her male persona aboard the ship. The moment she donned her captain's gear, she was Ara. Her persona at sea was no longer a role to be played but had become an identity. When Ara had first taken over from her twin Aran, it had not been her gender that concerned her crew but her youth. With each trip to the mainland, she had slowly won their trust. Today, with a cutter on their heels, there was no one better at the helm and they knew it.

She was tall for a woman, and slender. She prowled her ship with an agile physicality. If she could swing from the rigging to move about, she did. It was as though she relished the freedom from her inhibiting skirts. She wore a peaked felt hat pulled tightly over her head. The hat sported tattered frills at its back to disguise the bulge of her braid. A tattered red sash covered her lower face, its ends flapping in the winds. Her red faded long coat was fastened with one button at her chest; its lapels flapped open wide to reveal the cutlas and telescope attached to a sturdy belt. Fitted trousers were tucked into tall boots.

Arabella handed Jem her telescope. Jem stretched to his

full height of an awesome six foot seven and squinted into the lens.

His weathered and scarred face twisted as he focused on the ship in the distance. "She's a big one, Ara. And she's moving."

He handed Ara back her spy glass, and she raised it to her eye once more, focusing it on their pursuer. She estimated the distance quickly. Turning towards the English coast, she saw her deliverance rolling in from the north. Fog; a thick band of it hugged the rocky coast. And the sun was setting soon. But knowing the winds would still as they neared the foggy coast, Ara decided to make a separation from the revenue cutter now.

She turned to her first mate, Jem. "We'll make a hard run. Then I need to take her in close to the shore, to hide in the fog." Ara swore under her breath. "But the Bella can't be steered in until we clear Bergen's point with its rocky reef. We have a battle, and she's going to be a close one, Jem. Call up our spotsman."

Arabella grabbed the rigging and swung lithely across the deck. Let the cutter come. Her place was in the bow, at the helm.

She muttered, "Please god, let us get safely past the reef and into the fog before the damned cutter can catch up to us."

Her spotsman, Jamie, climbed to the stern of the boat and braced himself against the railing. His talent was essential now. She trusted him above her telescope. Jamie knew this coast better than his cottage on shore. He would holler when she could veer in towards the shore. Still, she trained her scope on the shrouded coast once more, trying to identify the exact moment they passed the reef.

Arabella spun around, raising her spy glass to check the cutter. She was gaining.

"Damn and blast!" she swore into the salty spray. Grasping the wheel, she swung the ship hard to starboard. A rush of icy water struck her full in the face, the salt stinging her watery eyes. Without taking her hands from the wheel, she rubbed her face against her sodden sleeve.

"Tighten her up, boys. We're going to take her to the limit! Full speed ahead." Arabella felt the hull beat hard into the waves, as they zigzagged into the wind. The port side hull was tilted dangerously close to the waterline as the Bella crashed into a wave. Water cascaded over the deck. She turned the Bella sharply starboard. With a head wind, they needed to zig-zag forward, executing tight turns to accelerate.

Timing was everything. It would determine the fate of all aboard. One wrong maneuver could mean death to the crew; first from the sea, and then, if they survived, from the law. Being boarded by the revenue cutters could mean that all aboard would be sentenced to death for treasonous smuggling. If they were lucky, they could be pressed into the British navy as a galley slave, a fate which too often was also a death sentence. There would be no defense. Now was not the time to be faint hearted; it was the time for extreme risk.

Though her heart pounded in her chest, and her stomach knotted, she showed no outward signs of fear. At each turn, Arabella pushed the ship to the edge of its capability. And with each turn, the water was inches from the top of the hull. The Bella raced forward at breakneck speed. Arabella kept a steely grip on the wheel.

She needed to clear the reefs to safety and soon. Her hands became slick with sweat. Arabella had to pull her right hand from the wheel to wipe it dry on her coat.

She urged her ship forward. "Come on, baby!"

Jem shouted into the fray, "Hang on, boys!"

A massive wave pounded the hull as the lugger took a sharp turn to starboard. Water rushed across the deck, forcing the crew to brace themselves against its fury. She was at top speed.

Arabella gripped the foremast with one hand and held to the wheel with the other, first peering coastward, then swinging to check the revenue cutter once more. She could see nothing of the shoreline through the thick fog to her left, but they had gained some ground on the King's men.

Another huge wave approached from the portside. She was just able to turn the bow into its crest before it smashed into the ship. The ship was precariously over-powered. So far luck and precision had been with her, but one slight error and they would capsize.

Thankfully, the load was tight. She carried a cargo of gin and brandy tubs, with some extras of silk and lace. Had the stock in the hold been able to shift, it would have been enough to tip them into the sea. Arabella was thankful now that she had carefully supervised the packing.

At last, Jamie screamed from the stern, "We are past the point, Cap'n."

"We'll pull her in," Arabella shouted to the crew. Though she could see nothing, even with her telescope, Arabella trusted Jamie's expertise. Jamie would not call it unless he was sure. Arabella swung the ship sharply to the portside.

The ship swerved into the safety of the thick fog. From here on, Arabella would rely on her memory to guide them along the coast. This was her home stretch, and she knew it well. Beneath her mask, she smiled in triumph. They had outrun the revenue boys. The setting sun would be further cover for them.

Arabella expelled a long breath. It had been a close one.

Jem approached her and laid his massive hand on her shoulder with silent approval. The spotsman stood on her right. His job now was to watch for the signal from the shore.

Jem leaned down and spoke quietly into her ear, "That was a near miss, Ara. That cutter was seventy tons at least. We have not seen her like in some time. I heard rumors about a cutter of that size in our midst but hoped the tales were exaggerated." He shook his shaggy head. "Worse, this is the third time we have been spotted on as many trips. Something's not right. There's a leak somewhere. We'll need to keep our ears to the ground. We don't want to meet her in the open sea. She's too fast for us."

"She was that. And you're right. The bastards were waiting for us." Arabella looked at the darkening mists swirling around her. "But he won't catch us today, Jem."

She would address the worry of the new cutter in time. Tonight, she had to concentrate on bringing the ship safely into port.

Her timing was right. They would see the signal light soon for the unloading. The night's smuggling job would not be complete until the goods were safely on shore and stored in the caves until Jem could arrange their transport.

As she suspected, the breezes had died closer to shore. The sea had calmed to an eerie stillness. The ship glided silently through the comforting blanket of fog.

Tremble Inlet was their destination. At high tide, the inlet allowed them to dock and haul off the cargo without the aid of beach crews. Tremble Inlet was a secret known only to the crew. It was tucked along the coastal cliffs of her

Yorkshire home, Harwood Place, safe from the prying eyes of the community and difficult to spot, even from the sea. The fewer people who knew of it, the safer it would be.

The Bella was built for speed not cargo. She was a mere fifty feet from bow to stern with a capacity for carrying only ten tons. It would be quick work to get her unloaded and sail her around to dock at the village.

Arabella knew the revenue cutter still prowled the coast, searching for her prey. She twisted her salt-ravaged face into an arrogant smirk. The fog and the dark would hide them.

Still, she sighed with relief when the spotsman hailed the signal flare and they maneuvered into the inlet. Grabbing a lead rope, she leapt to the ship's rail and hollered, "Drop the sails. She's calm. We'll dock her cliff side. Make fast work of it, boys. We can't have the damned cutters spot us now!"

Theo sat up and slowly swung his legs to the floor. By the look of the sun through the gauzy curtained window, it was already late morning. His head hurt. He ran his hand through his tussled blond hair, pushing it back from his forehead. He had consumed far too much brandy, again. His mouth was dry. The sweet smell of Dierdra's perfume mixed with stale sweat clung to his body. It nauseated him.

He squinted down at Dierdra. She was the latest in a string of mistresses. The morning sun was not kind to her. Her blonde hair lay snarled across her pillow, heavily pomaded locks now stiff and misshapen. Her rouged cheeks and lips stood out sharply in the harsh light. Her makeup betrayed her. Instead of enhancing her beauty, as it had in the soft light of the evening, it now emphasized her aging skin.

But it was not her age that concerned him. It was her cloying possessiveness which had convinced him the arrangement they had was over. Last night, she had irritated both he and the predatory mamas of the marriage mart by clinging to his arm all evening. Finding a suitable wife with Dierdra at his side would be impossible.

She stirred, looking at him through eyes opened in narrow slits, and groaned, pulling the sheet up over her head as if aware of her disheveled state.

He was bored with her. Knowing what would be next, he sighed. There would be the scene with its tears and recriminations and finally the gift. He wished he could simply walk out and never return. But she was a widow in good standing in the ton and could make life a misery for him. That she had begun to make claims on him publicly could only mean she had aspirations; she hoped for a proposal. Theo had made it clear to her at the start of their affair he had no intention of involving himself in a committed relationship with her. She had agreed. He resented her obvious manipulations.

Rising from the bed, he grabbed his shirt off the rumpled heap of clothing on the floor. The scene with Dierdra would have to be saved for another time. He had promised to luncheon with his grandmother. Getting home and making himself presentable before she arrived was his priority. Things would not go well for him if she saw him in this state.

As he buttoned his trousers, Theo smiled at the thought of his formidable grandmother. She had messaged him to inform him of her arrival to discuss a matter of great importance. He was not concerned. Every discussion was a matter of importance to his grandmother. He was fond of the old girl. She had taken the reins after his parents had died. He and his little sister Lizzy had been in firm, but loving hands.

Two hours later, Theo sat rigidly at the table in the breakfast room staring at the faded contract in front of him. It was outrageous.

"You cannot be serious, grandmother. This is positively medieval."

His grandmother had said little while they lunched, strategically waiting until the meal was concluded before presenting her case. Her silence during the meal had been suspicious but never had he suspected this bombshell to be dropped into his lap.

"It is a contract. It was signed in good faith by your parents and those of Arabella Forsythe. I have had it checked. It is legal and binding." She gave her cane a solid thump.

He winced. She used her cane like a judge's gavel. It had never boded well for him. Once the cane had hit the floor, her mind was made up. She would entertain no further arguments.

Theo's first instinct was always to resort to charm. It usually worked for him. He tried a winning smile. "Surely you don't think to hold me to this, Nana. And think of the poor girl. I have not laid eyes on the lass since she was a child. All I can remember of her is scraped knees and pigtails."

He laughed at the memory. The last time he had seen Arabella Forsythe, he had been fifteen and she was about eight. She had swung at him from a tree branch and plopped down at his side to ply him with questions. She was curious about everything—could he ride? Why had he been sent to school? Did he miss his home? Could he sail a ship? Indeed, his most enduring memory of her was thinking that she was the most annoying brat.

"She cannot be eager for this arrangement," he said.

"She is willing." Lady Osbourne rested her cane on the arm of her chair and laid her hands on the table. "Think of it, Theodore. You are thirty. It is time you took your responsibilities seriously. The Earldom must have an heir. You have scoured the town checking out the young ladies each season. None have appealed to you. Had you found a young lady to your liking, I would never have brought the contract to your attention. But you have not. It is time. Unless you have someone that appeals to you..."

She left the question hanging and looked curiously at him.

Theo thought of Dierdra. He gave a bark of laughter. "No. God, no."

He continued to smile as he thought of Dierdra's reaction to the news. It would certainly solve his mistress problem.

He had no idea who would best suit him as a bride. The responsibility weighed heavily on him. It had been on his mind since the marriage of his best friend Ambrose. Lately, he felt he was the last of his companions to find a suitable spouse.

Marrying was his responsibility. He needed an heir. He loved women, almost all of them, at least for a while. Each time he thought he found the one, he became bored. To choose someone to spend the rest of his life with was next to impossible for him. He had considered the new crop of ladies this year with interest, but soon found the games played by them and their mamas a burden. He could not stomach machinations and manipulations.

He was an earl and therefore a fine catch for every girl. And he had money. This season, Theo's attendance at the soirees and balls had signaled his interest in finding a bride. The mamas had gotten wind of his intention to seek a bride. There was no end to the line of eligible ladies who had thrown themselves at his feet. Literally. Last weekend, a young woman had actually fainted in front of him. He had been obliged to catch her and haul her to a chair while her mother smiled approvingly. It was too much. He had given the business of finding a wife a serious try but found the games impossible to tolerate.

"Theodore. If you must marry and you have no one in mind, then why not honor this agreement? Your problem will be solved."

Theo looked down at the contract once more. It was real. It laid out the marriage settlements precisely. "What do you know of her?"

His grandmother smiled. "She is twenty-three, neither too young nor too old. She is an intelligent, spirited young lady. Like you, she lost her parents as a child. And she is lovely. I have heard she takes after her maternal grand-mother who was an acclaimed beauty."

Theo was skeptical. "Then why has she not been snatched up?"

His grandmother shrugged. "She had many offers in her first seasons and declined them. Her grandmother has much indulged her. This past year, she has apparently been helping to manage her brother's estate and not moving in social circles. And then, of course, there is the trivial matter of money. She has none."

Theo glanced down at the contracts. Money was defi-nitely something the woman would gain if they honored this agreement. Theo considered the exorbitant price he would pay for this bride. He winced. But it would be worth it if this damnable search for a wife was over.

His grandmother appeared to read his thoughts. "And speaking of money, there is also the little matter of my inheritance for you. I would be willing to grant you half of my sizable estate. I must of course hold a portion back to settle on your sister when she weds, but it is a generous amount." She paused to let him consider the deal before adding, "Harwood Place is floundering. I think it may need a capable manager to bring it about."

Theo raised his eyebrows. It was not like his grandmother to offer up funds. She had always been tight-fisted and conservative with her money. Indeed, he had had a battle with her when the time had come to manage his inheritance from his parents.

He thought about the challenge of bringing an estate back from the abyss. It intrigued him. Over the years he had made a considerable fortune buying enterprises that were struggling for rock bottom prices, turning them into viable businesses, then selling them for a profit. It was both a talent and a passion. It accounted for a sizable portion of his considerable wealth. Certainly, when added to his inheritance, he would be considered one of the wealthiest gentlemen in England.

"You very much want this arrangement, Grandmother. Why?"

She gave him a rare wide smile. "Believe it or not, I want you to be happy. I know the young lady's family well. Her mother was a woman of strength and integrity. Her grandmother and I have been lifelong friends. I have an instinct for these things and am seldom wrong."

"When was the last time you saw the girl?"

"I knew her as a child. Her personality was set. Trust

me. She will be a lovely young woman and make a fine wife. Her grandmother assures me she is very much the gentile lady."

"I will meet her." Theo shrugged. "I will even offer for her if that is what you want. I need a wife. I need heirs. I seem to have had no luck managing the task so far."

His pronouncement surprised him. He had been flippant and hasty.

His grandmother leapt at his agreement before he could change his mind. With a thump of her cane, she announced, "It is settled then. We will leave for Harwood place next Thursday. I will send a letter to the countess today."

Theo glanced at his grandmother. If nothing else, he had pleased her. She now leaned back in her chair and sipped her tea with an air of satisfaction. Theo too, found himself relieved with the betrothal. If Lady Arabella were the demure, gently raised woman his grandmother described then his search for a bride would be over.

He pictured a shy young lady, raised in the country. She would be blushing with pleasure at the thought of marrying an earl, forever thankful for his proposal. He imagined a soft, gentle creature. A woman who would happily manage his household, enjoying her role as wife and mother. It might all work out for the best.

The Smuggler: Chapter Two

Arabella stood with Jem admiring the new colt. "It's been a damned good year for the stable."

Jem frowned. "Watch your language, missy. There is no need to play Captain Ara here."

"Sorry, but she is a beauty, Jem. Strong and healthy." As if to underline her words, the little filly wobbled to its mother to suckle. "We have four new foals this season. It is a fine start for us."

Arabella rested her arms on the rails of the pen and smiled. The stables with their carefully selected breed mares were the one part of the estate which was flourishing.

"Aye, it is that," Jem replied, his scarred face twisting into the hint of a smile. "But we have a long way to go to make this place stand on its own."

Arnold approached. "Lady Adrienne wishes to see you in the sitting room. She has asked me to fetch you."

Arabella frowned. It was not like her grandmother to rise early, especially having just returned from a trip to

London. "I best be hurrying then. I mustn't let her majesty wait."

She laid her hand on Jem's shoulder in farewell and turned to do her grandmother's bidding.

Her grandmother's request could only be trouble, she thought to herself, as she walked into the sitting room. The countess was reclining on the sofa. On the end table before her a tea tray had been set. She was sampling an array of chocolates. Choosing one, she used it to motion in Arabella's direction.

"Sit down, my dear. Pour a cup of tea. We must have a little talk this morning."

Arabella perched on the chair across from her and poured her tea. To her dismay, her hand shook slightly with the task. In her experience, the more relaxed and indolent her grandmother appeared, the more difficult the conversation would be. In the past, if a reprimand or command was to be administered it was always done with the countess in a reclined position. Arabella was sure it was employed as a tactic to distract her prey. This morning, her grandmother was stretched out on the sofa. Not a good sign at all.

Her grandmother patiently watched Arabella pour her tea and settle it on the end table, then began.

"I have been considering this ruin of an estate your brother and you have been saddled with. My funds are limited. I cannot be expected to subsidize this place forever." She waved her hand, with the chocolate still held in her fingers, in a circular motion. "It is simply not possible to pull it from disaster with the meager income I have."

The countess expelled a long breath, laying her head back on the cushions.

Arabella felt her stomach turn. Her grandmother had dived into the issue without the usual niceties. This could only mean she had a plan in mind. Arabella lived in constant fear of her grandmother discovering her clandestine activities. The countess was the one person who could destroy her thriving smuggling business and put her beloved Harwood estate in jeopardy.

She turned to Arabella. "With your brother away on his tour, it is my responsibility as your guardian to manage your future."

Arabella looked down. Her twin Aran, unbeknownst to the countess, was not on a tour, subsidized by her deceased father's old friend, Admiral Hews. He had been caught at sea smuggling contraband. Like many in that circumstance, he had been conscripted into the British navy. Only Aran was not serving as a sailor; he was serving as a spy. Admiral Hews was not his benefactor, but his captor.

"In my estimation we have only two alternatives. We can sell this place—"

"Never," Arabella gasped.

"Let me finish." Her grandmother gave her a stern look. "Or you can do your duty and find a profitable marriage. One which provides a sizable settlement which can then be invested into Harwood Place."

Arabella found herself looking at her slippers again. She knew she must do this duty. She was committed to Harwood. More than anything else, she wanted to honor her family. All her exploits at sea had been directed to this very goal. To lose Harwood Place was not an option. Her twin would never forgive her, and she would never forgive herself.

She could hardly tell her grandmother she planned to restore the place with funds from smuggling. She was caught. Her grandmother had the power as guardian to sell the place if it was in the best interest of the heirs to do so.

With the estate in the condition it was, there would be no argument to forestall her.

"Now then." The countess took a small bite of her chocolate. "The season is in full swing in London. I think we shall pack up and journey to town. You will have this one chance to find a husband to help you save this place."

Arabella felt a wave of panic. "Oh, Nana, you know the trouble I have had in the past finding a suitor. When it is discovered I have no dowry, any young men melt away. I am left with old men. Those men willing to dump a large enough settlement on me are invariably of the merchant class looking for a brood mare with good bloodlines."

Her grandmother looked unmoved, taking a bite from her chocolate, and then discarding it, to examine the tray for a more pleasing dainty.

"Please do not insist on this. I do not display well in town." Arabella leaned forward. "There is no one more awkward than me in society's endless soirees. I will fail."

Arabella thought of the evenings in London, attempting unsuccessfully to flirt with men she had no interest in, and shuddered.

"No, my dear. My mind is quite made up. I have thought long and hard about the responsibility I bear to the two of you, my grandchildren." She sighed, closing her eyes, and rested her head on the cushions propped behind her once more, before making the effort to continue. "You are twenty-three years old, darling. The choice is no longer yours. I have neglected my duty in not insisting you do yours."

Grab your copy…
vinci-books.com/the-smuggler

About the Author

I wish I could say that I wanted to be a writer my whole life, that it was my dream. But it wasn't. I fell into it on a whim and discovered to my surprise that I enjoyed it. What I always have been is a reader. I will read anything. During the times I could not afford books, I read whatever sat on the shelves of the secondhand store. Sometimes it was History, sometimes Romance, and sometimes it was how to make macrame hangers.

But I am getting ahead of myself. I grew up in Brightsand Saskatchewan, in an immigrant family with six siblings. We were a hard-working troop, scraping a living out of a rocky mixed farm. I look back on those busy years fondly. I have plenty of stories about walking through miles of snow to school, uphill both ways!

I went to the University of Saskatchewan, studying History and English, which I converted into a career in teaching. I love my job. I teach a wild crew of junior high students. There is never a dull moment. It has been a passion of mine which has truly made life worth living. Much of my time is committed to coaching. I can be found most mornings in the gym by six thirty, spending time with my teams. We have had some memorable seasons, winning basketball districts against all odds.

I was lucky enough to marry the love of my life. My husband and I share another passion, gardening. He does the vegetables and I do the flowers. Together we spend many peaceful evenings, enjoying the beauty and bounty we have created.

I squeeze my writing into the bits and pieces of the day that remain. In many ways it is my personal time. I have been surprised by the writing process. Though I start with a plan, my characters always surprise me with their antics. I look forward to every new book, with its host of characters leading me into places unknown.